TREASURE *of the* HOLY QUINCUNX

a Travis One-Shoe thriller

E. T. ELLISON

© Copyright 2019 by E. T. Ellison

ISBN 978-1-7348036-0-0

Book, cover, title page, coaster and map designs by E. T. Ellison. www.etellison.com

Published by Clownbox Press
216 Mt Hermon Road, Suite E-233
Scotts Valley, CA 95066

028090

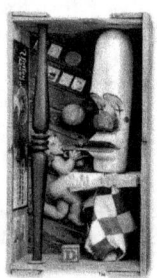

cLowNbox
P R ϵ s s

AUTHOR'S NOTE

The present story was inspired by a single paragraph in *Oddballs, Cults & Worldchangers* by Lavendra Cortioli, PhD.

> *"YOU MAY RECALL the so-called Pulp Revival of the 2240s. Lowbrow printlit was back with a vengeance and the Dark Mystery genre reigned supreme over even Sordid Lust, the distant second, with Tawdry Romance bringing up the rear. Among the dark mysteries was a short-lived series called Flickers in the Attic. The first book in the series was* Treasure of the Holy Quincunx *by Ace Falken and took place in a ruined IsoTown called St. Cumin. Treasure's popularity flared briefly when the* Village Global *reported that the fictional St. Cumin was actually the real, unruined St. Coriander with both great wealth and a real and towering Holy Quincunx. Father-Mayor Faunibeune deftly deflected or absorbed the spike of media attention and the storm passed. Almost."*

The "almost" refers to the so-called "Buzzard Invasion," an actual treasure hunt inspired by a speculative 'how-to' article in the October 2248 issue of *Soldier of Fortune*. It's one of those events that supports the notion that life too often imitates fiction. Rather than get into the details of the ill-fated raid by Bilko's Buzzards, I refer any interested readers to Chapter 27 of Dr Cortioli's exhaustive history of the IsoTown movement. That chapter was part of the original hardcover Chronicler's Edition of *The Luck of Madonna 13*, an edition that is out of print. Luckily, it's currently featured in *Genesis...and Then Some*, a free collection of adjuncts to the Last Nevergate Chronicles made available through special arrangement with the Transpoint Independent Archive (visit www.etellison.com to download).

Unfortunately, Transpoint has yet to unearth a copy of Ace Falken's original *Treasure of the Holy Quincunx*, so I decided to tell a first-person version of that tale to give me a mental break from the six-volume Last Nevergate Chronicles, which I'm happy to say is now more-or less complete and slated for publication sometime in 2020.

Since this story is set prior to the nastiness around the end of the 23rd century that isolated the Earth from the rest of the universes, you might wonder if it is in any way a prequel to the Last Nevergate Chronicles, which take place in the 26th century. Yes it is. Sort of.

What do I mean by sort-of? If you've read William Gibson's *The Peripheral* and *Agency*, you've encountered his idea of "stub" time-lines that branch off our own at some point, but develop differently after that. The Nevergate stub that Travis One-Shoe operates in has notable differences from the universe the Last Nevergate Chronicles is set in (which could be a stub itself, for all I know). Without giving too much away, the St Coriander in the Last Nevergate Chronicles is alive and well. Even so, it won't hurt you a bit to read this story prior to diving into the expanded 2020 edition *The Luck of Madonna 13*, if you haven't already. At least you'll know where to find the Falling Frog.

E. T. Ellison
April 1, 2020
www.etellison.com

DEDICATION

To the adventurous spirit of Varley Chan-Zita, whose eight-year-old self saw life as a treasure hunt, but died too young to test the grog at the Falling Frog.

Actual size Falling Frog coaster (unused), circa 2230.
Exhibit courtesy of the Transpoint Independent Archive's
St Coriander Everyday Artifacts Collection.

QUINCUNXIFICATION

QUINCUNX IS A WORD you'll encounter in this book ... and not infrequently. While it's picturesque as words go, it does not exactly make an elegant swan dive off the tongue. At least that's been my tongue's experience. Although it's pronounced exactly as it's spelled (kwin-kunks), the people of St Coriander took no more pleasure in its elocutionary gymnastics than you or I do. So they have been known to cheat. In everyday conversation they would often say "quinkess" or even "quinks." For a time, "kwunks" (they wrote it "qunks") was a fashion amongst the students of both Eastac and Westac, to the annoyance of school authorities, who feared the more formalistic members of the Fatherhood might take offense, although they rarely did. "Ah youth," they'd say.

Some readers don't even bother to mentally pronounce it; they acknowledge they know what meaning it stands for, and then move on to the next word. My authorial recommendation is to do whatever you want.

Simplified top view of the Holy Quincunx Plaza at the core of the St Coriander Town Center. To see multiple views of the original design blueprints, download the colorful 120-page Genesis...and Then Some *PDF from www.etellison.com. It's free.*

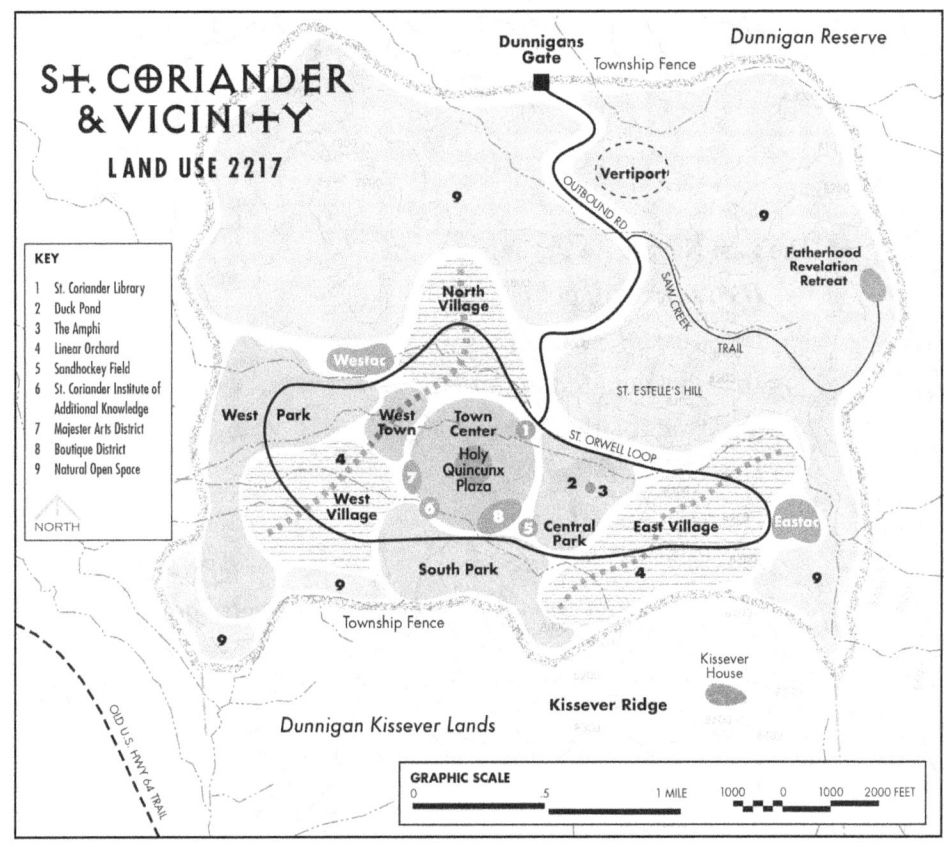

This plan is an accurate visualization of what is where
in St Coriander at the time of this story. The Falling Frog
Public House is located in the Majester Arts District.

NEVERGATE CYCLE BOOKS BY E.T. ELLISON

CONTENTS

0

....

THE WRATH OF HAROLD

SATURDAY, JANUARY 23, 2219 — Varley Chan-Zita hated being dragged to meetings. Normal 8-year old boys are like that. He would fidget, look a million times at his new timepatch, think about how cool it would be to leak out a silent-but-deadly and then look innocent while his parents and the others around him crinkled their noses.

What had made this meeting a little less boring was the voice. It was a deep, mysterious voice that showed up in his head about halfway through the meeting. It was loud enough to somehow drown out the shouts and the sharp whacks of the moderator's gavel, but it wasn't loud in the way that makes your ears hurt. *"Var-ley,"* boomed the voice, leaving a long trail of singsongy echoes in his head. *"Varley, I've got something to show you."*

The first time he'd looked around to see if anybody else heard it, even though he was pretty sure it was happening just inside his own head. When weird things happen, you have to be sure.

"Close your eyes, Var-ley, and follow the treasure bunny."

A new clue! Varley almost made a boyish gesture of enthusiasm, but caught himself in time. Instead, he grinned. He had been playing this new slate game for two weeks so he knew that when the treasure bunny appeared — which was a tiny red dragon, not a bunny at all — it would lead to a clue about where to find the key to the dragon's hoard, including a fabulous solid gold skull that had been featured in Varley's dreams last night. These clues had come to him strangely, almost as if whispered directly into his mind by the deep, mysterious voice. But he'd try them out wherever they came from. Varley was practical that way.

One clue required diving way down deep in the Moat. For that he'd need a gillmask, which was a problem because he didn't have enough game swag to get one. It was also a problem because the water in the Moat was probably frozen over right now and he'd also need to get a drysuit. But at least his pack included a multitool with an axe-head: he could chop ice with that. Varley didn't usually like games set in the Here and Now, but having a dragon and spooky treasure involved made this one okay.

Another clue would require him to find a hidden door somewhere in the room where the Elevation Stage was. That might be easier, although the huge stained glass windows had creeped him when it had been his uncle Frank's time to Elevate to a higher plane. But to win the key, he would brave it. And it was all just on his slate, anyway: not for real. Except that this game was so real in a way he couldn't describe that he had to keep reminding himself that it was just a game. Make-believe. A fantasy. Besides, there was nothing fun about reality right now; it was just adults arguing stuff that he was pretty sure meant nothing to him.

Twice he'd slipped out his slate to see if there were any messages waiting for him on Lurkentine, the magical rock in the middle of what was called Madonna Creek in the game: Lurkentine was his safety. The first time he saw a bright yellow bottle trapped in some branches. He zoomed in close enough to see the white label with a black skull and crossbones and some words on it, but before he could read it his mother put her hand into the image and shook her head. "Pay attention, Varley," she whispered. "This is important."

The second time he waited until there was a lot of shouting in the room. This time he snagged the bottle and saw the label on the back that said "ANTIDOTE FOR POISON" in big blocky letters. A chill rippled through his body and coalesced in his stomach, where it felt like a handful of icy rocks.

Once again his mother's hand wiped the image before he could read any more. This had felt really important and it made him so angry at his mother that he wanted to bite her hand. Or at least pinch her. But he just scrunched down and scowled.

When the meeting was finally over Varley yanked on his father's hand and popped the question: "Dad, can I play the new Dragon Hoard game when we get home? I'm at level 3 already and I'm getting close to finding the treasure. I know it. Really, Dad. I'm not just being a goofy gameboy. You'll see."

His father squeezed his hand and smiled a tight smile. "Sure son, but just for a little bit. This stupid meeting went way longer than I thought. I should have known better than to think Demetrius Krebs could ever be open to reason."

Mika Chan-Henry aimed a rueful smile in Varley's direction. Her son was shrewd enough to know who to ask for extra game time, but the extra game time probably wouldn't kill him. She silently echoed her husband's comment about the acrid editor-in-chief of the *St Coriander Times* and knew his comment had been edited for Varley: Krebs was a perfect asshole. Period. In all her 32 years, she had never seen the people of St Coriander so worked up about anything. But with Krebs fanning the fire and Father-Mayor O'Kelly away at a conference somewhere, the dithering Father Glinting had been hard put to keep the meeting under control. The result of all the acrimony was to form a committee to study the problems with the SI that managed their town. Did anybody really believe another committee would accomplish anything except allow the meeting to adjourn? Mika sure didn't. Buying this particular SI had been a bad decision and it needed to be returned or replaced or repaired or something. No committee needed.

The family of three exited the Convectory in the base of the Holy Quincunx complex and into a biting wind thick with gritty pellets of sleet. The weatherfield had been erratic lately and now it was clearly not working at all. To Mika's mind, the town should have gotten a proven Terra-made Dunnetix SI in the first place. Or just kept doing

3

things the old way without a central synthetic intelligence to manage all the various devices and systems that kept their quiet little Iso-Town in the high country running. That old-fashioned method had worked just fine for decades and she had said as much at the meeting.

This bargain-basement alien monstrosity from some godforsaken PU was surely turning out to be no bargain. And it wasn't as though St Coriander was poor: anything but, according to the last trust fund report. But the steady stream of editorials in the *St Coriander Times* had stirred up the old anti-Dunnigan sentiments and we ended up with this lemon, she grumbled to herself. In the three years since its integration, nothing had ever seemed to work quite right. She was still grumbling when the headache hit.

It was like a railroad spike being hammered into her forehead. Her knees buckled and she slumped onto the slushy path. Then some strange force tied her innards in knots and set her throat on fire. She pitched forward and only vaguely felt her husband's arms pull her upright.

Sounds were muted hazy things. Cries for help, screams and groans of pain were all around her, but all were thick and dull and distant as if they were buried under a pile of blankets. All sounds, that is, except for the hideous booms of laughter. Deep, cartoony bellows of evil glee exploded from inside her skull to shove all other sensations aside. With them came a blast of red light she could sense even through her closed eyes.

Mika forced her eyelids open and turned to see the Holy Quincunx towers engulfed in flames ... flames, but no heat. Her fractured mind realized the truth: the flames were just a projection on the mediaface that skinned the towering obelisks. But the writhing flames were no less horrible for being projections.

At the very top of each tower, the head of a monstrous dragon appeared through the flames. When the laughter trailed off, the blue-gray snout with hooded yellow eyes opened its jaws and spoke in a malevolent voice that was somehow both deep and shrill at the same time.

"Suffer, my faithless, whining subjects. Feel the wrath of Harold who you would betray! All of you — each man, woman and child of you — are now banished from St Coriander. At this instant! And I include your fawning, fleecing, fubbulent Fatherhood as well. So, my disloyal subjects, consider your citizenship revoked and the welcome mat rolled up and cast into my flames. Flee for your sorry lives ... if you can. You know the ways out ... maybe you will be lucky." Another peal of unholy cackles punctuated this idea.

"Run while you can, useless eaters. I will tolerate your draws upon my hoard no longer: flee into the night of punishment. Because Harold is a merciful being, know that I have placed antidotes for the agonies you feel on the other side of the Township Fence ... and also in a place known to my trusty friends as Lurkentine. But you will need to hurry."

The word "hurry" was consumed by an evil scream that seemed to drag on for a minute before the sound and the images faded away to nothing, leaving the towers free to reflect the swirling eddies of sleet that were painting every surface sparkling white. Then all lights in the town blinked out in unison and St Coriander's deepest, darkest night since the earthquake of 2174 began.

• • • • •

They'd taken a detour to their home in West Village where Carlos had the vain hope that they might find some kind of antidote. But it was a waste of time: they never even got inside. And Mika had nearly been electrocuted when she gripped the handle to open the door. Now she staggered along behind him, a snowball clutched in her burned hand, barely able to put one foot in front of the other.

As Carlos Chan-Zita started across the arched bridge over Fortunatus Creek with Varley clutched tight to his chest, his son looked around and became agitated. He squirmed and raved something about Lurkentine and yellow bottles, and then fell silent. Carlos ignored the outburst and his cramping guts, and kept pressing forward toward the Township Fence. A short distance past the bridge Varley lost consciousness and lost control of his bowels and bladder at about the same time. Carlos pretended not to notice the stench and the wetness; only in walking was there hope.

Five minutes later they stood in front of what was supposed to be the entrance to an escape maze. Carlos' head was splitting and his guts were roiling, but evidently whatever poison this was hadn't hit him as hard as some others, which was why they had made it this far. He supposed he should be thankful: his little family had passed many sprawled, unmoving white forms. Twice he'd stopped and tried to help, another waste of precious minutes on pulse-less gray bodies whose faces were so contorted he barely recognized them.

Mika dropped to her knees, anticipating the next phase: the crawl through the maze. Carlos just rasped a curse; the hole in front of them was almost completely covered by a mass of poisonous, high voltage thornmesh. The volunteer Fence Patrol was supposed to keep the escape mazes clean and navigable, but clearly nobody had tended this one in months. And he had none of the tools or protective gear needed to handle the stuff, so he just glared at it and cursed again.

Surreal echoes of the dragon's sneering guffaws rattled around inside his head and he couldn't avoid thinking that the whole situation was equal parts ludicrous and impossible. For the longest time he had hoped it was all some kind of dream, but the unquenchable thirst seemed real enough to be killing him. And his guts felt like claws had reached inside and were methodically shredding his organs. Had whatever poison this was already killed Mika? She was curled up next to him and hadn't moved in minutes. The snow was falling harder now and her fetus-like form was already coated in a fresh half-inch of white. He set Varley gently in a drift next to his mother and put a pair of numb fingers on his wife's neck in search of a pulse.

Nothing. Frustrated, he shook her shoulder. No response, not even a flutter of an eyelash. Although her face muscles were knotted in a parody of her natural beauty, her forehead had cooled. He ran the backs of his fingers along the unnatural rippled muscles in her cheek. Carlos tried to scream at that moment, but only a hoarse squawk made it past his cracked lips. He closed his eyes and felt his face muscles squirming against his will, as if infested with teeming maggots. He slumped to the ground.

He sucked in a frigid breath and wondered what had a wealthy IsoTown of pacifist vegetarians — descendants of lottery winners, all — ever done to deserve such a cruel, unlucky end?

A streak of acid pain in his abdomen dissolved any further wondering. His bowel and bladder control failed him then, but Carlos Chan-Zita was now beyond embarrassment. The last St Coriander resident was dead.

8

PART ONE

RAIDERS

10

1

DEATH, RESERVE STYLE

JUNE 4, 2245, 10:36 AM — My nose spotted it first. The rotting carcass was hidden under an animated umbrella of turkey buzzards in the new grass a couple feet off the trail. I was just outside the old St Coriander Township Fence about a mile shy of the gate. Nobody comes up here, so I figured it was probably the remains of a deer culled by a cougar. Whatever the dead thing was, it was stinking up what had otherwise been a routine Wednesday morning patrol in the south end of the Dunnigan Reserve.

The big ugly birds hovered over their treasure and hissed at me. I probably should've apologized and walked away. My life would have been simpler if I'd just minded my own business ... just let nature take its course. But I've always admired nature's way of tidying up messes, so I decided to watch for a while. The day was shaping up to be another sunny one, so why not enjoy it? A few minutes later one of the buzzards jostled for a better position leaving a gap that exposed something very un-deer-like. A boot.

"Meal's over ... buzz off, me uglies," I said using that cheery tone I reserve for creatures with genetic immunity to my voice of authority. For emphasis, I kicked some dirt in their direction and waved my arms. Still hissing, they lurched skyward in search of escape and the nearest thermal.

Mostly, the threatening signs posted in strategic locations and the obvious surveillance indicators around here work pretty well in keeping lost trekkers out of the Dunnigan Reserve. Plus, there's nothing worth stealing around here anyway. So why had this guy decided to get himself dead on my watch and trigger a bunch of extra paperwork?

His mangled right eye was the size of a baseball. How the chewed remains of it got to be dangling outside its socket wasn't something I wanted to spend time thinking about. But at least he'd gotten the snake: its head was just ragged shreds, thanks to the slivershot. And thanks to the buzzards, the snake's nearly 5-foot length was now just ragged shreds of scaled skin, flesh and tiny bones. Nice set of rattles, though. Without thinking too much, I flipped open my old fashioned monoblade and sliced off the rattles for a souvenir.

Then I took a closer look at the guy. Mixed race, mostly Asian and African with some NorEuro thrown in for spice. What was left of his face was a puffy, distorted mess. But something about him reminded me of somebody from my past: just couldn't place who. Considering all the unsavories I've run into, that worried me some. Maybe the guy had been waiting for me.

A slivershot lay a couple feet from the body, half-buried in fresh buzzard shit. Also one of those fancy buzzknives, half-buried in loose dirt. I left them both where they were. A bloody metallic cylinder that reminded me a little of an antique large-caliber pistol cartridge was lying next to what was left of the guy's neck. Curious, I picked it up ... and instantly dropped it like it was hot, which it was. I looked at it again; wasn't lying in the sun, so why would it be hot? Half-spooked and half-curious, I looked at it for a minute and decided I had a pretty good idea of what it really was.

But I squatted down and gave it a careful look-see anyway. What it *wasn't,* was an antique cartridge of any sort: no primer button and no bullet for starters. It had a machined ring at the back like a cartridge casing, though. This part was some kind of silvery alloy with a tangle of tiny wires sticking out of the end where a bullet would be. The case and the wires were crusted with what I took to be dried blood and brain goop, but the wires moved in this sort of slow random motion, kind of like miniature sea anemones in a tidepool.

I touched the ends of the moving wires with a fingertip, real gentle, just a little dab at it. Shouldn't have done that. Zapped me strong enough that I lurched back and landed on my ass. I still don't know how to describe that jolt; definitely like high voltage, but combined with a couple bee stings. And something else, a spike of jabbing, instant headache and a sort of mental hash that hung around for a while. I shook it off, but the headache stuck around.

Well, now I was pissed. So I got down on my hands and knees again and nudged the casing with a twig. No reaction. Then poked at the wires, which provoked some tiny sparks when I looked at it real close. There was also a small dent in the middle of the case, maybe where a hungry carrion-eater grabbed it before realizing it wasn't the good stuff. I figured it for an implant of some sort. Not too uncommon these days in tech professions. Made me think the guy wasn't just a casual hiker.

13

I decided against getting in trouble with my bosses by playing amateur coroner and digging around the remains of his cranium to see where this gadget might have plugged in. Not my job. Besides, the stench was roiling my guts.

Instead, I backed off and felt a sudden pang of sympathy for the guy. People do all sorts of dumb shit around lethal reptiles, but I doubted this guy had provoked the snake into a lethal strike on purpose. Whatever mysterious reason had brought him to the perimeter of a totally closed-off abandoned IsoTown, it was probably just bad luck that got him killed.

Or maybe his death had something to do with the implant. I had a weird sense about that thing. And I was still curious, even though the headache hadn't fizzled out yet. If I just let the ranger techs have it it'd be gone forever. But if I took it back to my hometown, maybe the Ishernot techs could tell me something about it. Decision made, I walked back a ways to where I'd seen some cowboy toilet paper, picked a handful of the biggest leaves and followed my nose back to the vic.

The implant was cool enough now that I could roll it up in a triple layer of soft green mullein leaves and stuff it into a little pocket inside the waistband of my official Dunnigan Ranger camo jumpsuit. Having willfully violated protocol for a possible crime scene — and gotten zapped for it — I got back to business, just not the part of proper procedure business that meant calling it in. Not yet.

Slivershots are common enough and a decent tool for self-protection up here in the high country. Unless you run into a bear. So finding an intruder with a slivershot wasn't surprising. And a lot of companies make them. This was a Mervix Z18, which is a sophisticated, expensive item capable holding up to a thousand tiny glass smart-rockets with explosive tips; not just any schmuck could afford one of these babies. But all that said was that the vic wasn't poor ... or that he stole it.

The guy's tattered clothes were city-bought stuff for hikers, with labels I didn't recognize, not fabrax stuff. His boots were good quality Stampedes, almost new. A cheap little daypack had been torn off and shredded by the vultures, evidently in search of food. But even whole it would've been too small to carry much; he hadn't planned on being gone long. And there was no ID that my quick search could locate. Interesting.

I rummaged through my own pack for a couple roaches and set them to work scanning the corpse, the snake and the immediate vicinity. For all of about ten seconds I was tempted to try to imagine all the stuff that crime scene investigators did before these brainy little bio-robots hit the market. Why even go there One-Shoe? I told myself. Total waste of imagination time, because I already knew the short answer: they had to find other jobs. So I left the roaches to their assigned tasks and switched mental gears; they'd be busy with that long enough for me to put a noze on the vic's trail and see if I could figure out how he got here and when.

Call me a modernist, but I prefer nozes over dogs any day. You don't need to pet a noze or scratch behind its ears and they don't have floppy tongues that fling drool all over your boot. And you never have to worry about stepping in noze shit. Sure, you'd feel stupid saying "good noze" to a half-alive thing that looks more like a two-foot long centipede. But they're sure good at following spoor. And they coil up in a compact little spiral that takes almost no space in a ranger's pack. So I let my noze loose on the job of following Mr X's trail back to where he came from and I just jogged along behind.

Mostly the noze followed the packed dirt road south around St Coriander, staying as far away from its thornmesh Township Fence as possible. Where the fence turned east at the southern boundary, the noze left the road and skittered through the brush, down an eroded cut to the bed of the Rio de Tierra Amarilla. The little river is shallow and sluggish here, with wide, muddy banks the color of oxidized Tabasco.

The noze had lost the scent temporarily and was skittering back and forth in the mud by the mostly buried carcass of an ancient yellow school bus. I picked it up and carried it across the water, only getting stuck in knee-deep ooze twice. It found the scent and was back on the case as soon as I set it down on the other side.

So far, me and the noze had tracked the guy back a little over three miles. Now we were about to cross Old 64, which is the south boundary of the Dunnigan Reserve. Technically, I should have stopped there and called the Rio Arriba sheriff. Technically. But since the Rio Arriba sheriff is a certifiable pain in the ass on top of being a moron, I forgot to do that.

The vegetation south of Old 64 is sparse compared to the Reserve and the noze was moving fast. It zipped up the remnants of an old dirt track that hugged the edge of a gully and climbed up to a ridge that gave me a good view north. From here the St Coriander Township Fence was an irregular ring of blackish green enclosing a grayish-green haze that blotted out all detail.

Weatherfield tech like that is expensive to operate and this was still working, even two decades and change after the blackout. Interesting. Made me wonder how I'd been patrolling in this vicinity for five years without ever getting curious about St Coriander. But actually, I knew the answer all too well: I was still mentally recovering from an incident involving too much curiosity, an incident that got me fired from the best gig I ever had, not to mention almost got me assassinated three different times. But here I was getting curious again. It felt good ... and the Dunnigan Reserve felt like a nice, safe place to get curious without having to look over my shoulder every second.

If you've never been to this part of the world, it's what's still called Navajo country in some circles, although WorldGov would rather you left off the reference to the tribals who still manage to scratch out a living somehow. It's all high country, mostly arid and hasn't ever made anybody rich. Before WorldGov, this mountainous part of it was in the north-central part of the old U.S. state of New Mexico (WG:US:NM). Here it's dense forest. Get out of the Dunnigan Reserve in any direction and it quickly changes. Go 300± crow miles to the southwest and you're in my previous high desert stomping grounds: Nirvanata and the delightful little town of Winslow (WG:US:AZ). Both are places I'll be happy to never see again.

From where I stood right now, almost everything I could see beyond the haze of St Coriander was Dunnigan Reserve forest, with the Brazos Cliffs poking up in the middle distance. The ridge where the track ended was just over 8,000-feet elevation, but the noze wanted to go higher, so I gave it its head. It slithered up a zig-zaggy deer trail to a small clearing at the top of a knoll surrounded by a jagged stand of youngish ponderosa pines. In the very center of the clearing it stopped. Interesting.

The clearing was a ragged oval, its longest dimension maybe a hundred feet or so. I looked for the usual telltale signs of a moller fan-craft or a heli landing and take off. Possibly one had dropped Mr X here and he had done a magnificent job cleaning up after it. Possibly, but not likely. Didn't really matter much though, because all such craft are monitored by the mighty local powers-that-be, the Clans Dunnigan. Dead end for me and the noze, though.

I called in the body's location, hoofed it back to babysit the scene until a crew arrived in a carryall and took the body, the other evidence and the roaches and noze I'd employed back to HQ. When they left, I finished my assigned rounds and finally ended up at the office. A half hour later I handed my report to Max Dalt, the pucker sucker in charge of day-to-day ranger activities. Then I checked on flight data, but the Dunnigan records showed no mysterious aircraft had been in that area recently. I filed that for future reference. My inner busybody was waking up and competing with that headache for attention.

18

2

BUMBUSKER INTERLUDE

MY NEW HEADACHE didn't survive the night thanks to a cap of CureAll, but it left me a brand new nightmare. The kind where something huge and nasty is chasing you in the dark and you wake up sweating. And when you look back to see what it is, you can't really tell because it's spouting flames that completely hide its body. Haven't had anything like that since I was a munchkin when I used to dream I was being chased by some kind of mechanoid transformy thing. Kid stuff.

I roused myself just before sunrise, a little groggy, but otherwise okay. Did the usual stuff, let the bunkhouse MenuMaster cough up my usual breakfast of fry bread and hash with too much syrup, put on some coffee and started getting curious about the dead guy. My turf, right? So three cups of coffee later I stopped by the office, just in case. Turns out the techs already had a genematch on the guy. Henry Ng was his name: Chinese, Kenyan and Irish extraction. Seems he was a top flight SI mechanic with high level WorldGov security clearance, mostly working with ThoughtDancers, which struck me as a little weird, on account of those alien SIs being so rare. Part of every Dunnigan Ranger's indoctrination is learning that this very neighborhood is the unlikely home of all the Dunnetix synthetic intelligence varieties that totally rule the roost. As in, total market domination. But this guy mostly worked with the oddballs. According to the file, the dead ThoughtDancer specialist had been lily white until he got sucked up into a political shitstorm during a military coup on a planet called Parsimony in some bumfuck parallax universe about a year ago.

The chief local tech got more than a genematch, which sometimes makes him a little cocky. This was one of those times.

"Hey One-Shoe. Your dead guy in the woods? Snake venom didn't do him in. Didn't help any, but didn't kill him. COD's gonna fry you," he said, grinning. "Guaranteed. Half a brain and you woulda figured it out yourself. Wanna take a guess?"

"Dunnigans pay us to act stupid, Conger. You know that. They can't afford to let you rare tech types start feeling inferior to us manly field men ... afraid you'll go all Nirvana on 'em."

Conger Tango went red in the face ... and I mentally kicked myself in the butt. His ex-girlfriend had taken the Soul Bus to Nirvanata just last week. It's free, but it's permanent; a bus ride from anywhere to Nirvanata or one of the other Nirvana transport centers is a one-way ticket. People who gate to Nirvana are never seen again. The price of bliss is forever, I guess. But with all the ways this world's little guys are getting squeezed, dumped on, chewed up and spit out like so much surplus phlegm, I understand the appeal. There was a time I was tempted. Really. Not just bullshitting you.

Conger knew all that, of course ... except for the part about me being tempted. We'll keep that a secret, okay? All I could bring myself to say to the guy was, "Sorry Conger. Forgot about Naria taking the Path." Conger Tango was a good tech and a nice guy. I felt for him. And I envied his surname ... although I doubted that even having that surname could make a dancer out of me.

Took maybe half a minute for the silence to dissolve. He still looked pained, but he did his job and coughed up the cause of death. "Yeah, okay One-Shoe. Not your fault. I'm still not over it, I guess. But your guy, something cooked his brain ... from the inside. Never seen anything like it. Looks like steam pressure popped his eyeball out. Not sure how else to explain it, particularly since the backs of both eyeballs were cooked ... along with a bunch of his graymatter.

From the cog rehash, it looks like the internal heat took him out before the snake venom could ... but neither would be a happy way to go. Chemtrace says most of his large muscles had suffered major cramping prior to death. Almost like with an electroshock. How would that happen?"

I had a midget of a clue, but I just shrugged.

"And there's one other weird thing: the guy had a port for an implant in the back of his skull, under his left ear. But no implant. And there was no ID under the port cover, which looks like a flap of skin behind his left ear, and the port was empty. You didn't happen to see a silvery thing about so long in the vicinity, did you?"

I frowned and scratched the back of my head. "I met a guy once — he was a diver — who had one of those things. During expeditions to explore wrecks and drowned cities and find sunken treasure and shit like that his implant linked up to the SI that kept track of everything. Showed it to me: about this long and this thick and had these fine thread-like things on one end ... they hooked into his brain somehow. That the kind of thing this guy had?"

"Yeah, something like that is pretty standard from what I can tell. But Ng's port was empty, so we don't actually know if he had something in there or not. You sure you didn't see something?"

"Sorry, Conger. I didn't mess with the scene. That kind of shit is way above my pay grade."

I paused, looked up like I was remembering something and said, "But wait ... I bet I know what might have taken it if it was actually there. Turkey buzzard. Seriously. There was a whole flock of 'em when I found the guy. Completely covering the body like there was a huge buzzard birthday cake under there. A couple were tussling over some little thing and one took off with it in its beak. I was looking at the bunch on the whatever-their-meal-was mostly, so I didn't pay much attention to the outliers, other than to shoo them off. Dunno, but that maybe coulda been your implant. You think?"

I shrugged, grimaced and held up my hands as if perplexed, the way would-be innocent liars have done since the first humans did it in the legendary Garden of Eden, when some godly authority busted them for eating an apple. They just shrugged and said, "Apple? What apple?" At least that's my theory.

"I dunno, One-Shoe. Nobody around here ever heard of a perp that kills its victims like that, so we're sort of grasping at every kind of straw. Thought I'd ask."

• • • • •

22   Yeah, I lied to Conger Tango. And I didn't even feel guilty. What did they actually need the implant for? From what I'd seen during my time here, they'd either send it along with the body if anybody claimed it ... or it would end up gathering dust in an evidence box along with the vic's ashes if nobody claimed the carcass and the personal effects. If I guessed correctly, the Mervix Z18 would become lost shortly after it made it into an evidence box. Or before.

And at least I only partly lied; I really did know a diver with an implant ... and he really did show me the actual gadget and the place it went into his head. Said it made all the difference in his trade.

Would the implant I'd absconded with do something for me? I couldn't see how, but it was too late to turn it over to Conger now. So it would just be my little keepsake. What was troubling me more at the moment was the vic's name. The sheet said Henry Ng had a sister named Maya. And I knew a Maya Ng. Very well.

The Maya Ng I knew was one of the smartest, toughest security techs I've ever had the pleasure to work with. A total Jill-of-all-trades. We did some good work together setting up systems for Nirvanata. Plus, we'd had a relationship that had once felt like the real thing ... except for being entirely impractical. Last I heard she was still working at Nirvanata, so I decided to look her up again one of these days.

It was almost three months before Maya Ng's name showed up again ... and through no effort of mine.

At first, I didn't want to have to tell her it was me that found a dead guy that might be her brother in a very messy state. She'd know I would've tried to trace him back to his point of entry and that I'd be wondering about a few odd things. Before any of that happened I wanted to do a little independent digging.

After a few evenings of after-hours research I didn't turn up anything. Nothing at least that would explain why a top notch SI mechanic would be trespassing in the Dunnigan Reserve, much less get himself offed in such a bizarre fashion. He wasn't a solitary hiker type from all the stuff I read; more of gadabout road warrior with expensive tastes and connections in high places. On the other hand, I didn't work very hard at digging into the guy.

About two weeks later I took a Tuesday off, signed out one of the spare rovers and made a quick trip down to my home town. Ishernot[1] is still the world capital of security tech and I wanted to take Tommy Whiterock to lunch. We agreed to meet at Mary Two-Feather's, which has the best barbecue in Ishernot. Tommy's a very smart guy I grew up with. These days he's an ace in the area of cognitive user/weapon interfaces. But before that he did all the coursework it takes to become an SI mechanic. But something about running the Circus spooked him and he elected to stay at home. In my opinion, Ishernot won big on that decision. Tommy's just too nice a guy to thrive in the outside world.

Halfway through lunch, after we'd gotten through the usual catch up stuff, Tommy wiped sauce off his mouth, gave me his patented wise man smile and said, "So One-Shoe. Why don't you just blurt it out and ask me whatever you came down here to ask me?"

Through a mouthful of heavenly pulled pork on garlic bread I sputtered out my first question. "In your almost SI mechanic days, you ever run across a guy named Henry Ng?"

He shook his head, maybe a little too quickly, but I really didn't care too much about that. I told him a simplified version of the crime

---

1 :: *Every once in a while somebody asks me if there's a connection between the very real IsoTown of Ishernot and the fictional weapon shops of Isher on account of the industry our economy is built around. I usually start with something smart-assy like, "Maybe you're not clear on the meaning of 'not'?" Then I smile and tell the truth: the town founders were neo-libertarian anarchists and big fans of the ancient mid-20th century scifi novels,* The Weapon Shops of Isher *and* The Weapon Makers *by A.E. van Vogt.*

scene outside of St Coriander then said I wanted him to look at something if he'd walk me back to the vertiport where I'd parked the rover. Might be something he'd find interesting.

It was just interesting enough that he agreed to give Ng's implant a techno once-over for me.

Two days later I had a secure message from Ishy (what we call the custom Dunnetix Superba SI that runs things in Ishernot); I needed to get back down there ASAP for a confab about the implant. Unfortunately, I couldn't get away on account of the annual Vertical Games; no extra-curricular activities for rangers when the calendar rolls around to the Vertical Games.

• • • • •

The Brazos Cliffs are about the only noteworthy scenery in the entire Reserve. The scarps rise about 3,000 feet above the Brazos River and have been a hot verticality spot for rock climbers since the 20th century. But back then, they were on private lands where trespassing was mightily frowned upon by the owners. When the Clans acquired the property, all that changed. In 2200 they put on the first Vertical Games. Big spectacle and enough of a media hit that they've been putting it on every summer since then.

Now a cynic might suspect a motivation beyond sheer public-spiritedness for the Vertical Games. Not saying I'm a cynic, but 2200 *did* happen to be the year that the Opus Refurburator Clinics were launched worldwide. And the list of folks invited to Vertical Games included several thousand rich centenarian-plus muckety-mucks: perfect refurb candidates. Naturally, since one of the Dunnetix SIs invented the refurb process the Clans get a piece of all the refurburator action. Not that I was even born in 2200, but I've been known to do a little workup on my employers-to-be, Dunnigans included. The biggest surprise in that little workup was learning that it all started way before 2200: 2178, to be exact, when their first SI invented their first appliance lifeform. Can you guess? I couldn't. But if you guessed

Puppy-Vac you'd be right. Launched the Dunn and Igan twins right into the economic stratosphere.

Nothing much about this year's Vertical Games to trigger my inner cynic this year. Well, maybe the Nike Hovershoe air-climbing demo was a little on the commercial side, but having the last day buzzed by Madonna 13 and the Bumbusker Bare Force, well that was a showstopper. Sure, the fetching Bumbusker ladies all wear transparent skinsuits, so they're not technically naked, but wow! My eyeballs won't forget that anytime soon.

25

Yeah, we rangers weren't supposed to be watching all the naked women cavorting in the sky while Her Luckiness did her singing thing, but not a one of us didn't do a little peeking. Trust me on that. Still, the whole gig is a four-day living security nightmare preceded by two months of maniacal prep which kept me from getting down to Ishernot again. But in a way, it's my kind of time: I live on coffee and spike during the entire event. Most of the time I couldn't sleep if I wanted to, partly on account of the recurring nightmare I'd acquired. Plus, I've become the Designated Worrier of the crew. My brain can't help itself. Not bragging, but I've stopped enough evil plots before they could hatch that my employers don't even call me paranoid any more. Or if they do, they use it as a synonym for something like Brilliant Anticipatory Realism ... which I take as a compliment.

Two days after the Vertical Games were history for another year, I got an invitation to a post-engagement party ... from none other than Maya Ng. That was when my placid ranger life started to go off the rails. I just didn't know it yet.

26

3

A COOL TRILLION

FOR ME, A PARTY is a lot like what I imagine an old-time colonoscopy would be like, only worse: just as uncomfortable, but way more public. This party promised to be off-the-scale un-fun: Maya Ng was getting married ... and to a woman named Sheila Vance. The invitation was one of those old-fashioned printed things, a white card with flowery engraved lettering that wasn't at all Maya-like. On the back was a note in Maya's tiny scribble: "You need to do this for me, One-Shoe. You won't be sorry. Love, your favorite chinkrican, M."

I read it twice; the second time, my normally immobile face erupted in a grin. Chinkrican. What kind of person jokes up their roots like that? That would be like me calling myself a navacelt. Or a mickajo. Never met anybody as totally irreverent as Maya. Yeah, the engagement announcement shriveled my cojones to the size of raisins, but given the history we had, how could I not go?

Dunnigan Reserve HQ is where rangers bunk if we don't have other living arrangements. Nice spot not far from where the Rio Brazos dumps into the Rio Chama. The HQ complex is near old Highway 84 and includes a faux rustic visitor center that almost nobody ever visits and a tidy little vertiport. The utility stuff like the motorpool, the shops and the private airfield are all hidden from the public areas by a dense stand of forest. The ranger HQ was where I was getting ready to go to Maya's party.

It was a Saturday night and most of the off-duty rangers were already in Chama doing off-duty ranger stuff. I've gone with them a few times, but it's not my thing. Max Dalt hadn't left yet ... and dressed like he was, he sure wasn't headed out bar-hopping in Chama. Our ranking honcho was standing next to me in the communal washroom, also getting ready for a party. Scuttlebutt said *his* party was with a bunch of regional hotshots up at North Castle on Dunnigans Wall.

"So, One-Shoe. Nice hat. And that silver hair clasp is ever so Injun. Never seen you go cowboy formal. What's the big occasion?" Dalt said it out of the side of his mouth while tweaking the angle of his green bow tie, even though it didn't need tweaking. He was dressed in formal Ranger Greens, a uniform that looked to me like a pastiche of military formal outfits from the last five centuries. Stiff and uncomfortable, but it communicated two concepts very effectively: "power" and "rank." Dalt loved wearing it.

"Party," I said.

Dalt nodded into the mirror and said, "Just wondering here, One-Shoe ... did you have to buy both boots?"

You want to guess how many times I've heard some variation of that jibe? My right leg is artificial from the hip down. Cycle accident when I was a big dumb daredevil teenager. When I was all doped up in the Ishernot medcenter, they gave me a choice of growing a new meat leg or splicing on a totally bionic leg. Bionic was faster and sounded cooler. Decision made.

The model I picked has no need for shoes: my right foot has all-climate, self-replacing pads on the highly articulated foot, kind of like on canine or feline feet, but better. Included some serious retractable claws, too. Great all-weather grip and incredibly tough: totally state of the art at the time. Plus, the leg's joint system lets me do stuff I'm not supposed to talk about. Works better than my left, actually.

Naturally, Dalt knew my whole story; he was just fucking with me. Dalt was a runner, a marathon sort of runner. In my experience, assholes who also happen to be long distance runners turn into super-assholes with a built-in superiority complex over anybody who's a non-runner, gimps like me in particular.

"Shit, Max. You ruined my surprise. The extra boot was going to be a birthday present for your nose."

"Very funny, One-Shoe. Wait'll you see your duty sheet for next week." Dalt is sensitive about his schnozz, which I've heard other rangers refer to as a potato stuck onto an axe head. His neck got a little red and I sensed we might get into it a little deeper tonight. But just then his pilot walked into the washroom and cleared his throat.

Actually, I was kind of envious. Dalt was getting flown up to North Castle in one of the Clans' brand new hoverbar powered Sumiyo-Brandé limos. Genuine antigrav — finally — just like in science fiction. Only titans of industry had been able to license the tech yet. Besides WorldGov, of course. Ishernauts had been crying foul so far, but I knew that if they couldn't get their hands on it they'd create their own. I wasn't sure what PU the tech came from and I didn't really care, either. But it was cool. And it got me wondering if I should start wondering again about the little clearing that my noze tracked the dead Mr Ng back to. Later, maybe.

I'd seen the pilot a couple times but never up close. At the Vertical Games, he's the guy responsible for keeping the Clans' rich and famous guests alive ... and he's been a decorated hero more than once. Among the ordinary class of ranger that I worked with, Duckworth Seupetto was a legend: kind of a super ranger. He'd been my level of ranger once, but now he headed up the equivalent of the Clans Dunnigan secret service. Up close, he was even bigger than his reputation. And me. Probably 6'-6" and 250 solid pounds, but moved like a dancer. Rumor was he didn't have much sense of humor ... not somebody you'd want to kid around with, like calling him Duck Soup to his face or anything like that. Rumor also said he'd been a cage fighter somewhere in CenAm before his Ranger days. Had to wonder why a hotshot like that would be schlepping around a yo-yo like Dalt. Orders, probably.

Seupetto ignored Dalt, looked me over and winked, a wink I barely saw on account of his really deep-set eyes that looked like they were little black cave mouths hiding under a rock overhang. But I winked back. Then he made a sort of imperious "come with me" gesture to Dalt, who walked out after him without a word. Just as well.

I walked over to the motorpool, checked out a green rover and let it drive me twelve miles west to the place on Heron Lake where the party was happening. Nice place on a wooded knoll overlooking the lake: a rich folks place.

The event was already in full swing by the time I arrived. I was ushered in by a tall man in some kind of formal uniform that I guessed made him part of the catering crew. Bad guess. He introduced himself as Morton Vance, father of Sheila, the other fiancée.

Mr Vance and I spent a few seconds sizing each other up. I said something small-talkish about what a nice place he had here and he responded with an it's-really-nothing wave of the hand and words to the effect that he was finding it a nice little getaway spot for escaping the hustle and bustle of the *continent*, a word he spoke in the audible equivalent of italics.

I opened my mouth to ask which continent exactly, then remembered it was what hotshot worldly types call the Eurostates.

My mouth was still hanging open when a sleek and strikingly glamorous young woman saved me.

"Oh, Daddy! You got to meet Maya's friend Travis before I did! Isn't he handsome? Did you know he saved Maya's life from crazed soul-trainers down in Nirvanata? Oh, Daddy, so many people are dying to meet him. Would you hate me terribly if I stole him away from you?"

Sheila was my savior's name: Maya's betrothed. She didn't wait for permission. She just took my hand and dragged me away into the crowd, aiming her huge flashy smile left and right, saying how great it was to see this person or that, all the while bulldozing her way out to a broad deck overlooking the lake. Then it was down a broad set of flagstone stairs to an intimate garden lit with strings of tiny glittering lights. Sheila stopped at a low wall. A slim, compact woman with short black hair sat in the shadows, her legs dangling over the edge of the wall, her back to us.

"I brought him, lover. Saved him from Daddy while I was at it. He owes me more than he knows." Then she flashed me her dazzling smile, planted a big wet kiss on my lips and sashayed back up to the action.

From the top of the stairs she shouted, "I'll see you later, big boy. Nice lips. He's all yours now, lover!"

"Fuckashitpiss, Mayarino! That's really your fiancée? Whew!"

"Nice to see you too, One-Shoe. Sheila's an actor. A real one: retro Broadway stage plays, that kind of thing. Dunno how she pulls it off. But we can talk about her later. Right now I desperately need to jawbone something with my favorite security gimp ... the one with the highly advanced worrying skills."

She must have read my awkward expression. "No need to say it, One-Shoe. I know you know that Henry Ng was my brother. So before you sputter around trying to express your condolences about his untimely death in your stomping grounds, you need to know that I hated the fucker. As in maximum detestation. Death by snakebite is too good for him. Maybe someday I'll tell you why. I'll probably never get over it, it's that ugly. And I don't wanna ruin an otherwise festive occasion."

She stopped, gave me one of her intense stares and then launched her wiry body at me. "Great to see you again, One-Shoe. Been way too long. You're looking reasonably good for a hero your age, but my crystal ball is telling me your time as a recluse forest ranger for the richest tech tribe on the planet may have about run its course."

She went intense on me again and dropped her voice to a whisper. "How would you like to score an astronomical payoff with virtually no risk? And it might not even be illegal."

"Score" has always been one of those words that makes me instantly nervous. I was currently an officer of the law, after all ... or at least an officer of the rules. And there ain't no such animal as "no risk." But I let her give me her pitch anyway. It was the least I could do for an old friend.

The pitch was a good one ... and right up my alley. Almost too literally. There was even a remote possibility it could succeed. Maya had even figured a safe place we could all gate to afterwards ... assuming I could manage to deal with my personal fear of having every atom in my body disassembled and reassembled by Nevergates that might be universes away from each other. And now she had the connections to make it happen: a mysterious somebody at Hildi's Palace who knew how to hook up with the renegade All Caribbean Freeboy Nevergate. The only hitch was that we'd need another accomplice. Somebody in the same profession as her dead brother. Big hitch in my book.

4
HELP WANTED

TWO DAYS AFTER her party, Maya, Sheila and I started doing some serious homework on St Coriander. I guess that means I'd accepted their offer to go after that crazy no-risk score. My worrier self knew it was doomed, but it seemed so clean and straightforward I let myself get suckered into it. I attribute it to the persuasive power of two smart, sexy women. That and the aesthetic appeal of having all-hours work sessions overlooking a lake instead of overlooking my fellow rangers in the bunkhouse or even reading in the library. And would you believe that my nightmares went away about then. Coincidence? What else could it be?

The winter of 2219 was bad up here in the high country, maybe even worse than it was in Ishernot, which is only about fifty crow miles due south of here and about the same elevation. Lucky for me I was in neither place at the time: I was doing security for the Royal Argent Nevergate down in Belize that winter. Tropical paradise, except for all the scumbuckets that hung out there.

That winter was not so lucky for St Coriander: that was the winter their lights went out. After almost sixty years of isolated, self-sufficient bliss, the place went dark. According to casual ranger scuttlebutt, not even the Dunnigans know exactly when, which is pretty amazing when you know that the Clans' World HQ is in one of the two faux-medieval castles bracketing that the huge dam they call Dunnigans Wall ... and that the whole complex is only a handful of crow miles from St Coriander. Then you add in the fact that the Dunnigans are pretty anal about knowing exactly everything around here. Based on all of that, my inner cynic was telling me that Ranger scuttlebutt might be wrong ... on purpose.

The Clans monitor all air traffic in the region and at some point somebody must have realized that there hadn't been any traffic in or out of the St Coriander vertiport for nearly two years. That's how I heard it, at least. But still nobody did anything. There's almost never any vertiport traffic in St Coriander anyway; the place was as self-sufficient as money could buy. And there was a long history of bad blood between the folk of St Coriander and the Clans, so the Dunnigans never even dropped a moller down to scout around. But, the Dunnetix Apex 3 SI that runs North Castle evidently made contact with St Coriander's ThoughtDancer Excel early on and was assured that nothing unplanned had occurred: the populace had just decided, en masse, to Elevate.

When I joined the rangers five years ago, nobody had been in or out of St Coriander in 21 years. If the Clans didn't care, why should their rangers care? After all, from a ranger's perspective it's just one small piece of geography in the Reserve: a tiny part of what we had to patrol. Nobody was very curious about what was behind all that nasty, overgrown thornmesh and the imposing black smartgate. And nobody included me: other than occasionally doing hometown smalltalk with the lonely gate SI, I just went about my patrols. Period.

Now that I had a reason to think about it, something didn't smell quite right about this. But I wasn't really in a position to dig into it at HQ without drawing attention to my previously incurious self. Fortunately, I didn't need to, thanks to Shiela.

What I didn't know anything about was what life had been like in St Coriander, but Sheila did. Sounded pretty boring, mostly, except for one very weird thing. Turned out people in St Coriander had a tradition of suicide, which they called Elevation. It was a built-in part of their culture and this is how it worked. When a resident reached the age of 48, they were supposed to "Elevate" themselves to a "higher plane" where they would live on in some more evolutionarily advanced form.

To make it work, the scientist who founded the town had developed a piece of proprietary tech called a psyfrac. One minute they would be standing on something called an Elevation Stage, the next minute ... poof, they're somewhere else. Kind of like being gated somewhere, except you don't know where and it's a one way trip. Yeah, a lot of bad old vids used ideas like that, but evidently this was for real.

Maya assigned me a book to read: *Lotto Loonies*. This explained how St Coriander became a hideaway for lottery winners "suffering" from something called Paraspiritual Wealth Trauma. So these poor abused big money winners come to this little hidey-hole outside of Nowhereville. Naturally they bring all their winnings along with them. Doesn't take a math genius to figure that the original 2,000+ lottery winners with an average of even a paltry 100 million teros in net winnings each adds up to a town with a lot of assets, assets that have been growing for at least half a century. According to the figures in *Lotto Loonies*, it's a huge fortune. And there's no place to spend much of it there. And no trips to the Riviera or Blisstown or Hildi's Palace for Cories; once you're in, you're in. Period. Cloistered, they call it. A bit more extreme than most IsoTowns, but that was part of the deal they all signed.

So you've got all these winners living like retired moguls up here. Where does their money go? Turns out it's in trust with the Holy Quincunx Church that runs this place. Or ran it.

I know you think I'm making this up. But, I'm actually being conservative. Even if they ultimately spent billions building this place with it's five transpaque obelisks that make up the Holy Quincunx, plus all the latest ucey and fabrax gear, there's an access key to probably way more than 100 billion teros stashed in there someplace. Sheila figures it at a cool trillion, give or take.

Here's where I've got to confess that a vast amount of teros doesn't mean that much to me. It's not why I signed up for this ca-

35

per. I signed on because of Maya: simple as that. Will I ever learn? Probably not.

End of confession, back to homework.

The Clans own the skies around here, but even they can't scout the place from above; St Coriander's haze generators — an accessory to their weatherfield — are still working just fine ... not even a flicker in more than two decades. Totally opaque to sensors from outside ... and flying into it might get you shredded if the rumor about armed micro-drones is true.

On the ground, the ten-mile thornmesh perimeter is only the first obstacle ... but it's a good one. It's like a hedge of high voltage poison-tipped razorwire, except it's biological. Even the electrical part: similar current generating scheme as electric eels. Here, the thornmesh has grown to thirty feet tall and about fifty feet thick in most places, but the thing is, there are all these one-way escape mazes grown into it for safety reasons, like in case of fire. No problemo, says Maya. She says she's pretty sure she can find a safe way through the godawful shit and I believe her. But I want to check it out with my own eyes.

But even so, that's only the first hurdle. Manage to make it inside, you're blasted into a cloud of messy molecules in ten minutes or less; the place is a landmine. Literally. In security circles you meet guys that know details like that because somebody had to install all that illegal ordnance. If you're not born in St Coriander or don't get a guest genebox, you're smithereens. All St Cories are born with some kind of cellular trace that protects them. You don't have it and I don't either, which is just one reason we needed a particular kind of fourth wheel for this mission.

After two more weeks of spare time planning sessions, Maya, Sheila and I had whipped up what seemed like a foolproof plan for the mission. Sheila surprised me more than twice; I had no idea that actor types could be both that smart and that devious. And for someone her age, she was very wise in the ways of the world. But I liked her spark, which was very Maya-like in some ways: I had to admit that Maya had picked a good one. Plus, her rich daddy had given her a generous allowance.

The problem with any plan is that it's only a plan; the old map-is-not-the-territory thing. At its current stage, our plan had too many what-ifs, holes you could drive a bus through. I argued for a simple scouting mission with just me and Maya checking out the lay of the land. The big hole in that idea is that none of the three of us could connect with the alien SI inside that probably still had control of whatever was functioning inside St Coriander's fence. So we'd gone about as far as we could go without a fourth wheel in the fold.

What seemed to make the most sense now was for Maya and Sheila to focus on the search for an SI mechanic with the right stuff for this mission. My part was to do as much worrying as possible about what could go wrong and what would help the mission from a technical and tactical perspective.

Thanks to a timely Ranger security assessment assignment in the vicinity of St Coriander, I got paid to worry about potential trespassers into the Reserve during the upcoming Huzbol marathon. When I was done with that, I figured I'd learned about as much as I could about getting inside the fence without more intel or actually doing it. I also got to think about what gadgets might help the actual mission, which was when I decided the time was right for a late summer shopping trip to my hometown.

5

DEAR DOCTOR FREUD

THIS TIME I WENT HOME by the slow route: regional bus from Chama to Española, then wait for the local to Los Alamos where I'd call for the Ishernot shuttle. It was a Wednesday.

On this particular Wednesday, Española looked shabbier than usual. Maybe there was a shabbification virus going around, because the bus had looked shabbier than usual, too. And it shook like it had a case of moller-palsy when it lifted off after every stop; you wouldn't want to have loose teeth when it was shaking like that. That was one surprise. Another was the pair of WorldGov's Finest who were eyeballing everybody getting on or off the bus. Made me kind of glad to be wearing my usual Dunnigan Ranger patrol uni. I stepped down, we nodded to each other, and that was that. Since I'd never seen Securitans in the vicinity before, I knew there was a story here that had snuck up on me when I was otherwise occupied. So while I waited for the Los Alamos local, I went to next door to Poquito Menos, a tiny café that's about the only place I've ever been in Española.

Tiny's coffee was muddier than I remembered but I felt obliged to drink a cup since it came with the latest issue of *Tiny's Rag*, the best source of unfiltered dirt and rabble-rousery in the whole county. Today's big news was the local outrage after the latest round of layoffs up at Los Alamos Research Center. Evidently Gov had "suspended" funding to yet another program, the third major cut in the last two years. No wonder there was shabbiness in the air: Los Alamos was where the jobs were, worthwhile and otherwise. Been that way for centuries. Made me think about the wisdom of planning to give up my ranger job with the Clans for a wild goose chase that would probably leave me unemployed ... at best.

I wondered about that during the ten-minute local bus ride to the Ishernot shuttle stop in Los Alamos at the old MedCenter. I got out to be greeted this time by a contingent of four Securitans, who wanted ID from all three of us who got off the bus, including me. The one checking IDs paid particular attention to mine, holding it up to catch sunlight at various angles, then squinting at the holocard, then at me and back to the holocard. He finally handed it back to me without a word. Asshole.

But I just kept my mouth shut and walked toward the bench at the Ishernot shuttle stop about fifty feet away. When I sat down I decided to amuse myself by trying to mimic the ID checker's Arrogant Dickhead body language. I thought I did a pretty good job of it ... and so did the guy in the gray business suit sitting next to me, who showed his appreciation by nudging me with his elbow and winking. I might have tried to outdo myself, but then the shuttle arrived for our short hop into the caldera. I was still on the steps when the pilot handed me a slate. "Let me guess," she said, looking first at my ranger uni and second at my shoeless robotic foot, which is all most people get to see of my leg. "You're Travis One-Shoe."

I smiled, nodded and made a gesture that would have been a tip of the hat if I'd been wearing one. "You have an appointment with our esteemed synthetic busybody, Mr One-Shoe. Details on the slate."

● ● ● ● ●

When your hometown is a dormant supervolcano you develop a healthy respect for uncertainty. Sure the volcano somewhere under the Valles Caldera hasn't gone off in a mere 1.25 million years, and you have to look real close to see evidence of its cataclysmic origins. But volcanoes have minds of their own. And so does the SI that supports this little town of cutting edge weapons makers.

Ishy's spacious digs are located an unknown number of feet below the surface in a place that could easily be called a hardened bunker. At least that's what I've heard. You'd never know it to look at it, though. To me, it's always seemed like a comfortable office type environment with only a dozen or so permanent staffers walking here and there.

One of the nods to office convention was having a desk for a receptionist in the elevator lobby. Usually, the only time there's a receptionist behind the desk is during a conference, in which case an advanced student at the Ishernot Thinkworks would be shanghaied for the job. To most of the outside world the place is the Institute for Defensive Studies ... except for our naysayers and detractors who call it the Death Factory. Thinkworks students generally detest receptionist duty, but they do it.

That day Ishy's receptionist was Sigmund Freud, which meant the human receptionist — if there was one today — was probably on a bathroom break. You've gotta appreciate an SI with a sense of humor.

"You're looking well for your age, Dr Freud," I said. A smallish semi-bald guy with stern black framed round eyeglasses, the life-size Freud Semblance was sitting on the corner of the desk with an unlit cigar in his right hand.

"Thank you, Travis," said Ishy-as-Freud. "It speaks well of your Ishernot education that you recognize the Semblance of a somewhat famous Austrian born back in 1856. One, you may recall, whose theories have been obsolete for centuries."

"So why ... "

"Why have I adopted this Semblance for our visit today? As you shall see, it has a somewhat facetious bearing on at least one of the topics we need to discuss. So if you will be so good as to join me in my study, we can get started."

With that, Dr Freud stood up and walked right through one of the two solid oak doors into Ishy's inner sanctum. Amazing how Semblances can do shit like that; I had to open it first.

• • • • •

"How much do you know about imported SIs, Travis? Specifical-ly, the ThoughtDancer line imported from Miotx 4 in PU 918?" Ishy had decided to stay in character and now stood in front of a wall of books.

"I know they exist. That about covers it." I'd dropped into a leather armchair and made myself comfortable. Ishy was going to drop some-thing on me so I might as well be comfortable while I'm hearing it.

"Henry Ng, the dead man you found, was an expert in working therapeutically with ThoughtDancers. The implant you left with Tommy Whiterock was designed specifically for communicating with the ThoughtDancer cognissery. In itself, this is not surprising. What surprised our best techs in this area — once they had disarmed it — were the nonstandard software elements that appear to be de-signed for surreptitious information extraction. This sort of viola-tion of 'doctor-patient' confidentiality would be an ethical violation of the highest order and any so-called SI mechanic convicted of such a violation would face not only a license revocation but also a prison sentence of up to 50 years.

"Were you aware that St Coriander had a late model Thought Dancer Excel managing its various systems, much as I do here in Ishernot? Well it is still there, even though the population of St Co-riander disappeared a quarter century ago. The implant you brought back contained a call for help: a plea to be rescued."

Dr Freud was now frowning at me, his hands tented under his chin. I didn't like that look.

"The Council has discussed various implications of this situation. On the one hand, Ishernot could benefit from the special talents of a ThoughtDancer Excel; something about their alien structure makes them unusually creative. Unfortunately, rescuing this trapped SI is highly problematic for all the reasons you can imagine. And then some. However ...."

The mushroom cloud moment hit me right then, blasting the scales from my eyes and flooding my brain with realizations. There have been rare times in my life when the mish-mash of random information and experiences and suspicions wandering around in my head all come together. This was one of those.

"They're in my state-of-the-art leg, aren't they? The spy gadgets that weren't part of the cool description I read, right? And I'll bet the fine print I signed while I was in a haze in the operating room that day gave you legal permission to monitor me. Probably forever. So I'll bet you've heard every word I've said or heard since the day I got the leg."

43

Dr Freud looked like he was about to say something, so I held up my hand.

"So the upshot is, the Council wants me to add rescuing an SI to the list of shit my team has to accomplish when we go on our little picnic in a certain defunct IsoTown in the vicinity. Oh, and I'll bet you want our relationship to be invisible, off the books, mum's the word. That pretty much cover it?"

Dr Freud nodded.

"And naturally you're prepared to offer me a huge bonus for pulling this off ... invisible and off-the-books, right?"

Dr Freud made a fatherly nod, as if he was proud of me for finally figuring this all out. But the only thing he said was this casual, offhand warning. "The Council suggests enhanced wariness going forward. Specifically, that you start paying surreptitious attention to the people you encounter. The man in the gray suit who sat next to you on the Ishernot shuttle bench had been waiting there for an hour. And he gave you a little gift that we neutralized for you while you were still on the shuttle. Word to the wise."

• • • • •

I was still smarting from my embarrassing encounter with Ishy, but at least I hadn't spotted any obvious surveillance on my way back from my hometown foray. Right or wrong, I decided to keep that incident to myself, along with several other factoids of an even more personal nature. One factoid I *did* trouble to mention was my visit to what we Ishernauts call the "kidrium" where I'd spent whatever early formative years I can remember. More conventional towns might call it an orphanage. I didn't learn until much later that Ishernot's Institute for Child Development isn't just some guilt-soothing charitable stewpot for abandoned kids from the territory ... which is all I'm going to say about it. Except that I spent half a day there, goofing with kids, telling them wild stories and letting them know that someday they'd really appreciate their time in the kidrium. Just like me.

While I was away, Maya and Sheila had narrowed the search for our fourth wheel to three candidates. I looked over the profiles and knew right away that only one of them had even a ghost of a chance working on the kind of caper we were planning. And I wasn't even too sure about that guy. A gut thing that I couldn't explain. And Maya was even less sure about him than I was. But it seemed like it was either him or nobody; if he didn't cut it we'd have to call off the mission and go back to what we were doing before this gig got going.

None of us were ready for that, so we decided to check him out in person, right in Chama. ASAP. No harm in that, right? He'd have a little personal meeting with Maya ... and I would be surreptitiously watching him ... and everybody else, of course. If this guy passed muster with her, the mission was on. Naturally, I worried about everything.

6

FLY SHIT ON THE WALL

THE BIG YELLOW BUS lifted off the pad and slid south in a cloud of rusty late summer dust. Blocky, soulless black lettering on the side said, "Soul Bus." Go figure. From the passenger shelter a few women still waved to the departing or dabbed their eyes. None of the men waved; they just stood there, stolid and dour, baking in the sun. I wondered if any of them were thinking they should've gone, too. My bet was that some of them would be on the next free bus to Nirvana-ta. Or if not, the one after that. Same thing was happening all over the world. Planet Earth was shrinking, one bus load of freepassers at a time. Gov and the titans of industry were fond of likening the process to parasites eating their host from the inside. From where I stood, though, it seemed more like fleas leaping off a drowning rabid dog. History will probably say we all had the wrong metaphor.

A single incoming passenger had gotten off; the exact passenger I was looking for. She'd boarded the bus at Pagosa Springs, the only stop between Durango and Chama. Her code gesture told me no tail spotted, human or electronic. And I know she knows her shit. So far, so good: but I still worried, which was not how people usually spend the first day of their annual vacation. And now in addition to the usual worries, I had to suspect everybody on the planet of wanting to monitor my movements.

I watched her from a nearby shadow in the doorway of the tiny terminal shack as she walked to the baggage rack. She didn't look around, just thumbed one of the rectangular cases on the rack, whispered something to it, then walked toward the road in front of the old trailer that passed for office and ticket booth for the Nirvanata shuttle. The rectangle walked along after her, its camo legs almost invisible.

An old guy with a wide-brimmed straw hat fanned himself in the driver's seat of a mule-drawn open cab that had once been a pickup truck. Both the hat and the cab had seen way better days. The guy waved at the woman. She nodded, said a few words, he nodded. His lucky day. Then she and her case climbed up to the passenger bench and the mule started walking, no hurry to get anywhere. It's one of the things I like about mules. But there's not much of anywhere to go in Chama, a reality that pretty much describes any other town between here and Santa Fe. Usually there's a place or two in each town that I'd spend more than ten minutes in. The place she was headed was one of these.

I left my shadow, hiked down to the tracks where the Cumbres & Toltec stores its inventory of antique rolling stock, and made my way up toward where I'd be doing my eavesdropping.

Most of the Chama businesses still operating are located on the highway that runs north-south along the eastern edge of town. The Triple Boxcar is one of these. I eat there a lot on weekends, but today I was just spying on the place.

At this time on a weekday it's cool, dark and almost empty inside. Good time and place for a meeting, if you don't mind the floor. The old railroad ties it was made from have left a permanent creosote stench inside the place. But most of the time the aromas of spicy food, ale and sweat are enough to overpower the lingering esters of wood preservative.

My stomach gurgled and I started salivating thinking about a plate of chipotle enchiladas with a mound of melted Red Man Ewe sheep cheese, chopped onions and a pitcher of local Firebox ale. But that would have to wait.

My cover was wandering around the ancient railroad miscellany that's the outdoor museum separating the station from the yard. I squinted and frowned at the explanatory signs just like any other tourist over the last couple centuries. And I watched other tourists like any other tourist. I was even wearing dark glasses and a well-worn straw cowboy hat, just like most of the male tourists ("pre-venerated" straw cowboy hats are a popular souvenir item at the Durango, Pagosa Springs and Chama stations). But now it was time to go to work and do my job as meeting observer. So I tapped my glasses, got a visual and started to eavesdrop on the Triple Boxcar.

47

My view of the scene was courtesy of the flea I'd attached to a weathered timber post earlier in the day. It didn't really look like a flea: that's just what they're called in the trade on account of their jumping ability.

If you didn't know what you were looking at, this flea would look like a speck of fly shit stuck to the edge of a thumbtack that's holding up an innocent job posting for a junior assistant kitchen helper.

Maya entered my field of view and walked to a booth in the far corner. She nodded to the current occupant and sat down on a padded bench with taped up red upholstery. Across from her sat a man with a tidy, bland face and a pale complexion. His soft-looking hands were gripping a frosty glass of horse piss, poured from the longneck bottle in front of him.

He'd arrived in Chama yesterday afternoon on the old Cumbres & Toltec steam narrowgauge looking like every other tourist making the scenic run down from Antonito. Even wore a well-worn straw cowboy hat. Except he didn't take the same day return trip back like most of them. Last night he stayed in the Firebox Inn and Pub, just like he was supposed to do. So far, so good. All night my fleas watched over him. As far as they could tell, he just slept. Tossed and turned a lot, but that wouldn't be unexpected. Something would have been wrong if he wasn't at least a little anxious about becoming involved in our short-notice hush-hush enterprise.

That hadn't kept me from worrying. I knew he had to have an implant to be able to link with the SI. Did he have other implants we didn't know about? I didn't have access to the gear and the bugs that could tell us. So part of my job was to watch his reactions to Maya's "job interview."

Mr Bland and Tidy signaled the top-heavy waitress with the yellow curls mounded on her head and said something. He seemed more impressed with the curls than the cleavage and I wondered if he knew Blanca wore a wig. Blanca suffers from some rare form of alopecia, so her eyebrows are fake, too.

Blanca signaled to the barkeep, sashayed over to pick up the order, sashayed back with a loaded tray and plunked down a schooner of draft and a bowl of popcorn. No woman in Chama can sashay like Blanca.

Maya gave Mr Bland and Tidy a nod and one of her patented hardass stares, then downed half the brew in one long swig. Then she leaned forward and said something. The guy nodded, said something back. Maya downed the rest of her beer and plunked the empty glass on the table with a resounding clunk. My sensors under the table could spot any electronic anomalies and we wanted to see if an acoustic spike would trigger transmission of a signal on a channel I could track, but if the guy was being monitored by some other agency, my sensors didn't register it. Didn't mean somebody else wasn't using better tech or was smarter than we were. Or whatever. So I worried.

In addition to the hat, Mr Bland and Tidy was wearing the sort of clothes tourists wear around here when they're trying not to look like tourists. Wouldn't fool a single local. Even yokels could tell he was an office kind of guy from a big city. And that he was nervous about it.

I watched him for tells and odd body language while he and Maya did the dance of checking each other out. They both looked uncomfortable now. That's good. Nobody should ever be comfortable about trespassing in the Dunnigan Reserve, much less trying to break into the mysterious empty IsoTown of St Coriander looking for treasure.

Of course, a lot of Maya's apparent edginess was an act, part of our scheme for vetting this guy.

The dance went on. After a few minutes Blanca sashayed back to the table and got two head shakes in response to her question. So I figured their session was almost over.

But I was getting a little nervous waiting for my signal. If Maya decided Bland and Tidy knew his SI stuff and had enough of the right vibe for a risky gig, she'd shake her head, shrug her shoulders, toss some counters on the table and walk out the door. If he's not right, she'll lean over and plant one on his lips. A big juicy one. Then they'll walk out together and head toward the Cumbres & Toltec station. If it goes that way, I'd be surprised: Bland and Tidy was looking solid enough to my eyes and my sensors so far.

Not easy finding SI mechanics that are willing to take a risk. And why should they? Most people don't know it but it takes the equivalent of three PhDs to become a competent SI mechanic and there are probably only a couple thousand on the planet. Plus, you've gotta get special wiring. Expensive.

Actually, according to Ishy there were exactly 2,214 people in his field on the planet at that moment: there were a lot more that have gated to planets like Onedinket or Nondescripto in some bumfuck parallax universe. The bumfuck PUs were where the big money was: keeping the planetbrains from going crazy managing terraforming ops, monitoring literally everything, negotiating with aliens. Shit like that.

But this guy was a gatephobe: totally unwilling to have himself torn apart and reassembled somewhere else by a Nevergate. Same as me. And he was a specialist in ThoughtDancers, the brand of alien SI that's been keeping St Coriander in holdstate after the residents suddenly disappeared. So he doesn't really have that many job options on this planet dominated by homegrown Dunnetix SIs.

While I was thinking all this I was crossing my fingers and wishing I were more of a what-me-worry kind of guy. I was also trying to look like a semi-bored tourist walking around the old railroad junk while letting my hatband surveil the neighborhood for out-of-place movement, suspicious characters and all the other usual bugaboos I've loaded into my brain over the years. It's always tough for me to be in three places at once ... and that's even though I've had a lot of practice. In the railroad yard museum, I was looking at a pier made of steel axles and wheels stacked in crib fashion. The sign said they were rare 3-foot narrow gauge units from the mid-20th century. I'd started to wonder what other gauges were still in use when movement in my sunglasses switched me back to the booth in the corner of the murky Triple Boxcar.

Maya slid out, leaned toward the guy's face, lips puckered. Shit! Then she snarled, gave her head a vigorous shake and knocked Bland and Tidy's still unfinished glass of horse piss into his lap. On purpose. Like the guy just propositioned her and she turned him down. She stood there staring at him and then stalked off in a huff. That whole little act was Sheila's idea to throw off anybody who might have gotten wind that we were up to something. I thought it was a little cloak-and-dagger-ish, but I got outvoted.

I grinned in spite of myself and hoped nobody was wondering what I thought was funny about a stack of rusting iron. Maya was fucking with me, but in a good way. In her eyes, the expedition — at least the recon phase — was a go. I hoped he was the kind of guy with enough of a sense of humor to think a lap load of lousy beer is a small price to pay for a shot at a planet-sized jackpot.

7

TRUST ME, TRAVIS

ON THE THIRD DAY of my vacation, I kicked off our recon mission by getting shitfaced ... for a good cause: flagrant duplicity.

I'd ridden an ancient stolen bicycle down from the north to the Broken Arrow, just beyond the south end of Chama. It's a shabby watering hole mostly patronized by tribal losers; I fit right in. Sheila had designed my costume, instructed me on posture and demeanor and done my makeup, including a very impressive scar and an even more impressive nose. I even wore a well-stuffed right boot for the occasion.

I carried on as loudly and offensively as I could manage about leaving for Nirvanata on the next bus. When I'd downed enough 'Apache sodapop' to be sidewalk lickin' drunk, I announced my intention to piss and wandered outside.

An ancient woman in an equally ancient electric pickup truck happened by and stopped just as I was about to relieve myself on the curb. She looked like a neotrad Jicarilla Apache elder, which was no surprise. Lots of old neotrad women play bingo every night in town. More bingo ladies than usual tonight with the High Country Huzbol starting tomorrow. We exchanged words through the open window, I got in, slumped onto the dashboard in a sodden stupor and the pickup bounced away.

The truck rattled down the road and I kept up my drunk act. Of course I secretly worried that maybe she was driving a little too fast or too slow and whether she'd get the pickup stashed in the right place later tonight and that she would get down to Santa Fe before sunrise as planned. In other words, my inner worrier was functioning normally.

We rattled past Monument Circle, which would usually look lonely and empty ... but not so lonely tonight with all the banners and hoopla going on. Tomorrow, something like a thousand insane entrants and maybe five thousand live spectators would start the two-day High Country Huzbol Double Marathon from here. Fifty-two miles along the Old 64, hitting 10,000 feet elevation at its highest point and ending in Tres Piedras, a little desert hamlet on the other side of the Tusas. Hardcore distance runners from all over the planet come out here every October just for the challenge of it. Some years the challenge includes frigid temperatures and snow. They got lucky this year; forecast is sun and temps in the fifties.

Have I mentioned that stuff like the Huzbol makes no sense to me? Actually, running for any reason makes no sense to me ... except if something nasty is chasing you. In that nightmare I still have off and on, I run like the wind. But I figured it would be a perfect time to practice our trespassing without attracting much notice.

I was still thinking about marathons when the old truck pulled off the road. The driver said nothing, just opened her door, crawled out and squatted in front of the left front wheel.

She'd parked next to a copse of thick shrubs and old oaks. Ahead was a bridge over a wash. It was the right spot, so I lurched out of the vehicle and staggered a dozen paces back, waving my flashlight like I was looking for a really special place to take a piss. What I found was a nice little path into the underbrush. While I was doing this, two shadows wriggled out from under a tarp in the bed, slid over the busted tailgate and crept into the bushes.

The old woman reentered the pickup and started off again. By the time her taillights were out of sight the three of us were already down the embankment. Under the bridge we shouldered the heavy packs we'd previously hidden under stealthfiber, donned our own stealthfiber cloaks, powered up and headed into the Dunnigan Reserve.

The first half of our route was along the ancient La Cañada Ditch, an irrigation channel built more than 400 years ago. When the Clans Dunnigan bought up all the land for the Dunnigan Reserve back in the '80s, they made a commitment to maintain in perpetuity all the old irrigation channels that routed water from the Tusas to the farms and ranches to the west. Fact is, they improved 'em, which ultimately made the various Chama ditch water associations happy.

What made us happy was the trail along the south edge of our ditch. It was smooth, flat and the only occupants were us. But it didn't take us long to work up a sweat even in the evening chill; we were loaded with gear and stealthfiber's heavier than most people think. And it doesn't breathe for shit, either.

By the time we had to leave the ditch trail and strike out along an abandoned dirt track for the second leg of our late night hike, Mr Bland and Tidy — aka Roston from Boston — was huffing and puffing and wanting to stop and rest every three minutes. I said no.

Before the Dunnigan Reserve was developed, our new route had been a cheerless dirt track infested with potholes and tangled underbrush crowding in from the edges. Only thing different now was that the potholes were bigger and the brush a little lusher. Clouds had rolled in to cover the nearly full moon, so I gave the signal to stop; time for night glasses and Roston's first rest. He got another rest five minutes later, thanks to me spraining my meat ankle in a pothole. Not only did it hurt, it was embarrassing. While I wrapped it, Maya went off in search of something I could use as a walking stick. Roston and I waited about ten minutes before she returned with just the right item. She's a gem, that Maya.

Even with my hobbling gait, we made it to the vicinity of the Township Fence only about two hours behind schedule, but it was a loose schedule, so no matter. It was a little after one. We made camp in a sheltered spot I'd picked out a week ago. It was on the lee side of the steep, rocky knob just west of the gate and far enough back from the perimeter road to keep us insulated from casual observers. While

Maya was setting up to do her investigation of the fence, Roston from Boston was trying to get remote readings on the state of the Thought-Dancer. We were going to be up for a while, so I whipped up a little snack and some cannonberry tea with a shot of spike: guaranteed to dissolve cobwebs. We could sleep tomorrow after we had some live data from our recon mission. Then we could plan the 'real' raid.

Maya had already prepped a pair of roaches and set them heading in opposite directions to map the fence and find the escape mazes. At about a mile per hour, she could be stuck here for as long as five or six hours just mapping the perimeter. Yeah, we could get lucky and locate a maze right in front of our little hideaway. But the plan was to locate each of the mazes; we wanted a choice of entry and exit points so we could pick the best route to the part of St Coriander where the Holy Quincunx Plaza is located.

The best route mattered. And it's not like we have a tight schedule, anyway. Normally, rangers only physically visit the place every couple days and they mostly focus on the areas near the Old Highway 64 road beyond the extreme southwest part of the perimeter. For the next couple days, they'd be busy keeping marathoners and sightseers on the designated road. Same with their drones. Way I figured it, we'd have the place to ourselves.

We had a powwow before I hobbled out on recon duty. Roston was already getting cogtraces from the SI in there, so it clearly wasn't dead. He said his readings were strange, even for a ThoughtDancer. I wasn't worried, though: he'd trained with people from Miotx 4 in PU 918 where ThoughtDancers are from, so if anybody oughta to have an inside track on dealing with their quirks, it should be Roston.

"There is an uncharacteristic patina of negative emotion," he announced, warming to his subject. "In human parlance, we might use words like guilt or paranoia." It seemed to me his proper Bostonian accent was a little thicker than usual.

"However, we should be cautious with anthropomorphic interpretations; it is far too early for me to be able to characterize such subjective qualities in an intelligence of this nature. Still, some manifestations of its persona seem somewhat suppressed ... perhaps even atrophied. And I get an undertone of something atypical in the interstices between nodes. More surprising, I only noted brief flickers that might indicate a 'panache.' Possibly this is an intentional suppression, which could suggest duplicity, an aberrance that could be troubling if it leads to hostility toward our enterprise. On the other hand, nonstandard responses may make some degree of sense if this place has truly been dark for 26 years. And ThoughtDancers are, well, ThoughtDancers."

Roston made a sound I interpreted as a snicker and turned back to his cogtraces. I just rolled my eyes.

Maya's homework assignments for me had included learning a little about ThoughtDancers. Their quirks include the virtual panaches they create as their personalities evolve. Kind of like costumes or jewelry or totem poles. To a savvy SI mechanic, a ThoughtDancer's panache could serve as a window into its personality and underlying thought processes. Evidently creating panaches was a behavior unique to them: none of the Dunnetix SIs do anything like that. But I didn't want to get a dissertation from Bland and Tidy right now. And I wasn't even starting to worry that the mission might be in jeopardy. Not by my standards, at least. Still, I felt Bland and Tidy might benefit from some encouragement.

"What we need to know right now, Roston," I said, "is whether you're gonna be able to work well enough with this SI to learn what we need to learn on this trip. There's a lot at stake for all of us here."

Roston held up a hand, flipped back his helmet and sent a contemptuous glare my way. "You're a compulsive worrier, aren't you Travis." It wasn't a question.

I nodded. No point denying it.

"It is not helpful. This is a delicate interactive procedure under any circumstances. But sitting in a dense forest infested with uncontrollable sensory inputs — not to mention poisonous snakes — makes it much more difficult. A million impingements. Your worrying looms over it all. I repeat: it is not helpful. Do your walkabout. Please. I may know something by the time you get back. Trust me, Travis. I'm very good at this."

I hate it when people say, "Trust me, Travis." But I gave him the benefit of doubt by attributing part of his testiness to the snake incident. I'd already forgotten about it. I may worry about a lot of things, but not much about rattlesnakes. Not growing up in diamondback-infested Ishernot. Never occurred to me to find out if he was a viperphobe, so I didn't think he'd freak when we ran across the big blacktail rattler about a hundred yards from where I'd sprained my ankle. Blacktails are night feeders when it's hot like it's been and I wasn't too surprised to see one since we were hiking through its hunting ground at night.

I think what troubled Roston most was that I didn't kill the one he spotted: I just gave it a gentle nudge with my new walking stick and let it slide away into the underbrush. That bothered Roston. He must have figured it would stalk us or call up the cavalry. But they're really not aggressive and they don't harbor grudges; they just want to be left alone, something I understand well enough. But Roston's really from Boston (if you can believe that coincidence): any snakes there are the human variety. Much more likely to push my worry button than a blacktail.

I bit back a few dozen snide comments, gave him my best ambiguous look and just nodded. He nodded back, raised a dismissive eyebrow and gave his head a little flip to make his helmet drop back down. Asshole.

Maya was leaning back against a ponderosa. She'd taken in the exchange but made no comment. Probably a good thing. She'd already gone back to watching god-knows-what on her big foldup with her usual intensity. She caught my gaze and said, "No mazes yet, One-Shoe. But maybe any minute now. You gonna wait around?" Maya's warm, rounded voice always surprises me. Judging from her wiry body type that's more straight lines than curves, you'd expect it to be thin and harsh.

"Naw, I'd better get started. I want to get past the gate and back here before the sun comes up. Ping me when you find something interesting."

"Travis? I'd still cop you, you know." Now her voice had dropped to a sexy whisper for my ears only. "Sheila won't mind. She'd cop you too, actually. Maybe both of us at the same time. Wouldn't take much to talk her into it ... and she's the type that'd want to do something really nasty with your foot. Not the meat one."

I caught her wink and had to grin at the pornographic two-handed gesture she was making. Part of me would love to take her up on the offer, but a wiser part prevailed: bad mission policy. Plus, she and Sheila were engaged ... and I'm still a little old school. So I just half-grinned, yanked off her baseball cap and kissed the top of the buzzcut she'd gotten just for this mission. Then I tapped on my nighties, checked my stealthfiber and slipped away into the forest.

58

8

ANOTHER SNAKE

FROM OLD PIX I've seen, a hundred years ago this area was all scraggly, brushy highlands. A few hundred years earlier it had been primeval forest, but a couple centuries of over-logging and then overgrazing by cattle and sheep had left it in sorry shape. Now it's all reforested and part of the Dunnigan Reserve. My hat's off to the Dunnigans for that; my lonesome ranger soul never feels more comfortable than in places like this.

I was thinking about the ranger life as I hobbled along the road next to the fence. My ankle was feeling better and I was tempted to ditch my walking stick. But it was a nice, unusually straight length of dense gambrel oak and I'd taken a liking to it, so I didn't. Good thing.

Meeting up with Dunnigans Gate is always a surprise. The black evermetal segments are a foot thick and swing on huge, black hinges hung from smooth, square webcrete columns that are ten feet on a side and about fifty feet high. Imposing, more like the gates of Mordor than the only portal in and out of a town of nonviolent vegetable eaters. In the center of each gate is a quincunx — a pattern of five dots like the arrangement on the fifth side of a die. Each dot is about a foot in diameter and recessed about two inches into the seamless metal of the gate. Nothing says what's behind those completely incongruous objects: no informative plaque with population and date founded, not even a signpost. The quincunxes are it. Very mysterious and foreboding and you can't not wonder what's inside.

What passes for a road leading down to the gate from the north is just a packed dirt track about twelve feet wide. If you go walking north on it, you can get to Old Highway 84 about five miles up, but only if you don't get lost in Circleton, which is what we rangers call the maze about a mile in from 84. Dunnigans put it in a long time ago with full St Coriander approval. It takes thirteen correct turns to get through it and I can tell you from experience that even rangers get lost if they're not paying attention or using nav. The only vehicle I've ever seen use this trail is a Dunnigan road grader that takes a pass over it every couple years. Makes me wonder why Dunnigans bother to keep it maintained.

I stood at the gate looking up that road in the dark. My inner paranoid told me that I should walk up the road a ways to see if anything else had used it lately, but I overrode that idea in favor of getting back to camp before sunrise. Turns out that was a mistake.

I turned back around and studied the gate. Time for a chat.

In five years of patrolling around here, this was the first time I'd seen it with nightvision. Something didn't feel quite right. Maybe the gate's thinker was degenerating. They do, you know. Nothing lasts forever. Not even stuff from Ishernot and Dunnetix that have built quality and longevity into their business models from the start.

The spot where the gate's thinker was hidden was a rectangle of ghostlight just a little brighter than the concrete itself. It sort of throbbed, almost like a pulse, making it seem more biological than it actually was.

The gate and I exchanged pleasantries in that way only fellow Ishernauts can. As SIs go, this one isn't exactly a rocket surgeon, but it has a great set of sensors and a flawless memory. Doesn't need to be a whiz kid. Possibly it knows the ins and outs of the Township Fence, but that could be just a wish on my part. Mostly, it just needs to know when to open every once in a while. And if it senses a threat, it needs to trigger alarms and get all nasty and defensive. Plus a few other things that are Ishernot trade secrets.

But right now, it was just an easygoing piece of security tech.

I was pretty sure it wasn't controlled by the St Coriander SI, but I didn't want to get too chatty in case it made reports to it. When it asked me if I had any recent news from Ishernot, I said something noncommittal, not wanting to get into my recent visit. Fact is, the gate probably checks in with the old hometown more often than me over the years. But it knew not to pry: there's an Ishernaut tradition about not asking each other possibly sensitive questions, so it didn't even ask me why I was patrolling at night.

So I just said a courtesy goodbye, hobbled away and got on with my mission.

I wasn't twenty yards beyond the gate when Maya pinged me.

"Two interesting things so far, One-Shoe. Westbound roach has found two mazes and seventeen dead bodies: eleven in the first maze, six in the second. Skeletons, actually, from what the roach is showing me. I'm having it leave a radax pellet at the exits to the mazes. You want I should continue the survey?"

Skeletons? That threw my assumptions a major league knuckleball. That was at the project level. At another level it was like a kick in the stomach. Why skeletons if the populace of St Coriander had all Elevated to a higher plane? It was one of those situations where if I had a drop of common sense I'd call this off, go back and regroup. But ....

"Still there, One-Shoe?" Maya was cool, matter of fact. She's not the sort of person who loses it over a bone or two and her thinking was probably way ahead of mine.

"Sorry. Wasn't expecting skeletons. Are they near the inside of the fence?"

"Check. All bunched up tight, none further than maybe fifteen feet in. Wild guess would be a panic response."

"What's across from your two mazes so far?"

"Forest and undergrowth. The roach hasn't even gone half a mile yet. Just passed the culvert where Saw Creek goes under the perimeter road."

"Your other roach find anything yet? And can you see where I am?"

"No strikes yet from the eastbound roach. Your icon looks like

61

you just passed the gate and are heading east; the roach is maybe a thousand yards ahead of you."

"Right. No need to ping me until I'm getting close to a maze so I can pay special attention. Unless I see anything interesting I'm going to about face and head back in about half an hour."

"Roger that. Oh, and not to worry you or anything, but I get the sense that Roston's glue might be getting a little soft. Or something very strange is up with the SI. Either way ...."

I worried about that for about five seconds. "Worry? Travis One-Shoe worry? Nah. But maybe you've got a spare flea or two you could flick in his direction? Unnoticed?"

"Good as done."

"Thanks, Maya. I could use a dozen of you."

"Nah. We'd grind your pencil down to nothing. One of me is plenty. Out."

Five minutes later, Maya pinged me again. "Two bogies, One-Shoe. Appeared out of nowhere on the east side where the road climbs up that hill. Coming your way fast. Get out of there."

"Clear," was all I said. I slipped off the path, bum ankle forgotten in the adrenaline rush. Five seconds later I was one with the forest like any worth-his-salt part Navajo.

Lucky for me, the two arrogant Securitans with nightvisors dou-ble-timing it up the trail were not one with anything. That's the way they're taught: you're WorldGov's finest; you own wherever you are. Sad thing is, they believe it. Then two more appeared. Only one of this pair was arrogant: the other was bleeding from a messy thigh wound.

My inner idiot was deciding the best way to take 'em out when a couple drops of wisdom finally caught up with my adrenaline. This was purely an illegal recon mission, not a military thing. And while I'm not a soldier, I've had more soldierly training than some soldiers and sometimes we over-trained security types can start to feel a little too soldierly for our own good. So I squashed my reflex and let the questions start popping in my head. Questions, but no answers.

What are Securitans doing in the Dunnigan Reserve? For sure, they weren't invited here by Dunnigans. Dunnigans pretty much detest anything related to WorldGov, Securitans included. Any special exceptions and I would have heard about it.

I boosted my goggles just as the first pair stopped not fifty yards from me. With this much magnification I could decode the stripes in the little bar on the leader's chest: SI Anomalies Investigative Unit. Cayoos, as they're called in the trade, although nobody ever told me why it's Cayoo and not Sayoo. Had some visit the Royal Argent Nevergate when I was there. Very smart, very nosy, off the scale arrogance. Worse, the word in security circles is that the "C" in "Cayoo" stands for "corrupt."

My brain — such as it is — went into overdrive. What were Cayoos doing here? Particularly at the exact time our little threesome was doing a recon mission. Coincidences this big smell like an open sewer in the wrong parts of Bangkok in high summer. I pinged Maya. "Four Cayoos on perimeter road, maybe 3,000 yards west your position. Shut down and melt. Roston, too."

"Copy bad boys. Back when done. Out."

The second pair of Cayoos had caught up with the first. While one tended to the bloody one's wounded leg, the other two held a confab. They seemed to be waiting for something and the something was not long in coming. I heard a faint whir and the skitchy sound of fat treads on packed dirt. The lead dog looked past my position. I followed his eyes and saw two guys on a standard issue forest gyroscooter emerging from the forest. One guy was a uniformed ranger: Max Dalt. My boss. The guy on the seat behind him was Roston Verloff: two-legged snake from Boston.

Ping. "Roston's gone. Never got to flea him, either." Maya's subvocal had a whispery quality with an undertone of fear. A good thing. Truly fearless people tend to be delusional ... and die young.

"Yeah, I'm looking at him. We've been gamed and are about to be loose-ended by the bad boys. Make for you-know-where and wait for me. Feel free to leave a couple Nasties for the bad boys. Out."

64

9
A CASCADE OF BONES

ONE UNSPOKEN benefit of being born an Ishernaut is a lifelong subscription to the Weapon Shopper, homebody edition. We home-bodies can obtain cutting edge stuff that nobody else can get for at least a decade. Okay, maybe a couple years exclusivity is all. It's one reason you see so many Ishernauts in security: we don't play fair. That's how I got the Nasties. They're smart, small and great for prop-agating unpleasantness, uncertainty and instant immobility among enemies that might be pursuing you on foot. When they work right. The ones I got are still in the beta stage, but Ishernot beta is like any ordinary techspot's third-gen models. So I wasn't worrying too much.

As my eyeballs zeroed in on the scooter guys slowing down to meet up with the Cayoos, the back of my brain was trying to process how complicated this little gig had gotten. My inner paranoid was thinking that the Cayoos have probably had one of their own thinkers keeping tabs on St Coriander since it went dark. But because there's never been a complaint filed about the town's ThoughtDancer, the agency had no official cause for an action, no excuse to go in with guns blazing and pull its plug. So it all got forgotten about ... except maybe by one of the rapacious types who was stockpiling a secure hideaway in some untouchable PU. That person had also done the math on St C's riches. So he watched and set out some flags of his own.

According to the theory I was hatching, one of his flags would have been SI mechanics that specialize in ThoughtDancers. After 26 years, something finally clicked and Roston Verloff showed up on his radar, courtesy of me and Maya.

Oops. Something else clicked and I realized I was wrong about Roston Verloff being número uno. Another SI mechanic came here first: Henry Ng. Maya's brother. Couldn't be a coincidence. The unsolved mystery of how he arrived in the vicinity suddenly popped back into my head. A wayward thought flew off in the direction of Maya. Would she be the next traitor I'd see here?

I shut that one down fast. After what Maya and I had been through together I'd have to see that to believe it. But however it came to be, a second get-rich-quick team had been formed. That one had a lot more resources than ours ... and it was now right in front of me. And unlike us, they weren't doing recon.

No idea how they turned Bland and Tidy, but with all the muscle the Cayoos could bring to bear, it couldn't have been too hard. And I'd wager they made him take a smoothie before he came down for his face-to-face with Maya in the Triple Boxcar. From what I'd seen of him so far, there was no way he'd pass vibe with her otherwise. Shit.

None of this had occurred to me until that moment. Pisses me off when my inner paranoid lets me down. Embarrassing, too. Wouldn't be surprising that one of the Securitan black units would have an undie or two in the Dunnigan Rangers, but no reason I would have connected the dots that they might be interested in our little St C scheme. I wondered if I'd let something slip. Or if Maya ....

Nope, already decided not to pursue that line of thinking. Better to be thinking about the presence of Max Dalt and the still-living bloody Cayoo. He hadn't shot himself and the wound looked like something inflicted by a Carver slivershot on hurt-don't-kill, standard issue for duty in the Reserve. So I guessed there might be a dead ranger down near Old 64. Probably half-decomposed already thanks to cellabugs. That's what I'd have done with the corpse anyway. By tomorrow the body would be gone, bones and all, and the bugs would have morphed into flyaways. Poof, no corpse.

While I was passing time waiting to see what the opposition was going to do, some little Pollyanna in the back of my brain was telling me this all might be a stroke of good luck after all. Maybe they'd do all the hard work and all Maya and I would have to do is tag along and time our cherry picking for just the right moment. It wasn't like anybody in that group was going to call the Rio Arriba sheriff's office with a complaint. Yeah, I was dreaming. So I just sat tight and watched.

Pretty soon there was a new vibe: an agreement had been reached. The injured Cayoo was now patched and boosted well enough to continue the mission. And I was getting curious about what was going to happen next; something about that group told me nobody was planning on wiggling past skeletons in one of the mazes.

My bet was on Dalt sweet-talking the gate so they could all just waltz through the front door. And Dalt had no doubt previously readjusted the drone routes ... or spoofed them, or both. I was also betting that Roston had already got the minefields turned off somehow. I would have lost that bet.

Maya pinged me right then. "Strange bogie just dropped into my field of vision. You know the mobile kitchens that travel along the Huzbol route? A big yellow one with a pair of dancing, taco-eating crocodiles and the words Azteca Grill splashed all over it is headed your way. Fast. Not kidding."

"You mean a roach coach like the ones they had all over Nirvana-ta? Seriously?"

"Yeah, like that. But this is way upscale compared to those. Made me hungry just looking at it. Order me a huge fucking carnitas chipotle burrito when it gets there."

"You want the pickled cactus on the side or inside it?" Maya actually likes that shit.

"The burrito was kind of a joke, One-Shoe; this thing is not a real roach coach. When I said dropped in, I meant it. Dropped straight down like a moller or a heli, except totally silent. And there's a blue glow underneath it."

"Hoverbars," I interrupted. "Very expensive new antigrav tech. Saw 'em in action on a Dunnigan limo the night of your big party."

"You thinking that's a Dunnigan thing? Tell me you're not."

"I'm not. But something like that wearing a roach coach disguise gives me pause."

"Well do your pausing fast. It's headed your way with its tires about a foot above the road. Be careful: I got a bad feeling about this. Check back if it shows up in your neighborhood. Out."

This is where I should shake my head and guzzle half a bottle of straight tequila and then eat half a fresh lime as a chaser, rind and all. Shit!

I checked my position and my camo. Still a couple days of power for the stealthfiber. Good. Then I went back to watching whatever was unfolding unfold.

The Cayoo leader seemed to be distracted at the moment. Maybe he was waiting for the roach coach to show up with coffee and a breakfast burrito. I can hope, right?

But then he said something and the injured Cayoo replaced Roston on the back of the scooter, and they all started moving up toward the gate. I followed them, first with my eyes, and then with very cautious movements, thanking the powers for the overcast that blanked out the starlight. They stopped at the gate and I stopped at the road down from the north, the one with the scooter tracks now showing on it. If I'd headed up the road like my inner paranoid wanted, I might have interrupted Bland and Tidy's meet-up with Dalt. But I might also have gotten dead. Oh well.

My musing was interrupted by the Cayoo leader saying something to Roston and holding out his hand. Roston shrugged, trying to act nonchalant. Then he pulled a small box out of a pocket and handed it over. The Cayoo opened it, nodded and distributed thin flesh colored tabs about the size of a large coin to each member of the group. He pressed his against his forehead and the others followed suit. I made a wild guess; those things were the equivalent of guest geneboxes. Roston had somehow encoded the things with data he got from the ThoughtDancer when Maya and I were doing our own shit. No wonder he'd been so anxious to see me gone.

Roston never told us he had those gadgets; he'd assured us that once we made it through a maze, the SI would disable all the mines until our business was done. And since he'd be at the same risk of being blown to bits as Maya and me, we bought the story. I felt dumber than whatever is dumber than a rock.

The Cayoo honcho gestured to Dalt, who dutifully went to work on the gate. A minute later he stepped back and the two halves started to swing open. The motion was slow and quiet and I took an almost reverent moment to admire the smooth Ishernot engineering. Then the clattering started. Malfunction?

Nope. Bones, showing up bright and clean in my nighties. First through the gap was a ribcage, but a couple seconds later the gates were open far enough that all I could see was a chaotic flood spewing through the gap. Some splintered, some bounced, some just clanked. When skulls hit the ground they started rolling in every direction, some bouncing off the legs of our hotshot competitors. One of the Cayoo grunts stepped on a tiny skull, slipped and whomped flat on his back. I stifled a knee-jerk laugh at the slapstick moment. I guess their info about what had happened 26 years ago hadn't been any better than ours.

But Roston from Boston had moved silently to the side when the gates started to open; he'd been expecting it, so I was betting he'd gotten in pretty tight with the alien SI. I watched him dodge a small skull with a coy little hop. Must have belonged to a kid. I hadn't really projected the implications of Maya's skeletons in the mazes. But now those implications were rolling around on the baked earth ... and in my head. I wasn't liking any of it, but the idea of kids getting stomped to death by panicked adults got to me big time. And the idea that we were here to rape and pillage the victims' trust fund? That was depositing a seriously nasty flavor on my taste buds. Not one of these skeletons had volunteered to die trying to escape whatever had spooked them.

Didn't seem to bother Roston, though: all in a night's work. His arms were folded and his narrow pasty face was twisted into a smug expression. I was really starting to hate that guy, but he would have been wiser to keep that expression off his face; smug is not a smart look for a civ to put on display for a Securitan of any stripe.

The chief Cayoo grabbed him by the shoulder, spun him around and got in his face for a hissed, one-sided conversation. Very short one. The guy was big, almost as tall as me, but without my Navajo barrel chest. Plenty big enough, though: Roston wilted. The big Cayoo gave him a shove and my current least favorite SI mechanic went flying into the pile of skeletons.

Meanwhile, Dalt and the other Cayoos were kicking and pushing the bones back inside St Coriander and out of the way. My wild guess at the time was that at least a couple hundred people died trying to get out of the gates ... that for some mysterious reason wouldn't open for them. I filed that item for later.

It wasn't easy getting them all pushed back. The chief Cayoo hissed again and Roston dragged himself up and got at it, too. Finally, the bones were all shoved out of the way and the place in front of the gate was clear. Then the chief Cayoo hissed at Roston again and pointed down the empty stretch of what must be Outbound Road according to Sheila's map. So Roston got to go first ... to test the water. For his sake, I hoped his genebox emulator wasn't another doublecross.

Chief Cayoo nodded to himself and turned his head toward the western leg of the perimeter road. I heard a whispery sound and followed Chief Cayoo's eyes: in a few seconds the Azteca Grill rounded the bend, its lightbar spreading a low, flat light in front of it that partially masked the blue haze washing the road from its underside. It skewed sideways a little as it came to a stop pointed at the gates.

Evidently the entire invasion force was now present, so Chief Cayoo gave the order to move forward. Roston was still in the lead, but the guys on the scooter were catching up fast. The other three didn't seem to be in a big hurry. The roach coach with its mystery cargo floated on through behind them.

The gates closed and I heard the faintest mechanical noises as the locks cycled shut. I sucked in a deep breath and allowed myself to indulge in a good minute of feeling very stupid. Our treasure hunt was over before it even got halfway through recon. These guys were doing the real deal. They had scooped us seven ways from Sayonara. Then anger walked in. Was it time to bail out? Regroup? From what I'd just seen, we'd be lucky to get out of here with our skins intact. Time to ping Maya and find out how much worse things had gotten wherever she was ... and see if she had any ideas.

72

10
WAY BACK WHEN

"FULLY BOOSTED, armored and armed to the nines," said Maya, the surprise in her voice unmistakable. "Heading toward the gate; current position between C and D. Got a plan?"

"You mean like a Plan X? I'm coming up empty on plans right now."

Maya knew me well enough to give me time to think, so she just waited. I was still processing her news that another pair of Cayoos had just showed up in range of the funnybees she'd sent out when we set up camp. Pretty sure Roston didn't know about those little buzzers. I didn't tell him, at least.

I'd figured the bad boys would be keeping eyes out for me and Maya, but that their current orders were to protect the exit routes. We'd be on the menu for later. Probably more were on their way to handle the little matter of us.

Getting out of the neighborhood and to the nearest Nevergate was what we needed to do right now. But being both embarrassed and pissed, I wanted to at least give them something to remember us by. But exactly what that might be escaped me. Like I said, I'm a security guy, not a soldier.

"About that plan?" Maya's as patient as she is subtle. But an idea was starting to hatch.

"You willing to take a shot at switching gears and going for it? Totally unprepared and completely out-gunned? Kind of along the lines of what you and I talked about Way Back When?"

"Hmmm. Way Back When, huh?"

Way Back When is a code for Plan Z ... the one nobody with half a brain intact wants to do. Maya and Sheila and I actually had a Plan Z. And now I had a little extra something that might give us at least a proverbial snowflake's chance ... assuming I could inflate my co-jones enough to give it a try. There also happened to be something I'd neglected to mention to my other team members that could maybe boost our chances. But really, why do anything this stupid? If I have to be honest, I'm not sure I could say for sure.

"Who wants to live forever? Let's hear your idea, One-Shoe."

"Only half an idea, so far, but here's a kickoff question. Your roach find any mazes near point C?" Point A was the gate. Point B was a mile counter-clockwise from the gate, etc. If I moved fast and was lucky, I might be able to get to our rendezvous in about twenty minutes from my current position. Emphasis on might. Well, not if I executed my plan-in-progress, but I was thinking it might be worth the delay. If I was lucky.

Maya answered my question. "First one I told you about is about half a mile my way from A. Eleven skeletons, all bunched up near the town side of the fence. Like I said."

"You think we can get through the maze with the skeletons in the way?"

"Pretty sure I can. Not so sure about you, One-Shoe."

"You saying I'm too fat?"

"I'm saying they're one-way mazes; the geometry is designed for getting insiders out safely and making it tough for outsiders to get in. Either way, small is better."

"Nothing ventured, nothing lost. We stay outside, it's gonna be a bitch steering clear of a thorough cleanup crew. And we're probably gonna need some bones."

"You want me to ask why?"

"Nope. But if it comes time for a maze probe, you might wanna be on the alert for a nice shinbone you'd feel okay having taped to your leg. You spot one my size, you could collect one for me, too. But I'd rather wait until we see if your roach finds anything great between C and D. I'll meet you at our hidey-hole as soon as I test out my idea for a distraction. Best get there as fast as you can. And try to be patient; I'm going to buy us some time."

"Better hurry. The first pair of drop-ins is now moving balls out; they should be at A in less than ten minutes. Break a leg. Out."

Only ten minutes? I was going to be cutting it close.

Ishernot "security" products often have undocumented features that can be useful to Ishernauts with the right creds. It's how we Nauts are able to do field mods for clients. Does wonders for our employability. When I was down in Belize, I took a little side job consulting with a gaming bigshot who'd bought a huge spread in the Maya Mountains, not too far from the ruins of an old Mayan city named Caracol. Word had gotten around Belize City that I was an Ishernaut, so he invited me out to his yacht to talk about his new hideaway. Best meal I've had in years.

Security for his new place had to be totally "fuck-with-me-and-die" (his words). I referred him to some topnotch people in Ishernot and promptly forgot about him. Turns out they designed him a system that included several miles of tropicalized thornmesh perimeter fencing and a pair of super-lethal first class smartgates. Awesome setup. But if I'd wanted to, I could have busted into that place just by having a chat with the gate ... and only because I grew up with Ishernot SIs. No need to tell him that, of course. Family secret.

Even with our recon gig blown and getting scooped by these bad boys, getting into St Coriander should be just as easy ... except for all the landmines. Flies in the ointment. But with a little help from World-Gov, maybe not insurmountable. So I left my hiding place, walked up to the gate and had some friendly chitchat that mostly verified my hope that it was an independent actor and wasn't obliged to report to the big gun SI. There was still risk, but what's life without risks? So I floated my idea for having a little fun and crossed my fingers.

Two minutes later, the first pair of Securitans trotted up and stopped. I was fifty feet away, but I'd swear I could hear the little gears grinding in their heads. Was the gate supposed to be open? Pretty sure they didn't think so. So their next step was a call to the Chief Cayoo to verify orders. Too bad they couldn't connect on their com channel, thanks to the broad-spectrum hash the gate was broadcasting for me. Then the two squibs I'd thrown over the fence went off about fifty feet inside St Coriander, which I hoped would be far enough. Boom-boom.

Now all kinds of shit had to be going on inside their brains. But if I were lucky, none of it would be properly devious thinking. They hit the ground and rolled toward one of the massive piers that anchor the gate, at the same time hauling out their main firepower. The last I saw of them while the gates of Mordor were closing was them blasting away at phantoms in the direction of my squibs. Phase One, bingo.

Phase Two was going to be iffier. To get them up off their bellies and into the playing field, I had the gate start making godawful mechanical sounds. The punch line was putting on its best robotic voice and booming out this classic motivational line: "Self-destruct sequence initiated: all personnel in the vicinity must depart the blast zone immediately. Zero minus thirty ...."

And so on. By zero minus twenty-eight both Securitans were up and running for the only cover available: the dark, overgrown woods that flank Outbound Road. The fastest one triggered a landmine at zero plus fifteen; the slower one at zero plus seventeen, probably set off when he hit the ground after the first one blew him off his feet. Phase Two accomplished.

I told the gate I was going to nominate it for a medal if I ever made it back to Ishernot and that it would probably have to figure out how to sign autographs. The rectangle of awareness on the concrete pier seemed to turn a pale shade of pink, but it was probably just some artifact in my optical nerves from too much time with nighties on. Then it asked me for a small favor.

Its loneliness assaulted me with needles of intense feeling that almost made my knees buckle. I hadn't known that gate-level Ishernot SIs could feel emotions like that. Over a few seconds the wave of raw, pent up feeling subsided and it was able to clarify. Loneliness was part of it. It was one thing to do gate duty in a living community full of people emitting the usual clouds of psychons. But it was something else to be doing a useless un-job in a community of skeletons. If it weren't for its relationship with the St Coriander Librarian, the gate would have self-destructed a long time ago. The ThoughtDancer was no company: it was alien and in the gate's opinion, it had mysteriously gone insane sometime before the plague killed off the people. So the gate had been stuck with an insane neighbor for more than two decades.

Another wave of intense feeling hit me. The gate felt guilty for its unwitting complicity in the deaths of St Coriander's population. It felt it had been duped by the ThoughtDancer, which had itself been duped by Father-Mayor O'Kelly. At least that's how it had all been presented to the gate by the Librarian, a Dunnetix Themis. My poor brain was trying to make sense of all this, but there was no time. More Securitans were headed my direction and the bad guys inside were way ahead of me and Maya. We were still outsiders looking in. We'd probably be wise to stay that way. Oh well. Like Maya said ....

Without thinking how I might pull this off, I promised the gate that if I somehow survived this little engagement, I'd do my best to take it back to Ishernot.

"I believe you, Travis One-Shoe. And here is some information that may help us all prevail."

What it shared with me after that changed everything. We might be able to pull it off after all. I reiterated my promise, gave the rectangle a love pat and left the scene of the crime about as I'd found it, sans two hulky bozos.

Before the next pair arrived at the closed gate I was back in the forest, hobbling west for my rendezvous with Maya. A maze from Hell wasn't the only way in. My brain now held the map to an entrance that even the ThoughtDancer didn't know about. And now we could just walk right in thanks to the gate: no deadly maze crawling and skeleton jostling required.

11
ONE SURPRISE TOO MANY

I WATCHED THE VAGUE shimmer of predawn light filter through the trees, outlining the mountains up behind St Coriander to the east. It's a time of day I usually try to appreciate, but not today. No time for beauty.

Hobbling through the forest as silently as I could, I was starting to feel better about our prospects. If we had any luck at all, the nice little explosions up by the gate would be giving our competitors pause. I found myself trying to imagine what the Chief Cayoo and Dalt would be thinking. Their first guess would probably be that the explosions were Roston's former associates. It would take them some time to determine that the blasts mysteriously obliterated part of their own crew that shouldn't have been inside in the first place. So really, I probably hadn't bought that much time. But the new info from the gate made it well worth the effort.

When the sun was high enough for decent visibility, Chief Cayoo would probably send somebody back up the road to check for remains. Then the truth might come to light. Or it might not. All I could do at the moment was keep moving toward our hidey-hole and hope that scratching their heads would slow them down some.

If we had even more luck, the remnants of night would be enough to hide the Nasties sneaking up behind the additional pair of Securitans headed north on the west side. Their colonies of a thousand legs would try to attach themselves to the boots of the hostiles. If they did, those boys would very soon be out of play. Unless they had the right scent markers, in 15 seconds the Securitans would be on their faces, immobilized by dehab injected by a hundred inch-long stingers that shoot out from their Nasty legs. Not deadly, but recovery time is at least 24 hours and there's no known antidote that will speed it up. So I was pretty sure these guys would be out of play for as long as necessary.

Sure, the Nasties had to find them, so this was no slam-dunk force equalizer. And since there was no immediate way to know if they were successful or not, I had to act as if they weren't until Maya could get a reading from her funnybees on those guys' locale. I tried to hobble a little faster.

Twice in the last ten minutes I'd been on the verge of pinging Maya for an update. Each time I held off. But I did drum up the nerve to make a connection I'd been hoping to avoid, just because the very idea scared me shitless. Not literally. After all, I'd seen what happened to the guy who had my new implant stuck inside his own head.

But the clever Ishernot techs had added extra shielding he didn't have. And since I'd just be acting as a sort of conduit between Ishy and the ThoughtDancer, maybe there was really nothing to worry about. Yeah, sure. I sat under a nice big oak and prepared myself just the way Ishy had told me to. Ishy handled it from there. For me, there was just this strange sensation inside my head, somewhere behind my left ear where the port was hidden. Kind of a hum that wasn't strong enough to classify as a buzz. It only went on for a minute or so, but Ishy had said it wouldn't take very long: SIs communicate with each other a lot faster than they can with humans. Ishy left me an eyeball message that was the equivalent of two thumbs up. I guess that meant that the Thought Dancer had been properly warned. Would've been nice if it felt it owed us something for the friendly warning about the invaders — like by being our eyes and ears — but as a certified optimistic pessimist, I wasn't about to count on it.

I was a little woozy when I stood up again so I popped a half-dose of spike. Also decided to take the long way around and approach the rendezvous hidey-hole from the south. I needed time for the spike to boost me ... and the extra think-time couldn't hurt.

The location we'd picked made sense originally. West of the Township Fence in the vicinity of point D, the topography slopes gently down toward the Rio de Tierra Amarilla. In this area the Reserve is mixed pine and oak forest and the undergrowth is sparse. Our hidey-hole was a four-foot deep trench about twenty feet back from the edge of the perimeter road. It hadn't been fun digging out the hard dirt and camouflaging the detritus, but I didn't feel right about asking Maya or Sheila to help with such time-honored manly work as using a shovel. But I did ask Maya to set it up, since that's her thing. She dressed it up with a mesh cover dotted with brush and sensors.

Across the road was the usual dense mess of Township Fence. Other than the fact that the fence and road made a curve just north of our spot, there was absolutely nothing noteworthy about the place we picked, which was the point. Totally innocuous, a hide-in-more-or-less-plain-sight sort of thing. But it was very well stocked with stuff we'd need for our "real" raid. Some of it might come in handy now.

I made a wide detour to the west. About fifty feet to the south the ground falls away in a steep embankment cut over the centuries by a stream running down from the mountains, through St Coriander and into the channel where I now stood. Under the perimeter road, Fortunatus Creek ran through three concrete culverts fitted with evermetal grates and all sorts of sensors and unpleasant deterrents that were monitored by my friend the gate. This time of year the water level was low, but it still flowed through all three culverts with that cheery gurgle that only water can make. In a few minutes I was going to tell the monitor a certain Ishernot code-joke, then Maya and I were going to walk that little creek right into the heart of St Coriander.

Nice work One-Shoe, I was saying to myself as I crawled and clawed my way up the embankment, noiselessly, almost like an old-time Navajo. At the top, I stopped patting myself on the back. Al-

81

though I couldn't see our hideout from this spot, what I could see was trouble. Big trouble.

12

UNSHAKEN

THE TROUBLE WAS a black, unmarked Sumiyo-Brandé carryall hovering a few feet above the road on a cushion of ghostly blue light. Hoverbars: latest tech from PU somewhere-or-other. But this was no limo like the one that took Dalt up to the Dunnigans' party. This thing was about twice as long and twice as high. It had wheels, but they weren't touching the ground.

Two uniformed Securitans were visible, one at each end of the vehicle. They looked just like the ones I'd gotten blown up with the help of my Ishernot bud, the gate. Except that each of these was guarding a cuffed, blindfolded and gagged woman. One was the old Apache woman who had been our driver, her wrinkled face now augmented by a gash across her forehead that hadn't been there when I saw her last. The other was Maya.

Was it possible that whoever was behind this little display hadn't penetrated Sheila's disguise? Made no sense. And if this were a setup to bring me in, why would they bother? Maya and Sheila had been the brains behind this raid. They knew the plan. And they were already bagged. There was something else going on here and I had no clue what it was. But it offends my nature as an Ishernaut to be outfoxed. At least not this easily. Then I heard the other guy.

He was just out of my immediate line of sight, up the road about twenty yards I guessed. He was on a com, talking to somebody. He had a suave, politico voice, but at the moment it was an I'm-not-too-happy politico voice. Not hard to guess he was hearing that things weren't going quite as planned in beautiful downtown St Coriander.

Nobody moved or made a sound during the time I prepared my demobilizers for duty. It's not boasting to say that I'm an excellent marksman with all sorts of weapons. But I usually don't need to be: marksmen are usually irrelevant in a situation like this. I loaded three fresh wasps with tiny canisters of dehab, linked up with the first via my goggles and sighted in on the target on the right. Click. Then I aimed the second wasp at the target on the left. Click.

I crept to my right until I could get a look at Mr Politico. My, my, my: a dapper one out here in the boonies. Bet he hated it here. Black suit, slicked back blond hair, average build, kind of short. In other words, a classic politico. I got a little extra pleasure sighting my third wasp at that guy. Click.

At my signal, there would be a barely audible hiss and the wasps would leave their launch tubes boosted to 30 mph. About double the speed of a real wasp ... or a running human. In around a second they would have navigated to their targets, homed in on a square inch of exposed flesh and planted their payloads of dehab. Game over, at least for the three targets.

One handy feature of dehab is how it progressively incapacitates its victim. In the first second after injection, the victim feels something like a high voltage electric shock. That disrupts its reactions. While it's stunned, the other ingredients take over and within five seconds it loses muscle control, including the ability to stand. Oh yeah, its consciousness flicks off, too. An interesting side effect is that the victim also loses control of bladder and bowels. It may be a psych thing, but people who wake up with a wet, stinky load in their pants just don't operate at maximum ferocity. No wonder Ishernot has such a diabolical reputation. If we didn't have our own Nevergate — and weren't so tight with the Clans Dunnigan — we'd have probably been snuffed by WorldGov decades ago.

Anyway, with my wasps ready to take out the visible unfriendlies, I had to make up my mind about what to do about whoever was hiding out of my field of vision. They were probably in our hidey-hole, but maybe not. What did I have in my pack that would do exactly the right job? If I acted in the next few minutes while the morning light was still low, maybe blindspot? This might be just the right tool if the ones I couldn't see were watching for me with nighties and in a highly vigilant state.

I sometimes have a tendency to think too much, so I tried to counteract that by acting maybe a little too rashly. In my defense, that last shot of spike was wearing off and I knew it. Plus, I couldn't see any clear way to survive this game without talking to somebody and getting some answers. So I triggered the wasps, counted to five and tossed the blindspot grenade next to the black vehicle. For good measure I'd triggered my last roach, which I'd instructed to zigzag through the underbrush by the hidey-hole side of the perimeter road, using its built in audio to amplify the noises it made.

The visibles crumpled right on schedule, releasing their holds on their captives. My eyes were closed when the blindspot grenade exploded with its triple flash. A couple seconds later there was a satisfying bunch of outcries from around where Maya and I had dug our hidey-hole.

I exploded into as much gimp action as my bum ankle would allow. In seconds I was charging through the understory behind our trench. Two Securitans were standing in it, tearing off their visors, making a racket and waving their ZR48s. They could hurt somebody if they weren't careful, so in thoroughly cowardly fashion, I came up behind the trench and compound-fractured their upper arms with that really nice oak staff Maya had found for me.

Whick, whack! The sound of moving air, the satisfying crunch of Securitan bones and the cheerful thunk of ZR48s hitting the dirt floor of the trench. Music to my ears. For good measure I swung my staff twice more; necks broke and the ex-enemies slumped into the trench. Then I heard a familiar female voice say, "Thanks for the heroics, One-Shoe. Now drop the stick or my fiancée is history. Time to give it up."

Was that a joke? I looked up from my task at hand, which was pretty much done anyway.

Across the road, the Securitans had folded as planned, but the old Navajo woman — no longer blindfolded, cuffed or gagged — had moved to the other end of the carryall. Maya was lying face down on the ground and Sheila had a foot on her neck. In Sheila's right hand was a Securitan standard Skotke slivershot aimed at my middle. Her left hand held its twin. At this distance, one pull on a trigger would release a spray of explosive glass slivers that would cut me into two not very neat pieces, sans lungs, stomach, intestines and the usual other organs. These parts would pretty much be vaporized. I didn't much like that picture.

"Well, Sheila, I guess you didn't make it to Santa Fe." I threw in a little rueful chuckle for effect. "Hafta say, as a fiancée for my best friend, you're a little slack in the trustworthiness department. You sure fooled me."

"Don't take it too hard, One-Shoe. I'm an old hand at foolery. Now drop the stick and step onto the road where I can see you, then get on the ground, face down, hands behind your back. And no more cute Ishernaut tricksiness."

While I was down, she pocketed one Skottke, borrowed a pair of cuffs from one of the unconscious Securitans and slapped them on me.

"Now get up. Somebody wants to chat with you."

Sheila rapped the butt of her Skottke on the rear door of the vehicle. After a few moments, the door slid open in the side of the carryall and a cuffed man stepped out. Sheila handed him a key she'd lifted from a Securitan guard. The man uncuffed himself and gave Sheila the cuffs, which she slapped over Maya's wrists in a well-practiced move, then stepped back. This was one scary woman and I'd completely missed it, something that didn't bode well for our continued survival.

I recognized the guy immediately: Sheila's father, Morton Vance. Instead of the formal penguin outfit he'd worn at the engagement party, he was now wearing a simple black cassock with a cowl drooping behind his neck. His once elegant face looked like it had been used as a test dummy for rubber hammers. He winced, rubbed his wrists, then held out a hand in my direction. "Thank you, Travis," he said. "It appears Maya did not exaggerate in the matter of your skills."

"Oh go ahead, One-Shoe, be nice. He won't bite ... and he's not really my father. But he is *a* father. Meet Dr Vincent O'Kelly, former Father-Mayor of St Coriander and chief architect of the little treasure hunt we're all involved in. There's much more going on here than you know and it's time to finish it." Sheila's voice had an edge of impatience that gave me pause.

The man she called Dr O'Kelly made a bow and indicated the open door. "If you will be so good as to enter the vehicle, we will all take a little ride in this marvelous craft. And then we will pay a call on a certain ThoughtDancer of my acquaintance."

I thought he was going to say something else, but Sheila interrupted. "Please excuse me for a moment; I have an urgent personal matter to take care of before we go."

At first, I thought she meant she was going across the road to squat in the bushes. Wrong. She walked to the fallen guy in the black suit. "Sayonara, Baker Hanley. You're way overdue for this ... plus, you're stinking up the territory. Literally." Then she blew his head apart with one shot from the slivershot.

Whoa. That was cold. Not that I hadn't just executed a number of enemy combatants myself, but it was a whole different thing to see Maya's foxy fiancée do an already out-of-play guy like that. Double cold.

Sheila walked back to the carryall and climbed into the driver's seat, stopping just long enough to give me a meaningful look, wipe down the gun and place it in the hand of the unfortunate Securitan she'd borrowed it from. I looked for Maya, but she was already climbing into the other front seat ... and seemed to be avoiding my gaze.

Having arrived at a firm conviction that my midsection was safer inside than outside, I walked past the guy with the pulpy face and started to climb aboard. Then a stinger tapped my neck and I went out like the proverbial light.

87

88

13
CIRCUS

I WOKE UP IN FRAGMENTS, my senses gradually identifying themselves to a mental controller who was still half asleep. My nose and ears and skin prowled around first, sending little messages that started to jog the controller out of its lethargy. For some reason, my eyes stayed closed. Skin says I'm somewhere different, somewhere indoors, coolish conditioned air. Nose says no vegetation aromas, strong smell of musty concrete, weaker smells of fabric, people, dust, lubricants. Body position: seated, leaning back against a cushioned surface, hands and feet unbound, a tiny spot of sensation on the side of my neck ... probably, where the stinger hit. Oh yeah, the stinger. Memories flood back.

Faint sounds filter in: breathing, multiple sets of lungs, rustlings of cloth, an almost imperceptible whir, then a voice I recognize as Sheila's breaks up my wake-up reverie. "Open your eyes, you sleepy little kiddies. We're out of time and we've all got work to do. And be nice." Her voice is faux cheery, but "be nice" gets extra emphasis.

Be nice? I blinked my eyes open and took in the setting in a single glance: easy, not a lot to see. We were in a big-but-not-humongous rectangular room with white painted concrete walls and a lofty ceiling. In one wall was something that looked like the doors of a cargo slidewell. I had no memory of going up or down in it, but why would I? That's one cool thing about slidewells, after all: no sensation of vertical movement.

Anyway, the place we were in seemed like an anteroom or lobby for a warehouse. In the wall across from it was a heavy door that looked like an old-fashioned bank vault door, but big enough to let a train through. The room was empty except for about half a dozen cartons piled against the wall by the vault door. I would love to say that thanks to my masterful intuitive and deductive powers I knew exactly where we were and why. Fact is, I was totally baffled.

Four humans occupied the only furniture. Maya sat next to me on a comfortable white sofa. Her face was tight and hard with bottled up anger. Sheila and the guy who may or may not be her father and may or may not be the former head honcho of St Coriander sat across from us on an identical white sofa, both still looking worse for wear, but better than my last memory of them. Each had a Cayoo-issue slivershot held loosely across a lap. I didn't think either of them was anxious to use it at the moment, which was a point in our favor if things got ugly. Besides, after watching Sheila execute the Cayoo honcho, I'd recalibrated. Now I figured her for the cold, calculating type: we wouldn't be here if they didn't need us.

Disguise gone, Sheila no longer looked like an ancient Apache woman. But even discounting the healtape on her forehead, she didn't quite look like the Sheila I remembered from a few days ago either. Older somehow. But the age was in her eyes, not her face.

She was in charge here, no doubt about that. But she hadn't said anything since our cheery little wake-up call. She seemed unsure of how to start but finally shrugged, rolled her eyes, leaned forward and aimed her voice at Maya.

"I love you Maya, really I do. I hadn't planned on that happening, but it did. But our marriage would never have worked; technically, I'm old enough to be your great grandmother. And although I am truly a professional thespian at the moment, in the past I have worked in far different capacities ... one of which is how the good Father-Mayor and I came to first meet each other many years ago. I would explain everything, but we have no time. So all I'm going to say is that you need to trust that I mean you no harm. And we are not trying to change the deal: any massive financial accounts we can gain access to will be shared equally among us. But the original structure of the mission has, shall we say, become fubarred, thanks to the inconvenient Forces of Darkness ...."

"Which, if not dead already, are about to join the rest of the St Coriander populace, thanks to Harold the Conqueror." The former Father-Mayor — if that's who he really was — was trying to hold his deep, rounded voice steady. It was a voice used to power and authority, but a tremor in his neck and the red flush rising up from his collar were dead giveaways that he was rattled. Assuming Harold the Conqueror was some persona of the ThoughtDancer, the thing was a major hot button for him. Interesting.

"You don't know that, Vincent," snapped Sheila.

"You don't know Harold, Sheila," countered the possible former Father-Mayor. "I've said before that it is the brightest, most creative and most deranged sociopath on the planet. Not to mention being unstable. But if anything, that's an understatement. And it has a remarkable ability to read emotions in humans. What's even worse is that it had become a master of psychon manipulation prior to the event."

The Father-Mayor gave Maya a meaningful look and continued. "Three years before it went on its rampage I tried to tell the Technical Council to send it back to Miotx 4 before its warranty ran out. But instead, they dithered and argued and defended their decision to license it in the first place ... instead of a proven local product. The result was a steady stream of operational problems. Finally, they brought in an SI mechanic to help 'work through its issues.' That certainly worked well: two weeks later every man, woman and child in St Coriander was dead. I am only thankful that I was attending an IsoTown conference in Milan at the time."

I thought the guy was telling at least some of the truth. But he was also leaving out inconvenient parts. Nobody runs anything without being a pretty good liar, but evidently his deception chops had gotten a little rusty since he moved to Europe. Or this was all an act and he was off-the-charts good.

"That's all old news, Vincent. And whether our Cayoo freelancers and the mechanic are dead or not has nothing to do with our mission. So let's focus on the present, shall we?"

Sheila's voice had taken on a snide edge that grated on me. I was thinking that if we could keep them at each other's throats Maya and I could jump them and get things properly straightened out. But Maya had other ideas.

"Would you two stop your fucking bickering? This is so-o-o-o unprofessional. Me and One-Shoe are trying our very best not to jump you and take you out, but it's really fucking hard when you act like five-year-olds in need of a spanking."

A corner of Sheila's mouth moved slightly. A tiny smile? I thought it might be in appreciation of her fiancée's spunky take-charge attitude.

Maya paused, eyeballed the two Vance's — or whoever they were — then continued her rant. "So take some deep breaths and get your shit together. While you're doing that I'm going to clear the air a bit. So let's start with a little team background information that has come my way.

"Ruella Velikovsky, born June 6, 2146 in Moscow to unknown wealthy parents who were possibly assassinated. Raised in an orphanage until age four when her precociousness got her transferred to the Meridian School for the Gifted in Abingdon-on-Thames. At age fourteen earned a scholarship to St Hugh's College at Oxford. After graduating with high honors at age eighteen, she went on to earn advanced degrees ... something to do with synthetic cognition theory and something else I can't remember right now. She settled into a nice career in Kirlian therapy for high-brows. No marriages, lots of liaisons. In the late 70s got interested in SIs and worked with Dunnetix prototypes for the original Nevers 1.0, in the process becoming one of the first of what we now call 'SI mechanics.'"

Sheila started to open her mouth, but Maya just said, "You can talk when I'm done. Meantime, don't.

"So Ruella was recruited by WorldGov to assay the potential impacts of the SI explosion. In 2105, she founded the SI Anomalies

Investigative Unit and headed it until '25, when she dropped out of sight, possibly due to hazardous Cayoo politics. Some rumors say she's a good friend of Hildi Mazarian and has spent more than a little time at Hildi's Palace on Dinero Dinero in the Caribbean doing things of questionable legality."

Maya paused, winked at me and took a few breaths. Sheila still looked more or less amused.

My favorite chinkrican continued. "Six months ago a refurbed and repersonated version of Ruella Velikovsky shows up in my life as a pampered, hot-to-trot thespian named Sheila Vance who just happened to be the daughter of my client here. While I'm upgrading the security system at his new Heron Lake vacation getaway, we get cozy and you pop this treasure hunt idea on me. How am I doing so far?"

93

"See what I mean? How could I *not* fall in love with a woman as clever and diligent as she is delicious?" Sheila was making a game recovery gambit, but Maya wasn't buying it.

"Nice try, Ruella. Truth is, I still think you're a fox even if you're a lying, double-dealing centenarian Cayoo bitch, but that has zip to do with this mission. If there still is a mission. So why don't you give us your concept of a situation report and where you see things going from here."

Maya was in her steely, don't-even-think-about-fucking-with-me mode, which even scares me sometimes. But not now. Now I was pissed at her. When had she planned to tell me about the real identities of Sheila and Morton Vance? Sure, I had my own secrets I hadn't found the right moment to tell her, but I had my reasons. Good reasons. We all have good reasons for our secrets, right?

I watched the Not-Vances. Their brains were up to their hair follicles trying to recalibrate the circumstances and were in a highly unstable state at the moment. So I decided now would be a good time to relieve them of their slivershots. I was a few milliseconds into my lunge when it hit me that my muscles weren't cooperating. Shit! They'd hyped us while we were knocked out. "Be nice," she'd said. My perfect hindsight told me that had to be a trigger phrase.

Hyping us made perfect sense, but with all the interesting disclo-sures since I'd come awake, I hadn't quite gotten around to thinking about that possibility. Stupid, stupid, stupid! Was I losing my edge? Or had I lost it already due to five years of low-stress routine pa-trolling the woods and licking my wounds?

Wasting time asking stupid questions about stuff that's already history might be another example of getting duller instead of sharp-er. I relaxed and looked at the opposite sofa to see if my stunted at-tempt to lunge had been noticed. Evidently not: all eyes were still on Maya. But knowing we were under hypnotic compulsions of limit-ed activity, why would they even give it a thought? Most likely, they wouldn't. If true, a bit of luck. But right now luck meant time; would I have enough time to run the Circus? That would take a bit of luck ... and then some.

94

14

PLAN C

CIRCUS NIGHTMARES still wake me up sometimes. But the occasional bad dream is a small price to pay for the benefits of Ishernot's trial by fire. You don't leave home without getting through it. No exceptions. It's also one of the reasons some Ishernot natives decide to never set foot outside the caldera.

I went through the Circus when I was 16 and wasn't my pre-Circus self for a month after that. Or maybe ever, now that I think about it.

The first part of it is getting linked up with a remote Cognitic Panalyzer. Nothing bad about a hundred autoprobes burrowing into your scalp and casting a dynamic scan of your normal brainstates for a week. That's nothing. You don't even know it's happening; you're just doing your usual stuff. But the next part — a solid week in the Circus — that's different. It's where Ishy runs you through every known situational sim ... plus a bunch of Ishy's made-on-the-fly improvs based on what it figures your vulnerabilities are.

People who think sims are "just sims" have never been through the Circus. Not even legendary paingames like *The Great Nevergate Hack* can hold a candle to the Circus. It's the gantlet of gantlets, but it's one of an Ishernaut's most powerful defensive weapons ... and the implants teach you lots of countermeasures during the process. Very few psych tricks work for long on an Ishernaut. And I'd had a wetware update on my recent home visit so I was totally up-to-date.

For Circus vets, getting around the average hyp isn't that hard; you just let your Circus cogmodel take a run at it. It takes about two minutes for the little kernel wired into your gray matter to work out what the hyp is doing and bypass it. Downside is you're incredibly vulnerable while it's doing its thing. And until you're running the cogmodel, there's no way to know if the hyp is average or off the charts deep.

Now was a lousy time to be that kind of vulnerable, but I figured being hyped was worse.

I tried my best to look like I was studying Ruella's face, but if she was as smart and psych-savvy as Maya's profile said she was — and if she decided to pay attention to me for even a millisecond — she'd know by a certain emptiness behind my eyes that I was faking it and would instantly try to knock me out of it.

Lucky for me, Ruella had started talking. At the beginning, I only heard about every fifth word because the Circus cogmodel was sucking up a lot of sensory processing power. But she warmed to her subject and was going strong even after I'd cracked the hyp. I could now take them out whenever I wanted to, but I held off out of sheer fascination. Here's the short version of her pitch.

Bear in mind that I'm only replaying what she said to me and Maya. Not saying if I believed it was all right out of *The Holy Encyclopedia of Irrefutable Truth.*

According to Sheila, the plan to raid St Coriander had been hatched in a café in Bolzano, Italy, where the actor Sheila Vance had been taking a break after Romeo and Julio's six-week run in Innsbruck. Vincent O'Kelly, the former Father-Mayor of St Coriander, was munching a pastry and sipping an espresso taking a little break after the Innsbruck X2 run. I hadn't figured him for a runner type, but I'm sure he had a bucket of hidden surprises. Anyway, this sleek, vivacious blond plunks herself down and whispers, "I know you; nice refurb, Dr O'Kelly. Mind if I join you?" Something like that.

If you've ever known many refurbed people, you know that they can get a little awkward around the subject of their refurb. Gets worse if there's been an appearance tweak as well, which is about as far as WorldGov's rules will let you go in altering your appearance. It's not laid out like that, but all the appearance pracs know how far they can go without crossing the line and having the ID fraud hounds yanking on their licenses.

So you can imagine O'Kelly was a little nervous at that little café table, particularly since all his current circle of acquaintances knew him as Morton Vance, the silver-haired semi-retired owner of The War Hole, a fashionable gallery/museum of military arcana in Zurich, Switzerland.

Sheila fed him enough clues for him to finally figure out who she'd been when they last met, which leads me to believe that she already knew some part of the story of St Coriander's missing population before she even sat down at that table. Not that she actually said that. All she said was that one thing led to another and eventually an outrageous plot coalesced.

Before she'd even met Maya she'd tipped off a former Cayoo colleague named Baker Hanley about a possible score. Right up his alley, she'd said. They danced around it for a while before making a deal and laying proverbial cards on the table. He would put together the muscle and he was the one who recruited Henry Ng, the SI mechanic spy, to make contact with the ThoughtDancer and learn how to access the hidden treasure. A mental smile flitted across my brain: the minor mystery of how Maya's brother had arrived on the scene with no tracks was now explained. He was probably ferried in by a black Sumiyo-Brandé fitted with the latest stealth gear and — most important of all — Hoverbars.

That was Plan A, which fell apart when Ng ended up dead in a very ugly way. Hanley was getting nervous about risking his other sure-thing extracurricular activities on a high-risk gamble in Dunnigan territory. And Sheila started having second thoughts about partnering with a guy that gutless. So she and Hanley had a supposedly amicable parting of the ways. Sheila/Ruella was okay with dropping things there, but O'Kelly didn't want to ... and he was the guy who knew where the crypto key was stashed, a little fact Ruella had neglected to mention to Hanley. And because it was hidden in a physical location inside St C, somebody had to get in there to get it, which meant both getting inside without getting blown up and getting past an insane ThoughtDancer. So a new plan took form.

First Maya got sucked into it, then I got tabbed. Since we needed somebody who could communicate with — and hopefully subvert — the ThoughtDancer, we brought in Roston. Innocent as new lambs, we timed our recon to coincide with the Huzbol marathon for cover. And promptly got suckered by Hanley, Dalt and company. But you knew that already.

That was the summary version: the longer version included way too many personal details, particularly about Ruella's bootleg refurb and highly illegal new physio/ID that she got at Hildi's Palace on Dinero Dinero. As every crime drama fan knows, when criminal types proudly blurt this kind of shit, it pretty much means they've decided you're roadkill as soon as they're through using you. Exactly how me and Maya were going to survive the roadkill phase was still a mystery to me. But maybe Maya had something up her sleeve besides tattoos.

The longer Ruella talked, the more antsy the good Father-Mayor looked. His facial expression remained bland and benign, but his pupils had become tiny dots, his neck muscles had tensed and a faint flush had gradually come over his face as Ruella told her story. Looked to me like he hadn't realized until now how far over his head he'd gotten. I didn't know if that knowledge would make him more vulnerable or more dangerous.

O'Kelly interrupted the story. "This is not just about wealth. Harold the Conqueror is a danger to this entire planet. He must be destroyed. Must! If you don't believe me, his plan is all in here. He flaunted it, put it right in front of the community. But they thought it was just a game." He had unfolded a garden variety slate from his pocket and held it out.

"Not now, Vincent! There's no time to go through your pet theory at the moment. And even if you're right, it doesn't matter. You know that as well as I do."

Clearly unhappy, O'Kelly folded up the slate and shoved it back into his pocket.

Sheila/Ruella leaned forward. "Sorry about the sideplay. I fucked up in thinking Hanley was done. The fucker was more devious than I ever gave him credit for. I apologize for that. But I don't apologize for turning his head into bug-splat ... he's had it coming for a lot longer than you know. Believe me, I did the world a favor."

Sheila was probably right about that part.

My guts told me the situation in the concrete room was approaching a flash point. I was trying to decide the best way to make some radical readjustments to the organization chart when Maya interrupted Ruella's spiel.

"Very sweet, Ruella. And now you want us to bend over some more and play whatever end game you have in mind?"

Ruella laughed, a big enough, hearty enough laugh to bust open the tension that had been spiraling upward. "Bending over for the end game, huh? Very cute Maya: I just love it when you talk dirty to me. Naturally there's more bending over. But not too much ... and it won't hurt a bit. I promise. And isn't a quarter of this humongous payday worth a little more bending over? Of course it is. Now here's my idea for Plan C and exactly what we all have to do to get it."

I decided to hold off disabling the pair across from me until we'd heard Plan C ... which had to be better than the Plan Z I had in the back of my head. No way I wanted to activate Plan Z on account of the idea scared the shit out of my sensible self. To my vast surprise, it was O'Kelly who pulled a little something out of his hat that would maybe give us a way to escape this fubarred gig still breathing and with all our limbs intact: current intel.

99

15

PLAN 36DD

IMMEDIATELY SOUTH of St Coriander is an area known as the Kissever Lands. It's technically within the Dunnigan Reserve, but rangers don't patrol it. Never have.

The only structure in it is Kissever House, a rambling mansion built on a high hill at the east tip of Kissever Ridge overlooking St Coriander. The four original Dunnigans built Kissever House back in the 70s before their Dunnetix business took off. When they finished the Dunnigans Wall dam bracked by its famous twin faux medieval castles in the mountains northeast of the Brazos Cliffs, Kissever House was turned into an admin center for Dunnetix. That was back in '91. The company quickly outgrew it and moved away, so for the last three decades it's been an empty shell, visited only by caretaking staff.

This much is common knowledge: they teach all that as part of Ranger indoctrination. The uncommon knowledge was that the abandoned Kissever House contains a secret route into the heart of St Coriander ... so secret not even the ThoughtDancer knew about it. Or the gate.

Sheila/Ruella explained this just before she opened the seemingly antique lock on the vault door. I was getting more impressed with this woman by the second: Sheila/Ruella had been — and maybe still was — very tight with some very powerful people in the Clans. I couldn't imagine any other way she'd be able to access this route into

St Coriander, one even the former Father-Mayor hadn't known about until the two of them got together a year ago.

The concrete room we were in was at the bottom of an industrial-size 1,000' slidewell shaft with its top end somewhere on the Kissever House property. On the other side of the vault door was a tunnel. A maglev monorail occupied the right half, with the rest of it a walkway with some sort of rubberized pavers. The tube was oval in cross-section and was about 20 feet wide. Looked well maintained, but not well used. My head was full of questions, but I just sat in one of the comfortable seats and went along for the ride, which took about two minutes. Smooth, almost silent, very comfortable. Overdesigned, understressed tech. Just the sort of thing I've learned to expect from the Dunnigans.

The monorail slowed and Ruella spoke. "Next stop, Library. We'll get you your patches and then you get to earn your keep, kids."

A few minutes later some kind of multifunction remote of the St Coriander Librarian spat out genepatches a lot like the ones Roston from Boston handed out. We stuck them on our arms and then studied diagrams of places we needed to know about. Ten minutes and we were ready.

"Good luck," said Father-Mayor O'Kelly, who might have even meant it.

Sheila/Ruella was more practical. "We'll reconvene at the Elevation Stage at the appointed time. And keep your thumbs intact: InterGate Commercial Escrow will need your prints on the slate before they'll open and fund your off-planet accounts."

· · · · ·

"So much for Plan Z, huh One-Shoe? I was sorta looking forward to going in with guns blazing and ... no wait, was that Plan T Minus 14 ... or was it Plan 36DD? I just get so confused about this shit." Maya rolled her eyes and grinned her special what-the-fuck-are-we-doing-here grin.

I chuckled and rolled my eyes, too. Sometimes Maya can be a little hard to read. Like now. I was pretty sure our partners were listening, so I didn't share what I'd been thinking. I knew from the alien echoes in my head that Harold was listening ... made me grateful for whatever Ishy did to take the oomph out of the agonized sendings while it was being tortured upstairs by the bad guys, however it is that you torture an SI.

But the Harold in my head was my little secret and I saw no reason not to keep it that way. So I shrugged and continued to walk toward a secret slidewell in the deep stacks of the St Coriander Library, where our new passkeys and the correct button took us to a landing that was supposed to be about 50 feet below the surface. From there we were supposed to walk a couple hundred yards to where it made a left turn, then climb a ladder that ended under a trapdoor in a public restroom in Central Park not far from the Duck Pond.

If what Father-Mayor O'Kelly's private spycams — ones he'd kept out of the systems managed by the ThoughtDancer — showed us was still timely, we'd almost be within shooting distance of the enemy's mobile HQ. You guessed it: the Azteca Grill roach coach. That was where Cayoo techs with psych shields were currently trying to reduce the ThoughtDancer's nanobio hybrid brain to putty ... in the service of certain secrets. That might be okay with O'Kelly, but it wasn't okay with me.

The trap door in the restroom floor opened up in a dark utility closet. A quick flashlight scan for threats yielded a wetvac, two brooms, a rag mop and bucket, and assorted cleaning supplies, toilet paper, etc. No threats there. We opened the closet door with Skotkes in hand but saw no perps, just a typical multi-gender restroom: no urinals, half a dozen stalls. Maya and I looked at each other. "You thinking what I'm thinking One-Shoe? Take care of urgent business before taking care of the other kind?" We both saw the skeletal legs and remains of a skirt in the cubicle closest to the wall, but ignored it in favor of biological urgencies.

I was half surprised — but fully grateful — that the toilets still worked. Now we could get down to the mission. Before I could say how wrong I felt being in there, Maya looked at the stall with the closed door and the skeleton and whispered, "You still thinking we need bones, One-Shoe?"

I nodded. "Maybe we flip for the job?" I mumbled, trying to not look as grim as I felt.

"Nah. Visible skirt means it's a girl job. I'm on it."

While she visited the skeleton I occupied myself by checking the closet for something like duct tape. No luck on that but I hacked off some strands from the mop instead and tied them together to make a couple strings about six feet long. While she was bone-wrestling and cursing under her breath, I studied the well-preserved ladies' overcoat hanging from a peg on the wall. Must've been cold the night of the plague or whatever killed off the population in such a hurry. The stall's door closed and I turned to see Maya brandishing a grim expression and a bone in each hand. Not that we didn't trust the little genepatches, but insurance never hurts.

A minute later we were ready to head out. "That was not at all fun, One-Shoe. The woman I stole these from pretty much had her head buried in the toilet bowl. Vomiting ... that or trying to drown herself." She shook her head, trying to shake that memory away. When that didn't work, she went the fake callous route. "You look really cute wearing a barfing woman's femur taped to your calf, One-Shoe. Very intimate. Now just hook up that Plan 36DD and you'll be good to go." She cupped her hands about a foot in front of her chest, bugged her eyes and did a little shimmy. "Woo-hoo bay-bee! But I think my new tibia accessory is a lot sleeker. Goes perfect with a ZR48 and this hot pair of Skotkes. Who needs big cachongas if they've got these big Skotkes?"

I just nodded and rolled my eyes. Yeah, I was grumpy and not much in the mood for Maya's banter ... even though I know she was doing it to shred the memory and to loosen tension. A subspecies of whistling in the dark, maybe. "What say we get out of this place without getting blown up or shot."

I admit that Maya's first mention of bones in the labyrinths had taken a while to sink in. But it finally got through my well-shielded cranium, and it was bothering me to be joking about strapping on a femur or a tibia that had once belonged to a murdered human being. The truth behind the bones had been gnawing on my conscience since the jumble of skeletons came pouring out of the gate. Either the Thought Dancer or O'Kelly was a large-scale mass murderer. Maybe they'd somehow schemed it together. Now Maya and I were helping them get away with it ... and haul in a huge fortune to boot. And then we were going to let them murder us too? Nah.

Once we pushed open the door and peered outside, the territory looked a lot like O'Kelly's pre-catastrophe pictures we'd studied. I mentally painted in a couple of decades of rampant vegetation growth and the smattering of skeletons for seasoning. But at least our major landmark wasn't about to get lost in the rank underbrush.

The so-called Holy Quincunx is five silver obelisks arranged in a quincunx configuration. Just imagine the "five" side of a standard die and you'll know what a basic quincunx is. The cluster of five glittering obelisks was surrounded by a ring of water, a reflection pond called the Moat. Size-wise, the central obelisk is a little taller than the Washington Monument; the four that surround it are a little shorter. We'd seen it in pictures, but in actual daylight and less than a thousand yards away, it looked alive: reflections and reflections of reflections, fragments, shards, all in almost imperceptible motion. For some reason, I couldn't see the order and beauty of it. All I could see was the chaos. And there was something wrong with the sky; even the wispy cirrus looked too fuzzy, lo-res. I looked at it trying to remember something. Ah. The haze generator I saw from that hill must do that. Was the aerial privacy they gained worth the sky they lost? Maybe I'd ask O'Kelly about that. Or not.

"Hey One-Shoe," whispered Maya. "This place creeps me. Let's get going."

106

16

PURPLE PEN

ACCORDING TO PLAN C, our job was to get up to the Moat, don the gillhoods and take a swim. Actually, Maya was going to do the swimming since the only thing One-Shoe can do in water deeper than a bathtub is sink like a guy with a lead leg. So I was going to stand guard while the homing device guided her to a spot some fifty feet down. That's where she'd find a sealed codebox with half of the account key that had been hidden by Father-Mayor O'Kelly on one of his daily long swims in the Moat. Then all we had to do was meet up with our partners at the Elevation Stage. Piece of cake.

During our white sofas convo I'd stopped myself from asking him the obvious "why don't you do it yourself" question. Just the fact that this slimy jerk had hidden it at all meant he'd been scheming against his "flock" for a long time. I was pretty sure the people of St Coriander hadn't begged him to hide the community treasure chest from them. The part of me that hates slick psychos had already decided O'Kelly wasn't going to skate away from this as one of the richest shitbags in the universes. It was just a question of how and when.

Meanwhile, here we were in Plan C. O'Kelly's latest video intel showed the Azteca Grill parked in front of a blocky, nondescript building to the rear of the anything but nondescript St Coriander Library. The blue glow underneath the vehicle was gone and it now rested on its wheels. The corners we could see each had a bored looking Cayoo sentry, but nothing seemed to be happening outside.

Wanting to keep as much space as possible between them and us, we were going to reach the Moat on the south through the Town Center. That would put a half-mile and a hundred-foot berm in the way, but we needed to get to the top of it so Maya could go swimming. If we took the easy way — the paved trail that wound up the berm from the plaza to the Moat level — part of that little hike would be visible to any sentries or sensors looking our way. So we'd have to do it the hard way.

Leaving the sanctity of our public rest room and its skeleton, we made our way through what had once been Central Park. When I think of park, I think of grass, but any and all grass here had been thoroughly colonized by two and a half decades of rank native underbrush and small trees. Not many species I recognized from my patrols as a ranger, but that made sense; the Reserve was well on its way to being a climax forest, while what we were seeing here were all pioneer species. In the interest of minimizing the impact of my gimpiness on our speed, we kept to the remnants of paths. Keeping us company was a faint whish of a southerly breeze rustling the leaves.

Grainy sunlight glinted off the occasional weathered skeleton in the park, but otherwise nothing to bump us to higher alert than we were already. Within ten minutes the trail fork we'd taken ended at a couple acres of sand dunes that had been colonized by grasses. A sign said it was the "Earthquake Memorial Sandhockey Field," whatever sandhockey was. The fence around it was still intact and the three banks of steep bleacher seats were also still intact ... just bleached looking. Nothing to see here, so we backtracked to the last fork and looped around it on the east.

Like good children, we looked both ways before crossing what had to be St Orwell Loop. This took us into South Park, which didn't look at all different from Central Park. It was the long way to get to where we were going, but we were betting there weren't enough Cayoos left inside to mount any serious patrols. About ten minutes later we took a fork north, crossed St Orwell Loop again and found ourselves on a wide ring of green pavement that surrounds the actual commercial center. Feeling far too exposed, we zipped across that, trying to avoid smashing the grasses growing up in the pores of the pavement, and into what would turn out to be a maze of tiny streets that were little more than alleys.

"Jebus H, One-Shoe." Maya's awed whisper took the words right out of my mouth.

At the entrance was a still legible monument sign of heavy timbers trapped between two miniature concrete obelisks. It had carved gold letters that said only "Boutique District" in a style that was heavy on quaintness. Shops lined both sides of the alleys. Nothing taller than three stories, but each one was a different design and color. If I squinted I could almost imagine it before the structures had become streaked with grime and decay and lichens. Except for the extreme unmanliness of the word, I could have called the Boutique District "cute." I settled for "charming." I looked at Maya: tears leaked down her cheeks.

"It's so 'human,'" she whispered. "People here may have had it easy, but they cared about their pretty little microcosm. Look at all these places ... each one had love in it."

I'd been looking at the alley pavement and the weeds of every description that had invaded every available crack.

Maya ambled — I've almost never seen Maya just amble — down this alley and that, turning at random. I followed, knowing we needed to get on with our mission, but unwilling to drag my partner out of her moment. Then I found myself looking more closely at the fading signs and the store windows that were like little museums of this place and trying to imagine it alive, unfaded and unmolested by time.

Maya stopped ambling in front of Melissa's China Doll House. The place had a white storefront in some architectural style that featured ornate curlicues. These were now covered by layers of dust and moss, but instead of making the place look forlorn and dingy, the grime deposits and streaks gave it an air of almost stately majesty. The windows were full of intricately crafted and dressed figurines in dozens of styles that would never be bought, never be gifted, never be played with. Maya signaled me to stop. She stared for a minute, then shrugged and started to move away. I was about to follow, but one of the dolls in the back row caught my eye. I put my hand on her shoulder and whispered, "Hey, chinkrikan. Check this out."

The doll I pointed to was in an exaggerated martial arts stance, wearing a baggy-sleeved red costume with tiny gold dragons painted on it. Nothing else like it in the whole window, but it was almost hidden by more ladylike dolls with fluffy skirts that wanted to take over the whole window. And it was the only one with Maya's mocha-cinnamon coloring. If that weren't weird enough, its face had her eyes and high cheekbones ... and one corner of her mouth curled up into a "don't-fuck-with-me" expression.

"Tell me that's not my favorite chinkrican," I said.

Maya looked at the doll for a few seconds, then just shrugged and turned away. "Yeah, kinda. Couple things you don't know about me, One-Shoe ...."

"Guess so," I mumbled. There was a story here, but this wasn't the time or place to dig into it. So I just nodded.

It was me that stopped next. The Waft was a smoke shop with elaborate carved pipes and hookas claiming to be fabbed from secret axodymes. The moss green facade had thick, manly fluted columns flanking a heavy wooden door topped with a massive lintel that looked to be carved timber. The windows also displayed open sample boxes of cigars made from — according to the sign in the window — premium tobacco leaf grown by St Coriander's own Horticultural Society. I'd never understood the whole smoking thing, but I found myself wanting to try one of the greenish Pure Mallardback cigars with the elaborate bands. Maya nudged me and we moved on.

We kept to the shadows, but more out of habit than actual fear of encountering an enemy in here. Or a friend, or anything living at all besides plants and insects. Well, probably rats and squirrels, which would account for the occasional something that skittered in the shadows, breaking up the purity of the silence. Part of me wanted to linger, casually wandering around in the wan sunlight like a tourist. But we had work to do and it wasn't in this graveyard where the dreams of St Coriander were buried, above ground and in plain sight. Spooky.

Eventually, our latest alley merged into a wide ring of flagstone pavement that ended at a steep, overgrown embankment a hundred feet tall. According to the pix, at the top was the Moat, a perfect circle of water surrounding the five mirror-surfaced obelisks. Although invisible from where we stood, we could see the shimmering water and parts of the walkway at the top in the reflections from the towers. The broad flagstone plaza in front of us was dotted with trees in round planters and a few sprawled skeletons dressed in the tattered remains of their garments. The only tree I recognized was the single apple in the very center. Decades of fallen fruit had stained both the flags and the skeletons a mottled melange of colors with no names.

To our right was the spot where one of the two spiral paths cut into the Moat's outer wall connected to the plaza. A quarter century of weather and roots had displaced enough of the stone paving of the slope that shrubs and scrubby trees now obscured most of the stone ... and most of the spiral paths, as well. The one I could see was only about three feet wide and had no guardrails. But O'Kelly had said we shouldn't be daunted by the starkness of the paths: he'd walked up and down them every day to hobnob with his fellow citizens at one of the cafés ringing the plaza. But he hadn't thought about the guards. We wouldn't be exactly bare-ass-naked exposed in the northern parts of our route, but we'd be too exposed for my cautious self. By my reckoning, the Azteca Grill and its Cayoo sentries couldn't be more than a couple hundred yards north of our current location. Or less. Too close for comfort. At least they wouldn't hear our whispers.

At the moment we were lurking in the shadowed doorway of one of the cafés he'd mentioned: The Lucky Lady of 13th Street. Its exposed walls were painted with a mural depicting various famous scenes of Madonna 13. Fascinating, but we had no time for any more mental side trips. Even as I forced my eyes away, I found myself wondering why this timeless pop star was so idolized by a citizenry of lucky vegetarian pacifists. Made no sense to me, but I'm sure there was a reason. There's always a reason[2].

I turned away and forced my brain back to the mission. From here I couldn't see where the spiral path intersected with the plaza, but it didn't matter now: I'd made my decision. I signaled Maya to follow me, but she didn't see my signal; she'd wandered to a different café and was staring through the window at something.

This place was called the Apple Pan. "Famous for Pies" was under the name in smaller letters that were still an unfaded apple red. "Hey One-Shoe. I'm thinking about apple pie," she whispered. "Not gonna make a pie or anything, but could we at least grab a few ripe apples off that tree?" I looked where she pointed. The area around the tree was littered with half-rotted fallen fruit. The low-hanging apples had either fallen or been picked off by local deer — maybe even bears — by now, but there were still ripe ones that might be within my reach. I looked at Maya and she half-shrugged, grimaced and cocked her head in a way that I knew was an unspoken "pretty please."

I stood under the tree. Nothing to it if I still had that nice oak staff. The available ripe fruit was a minimum of two feet above my outstretched fingers. Maya pointed and whispered, "How about that?" The "that" she pointed to was some sort of refuse container. UCEY it said in stenciled white letters on the forest green container. It was the nearest of several I spotted on the plaza. Could I use that as a step stool? Maybe. It had a gently rounded top with a hole in it. With my bum ankle I didn't want to try to climb up and balance on top of it. But if I could drag three of them under my apple tree, I was pretty sure it would be plenty stable. So we gave it a shot. They were metal and not very heavy, but they had weighted bottoms. Good for stability.

2 :: *Mr One-Shoe is correct. And the reason can be found in* Genesis ... and Then Some. *This colorful 120-page PDF file can be downloaded at no charge from the author's website: www.etellison.com. The reason for the St Coriander fascination for Madonna 13 will be found in the chapter of Oddballs, Cults and Worldchangers that appeared in the hardcover Chronicler's Edition of* The Luck of Madonna 13.

Maya helped me claw my way to the top of our tripod of Universal Converter collection receptacles. I stood up and reached for the nearest branch for stability. Better. I got myself situated and started reaching up for ripe apples. If I remembered right, you shouldn't have to pull very hard to detach the fruit from the stem if it's ripe. I grabbed the closest prime candidate. Victory! I tossed it to Maya. "How many more do you want?" I whispered. She'd already bitten into the one in her hand and looked up, chewing, with an exaggerated blissful expression. She shrugged, then held up five fingers. No problem.

113

The next candidate was a little higher. I put some weight on my sprained ankle and winced. But I stretched up and got my other hand around the apple, leaning away from the branch that was keeping me balanced. It flexed, broke and the useless piece came off in my hand. My stability crutch was gone and I started to fall forward. My feet jumped back a little to keep me afloat; not a good solution as it turned out. One receptacle tilted when I tried to push off. Then me and the receptacles all came tumbling down in a masterful metallic clatter.

Every bird in the plaza immediately took to the skies. I'm sure the sound pressure rocked the Azteca Grill and caused any Cayoos in the vicinity to say WTF or equivalent and instantly come to high alert. I wouldn't be surprised if people in Chama heard it and scratched their heads. While I was still in the air I found myself on the verge of insane laughter.

My landing wasn't pretty, but old training helped me do a very sloppy forward roll instead of a face plant in the layers of vintage and brand new fruit slime under the tree. I made it back to my feet as fast as I could, grimaced and tested my bad ankle. Shooting pain was back, but nothing broken. I'd live, but I'd be back to hobbling and popping CureAll. I looked at Maya, shrugged and held up the second apple in absurd triumph. Then we beat a hasty retreat. The busted Plan C flashed before my eyes and I saw a shootout that we couldn't win in our immediate future. Shit.

114

17
PLAN Z

FOR FIFTEEN MINUTES we waited for the inevitable. We'd gotten ourselves behind protected corners of the shops on the plaza, ZR48s scanning for any sign of Cayoos from any direction we could see. I watched the openings into the plaza at our level; Maya focused on the top of the Moat. Nothing. Were we lucky or were they circling around behind us? If so, that could take them a little more than we'd allowed so far. So we watched for another ten minutes. Still nothing, so I called it off. Time for a change of plan.

We backtracked a few alleys until we found the shop I remembered seeing: the Purple Pen, a storefront whose name appeared to be written by a 5-foot long quill pen that still hung cantilevered in the air over the door. The quill sagged now, possibly from the encrustation of pigeon shit. I shooed away a trio of sleek gray birds and opened the door with more caution than necessary. We hadn't encountered a locked door yet, which told you something else about either the shared values of the late citizens or the quality of their security sensors. I felt kinda bad about entering uninvited and even worse about pilfering a vintage Mont Blanc Skywriter replica. But I rationalized that my need was greater than the skeletal citizen in the well-preserved black waistcoat and bowler hat who'd evidently elected to go down with the ship. And go down writing, actually. He'd expired while inscribing a letter, which I was tempted to read, but didn't. Maybe later, if we survived.

Maya kept watch for Cayoos while I shamelessly pilfered some very toothy paper I found in a display cabinet. Fully prepared now, I dragged Maya to the Purple Pen's darkened office where I whispered "trust me" in her general direction, then stared up at the darkest corner of the ceiling and wrote her a scribbly three-page note detailing how we were switching from Plan 36DD to Plan Z. Also mentioned why I was writing in the dark, which took a little longer.

When I was done, she took the papers out into the light and read them. When I came out, Maya had already tucked the papers in a pocket. When we were outside, she winked, stood on her tiptoes and whispered in my ear: "About fucking time, One-Shoe."

● ● ● ● ●

I decided the fiasco at the apple tree was a stroke of good fortune. For whatever reason, nobody had come after us: now we were going to find out why. Time to take the war to the enemy. So we circled around the town center and the Holy Quincunx and reconnoitered the Azteca Grill from opposite directions.

Before Maya got into the tech side of security, she'd been a local cop in Los Angeles and a five-year vet of their crack SWAT team. She'd been through the bloody riots during Errigaspovarrial's tenth Nirvana Soul Train Tour in 2232. So she's seen a lot. But one thing she hadn't seen was what we saw that afternoon: jūmonji-giri.

I hadn't actually seen a jūmonji-giri event either, but I'd once been head security advisor for an expensive holo remake of Chūshin-gura, the classic Japanese story of the 47 ronin. Maybe because I look a lot like a Native American (for good reason), the project curator took it upon himself to assuage my total ignorance of samurai culture. He was particularly adamant that I learn too much about ritual suicide: seppuku, also called harakiri. In the basic form, there's usually an assistant — a kaishakunin — who neatly lops off your head with a sword after you slice open your own belly.

Jūmonji-giri is a little more rigorous and a lot slower: you slice open your abdomen with two deep cuts in a cross shape. Then you

TREASURE OF THE HOLY QUINCUNX

pretend that didn't hurt at all and set your blade across your lap just so. The last part is holding your hands over your face until you bleed out and croak. And because you're doing this in front of an audience, you don't want to besmirch what's left of your honor by letting out even a whimper, much less a moan or, gods forbid, a scream.

What Maya and I saw was some modernized combo version that involved blowing your own head off as the capper instead of having a neighborly kaishakunin handle the decap part for you. This do-it-yourself version was quicker than waiting to bleed out, but a lot messier.

One Cayoo Securitan had been standing guard at each corner of the roach coach. Now all four were on the ground, unrecognizable mush for heads and with red leakage still dribbling up out of their middles. You can probably visualize the associated fluids and spew well enough. The dead four included the guy with the patched up thigh wound.

The way I figured it, each had pulled off the combat armor that covered his belly and carved the slashes with his own combat blade: one horizontal, the other vertical. If my guess was right, each guy left his knife lying crosswise about where his navel had been, then stuck his sidearm under his chin and pulled the trigger. If I had to bet, I'd put my money on Harold the Conqueror as the inspiration for these suicides. So I guess we should thank him (I'm having a hard time thinking of an entity that calls itself Harold the Conqueror as an "it") for taking out the sentries.

Maya and I had scoped the suicides from opposite vantages as far away as we could manage, then communicated by our private hand signals to rendezvous at the back of the building the Azteca Grill was shielding. O'Kelly had said it was where the ThoughtDancer's core was located, but one glance and I was pretty sure the SI had been forcibly relocated; the heavy metal doors of the building had been ripped open and were now dangling from one hinge. A flexible tube the size of an anaconda snaked out of the open doorway and was plugged into a port in the side of the coach. I pulled out the Mont

Blanc and Maya and I had a little planning session in the dark on some of that arty paper made by St Coriander's Fibrous Reality Society.

Plan Z was facing a little dilemma. We had no idea how many hostiles were inside the roach coach. Unaccounted for were three that I knew of for sure: Max Dalt, Roston from Boston and the big Cayoo field commander. But somebody had piloted the vehicle and I was betting there had also been Cayoo techs inside. I was also betting they had ways of monitoring the immediate vicinity, so they might already know we were here. But I hadn't seen anything that looked like firepower.

"STALEMATE?" I wrote in big letters.

Maya took the pen out of my hand and wrote "Smoke 'em out? Old fashioned, but … "

I leaned over and kissed the top of her psychshield.

• • • • •

The back end of the roach coach was the only side with no windows or doors, but there was a big exhaust vent near the top that ran its whole width. It was emitting a low hum and the infrared signature of my nocs clearly showed it as hot, so we knew it was working. Had to be optics hidden in the grille, but at this point I didn't much care.

Maya and I worked our way around the angular Library structure to a spot that let us see Central Park and the restroom where we'd filched the bones. Whatever you might think of an out of place structure inspired by an award-winning 21st century library in Vennesla, Norway, it did a nice job of visually protecting us from any surveillance from inside the coach. While I made a foray to gather a supply of green fuel, Maya snuck back to the Stitchery Cooperative, a sunny yellow place we'd passed that billed itself as a showplace for homecrafted garments. She must have sprinted, because in a couple minutes she was back with a pair of voluminous skirts made from recycled ladies' undergarments originally compiled by the Central Fabrax. Good to know all that.

I set an armload of shrubbery on each skirt and started to piss on the first smokebomb. You may not know this, but burning urine is right up there with skunk fragrance for gagworthiness.

Maya grinned and made some amusing sign gestures. I was to turn around while she pissed on the other pile. Not like I hadn't seen her pee before, but fair enough. As soon as she'd pulled her pants back up we made nice bundles that I figured I could fling at least thirty feet. We also figured the safest way to run this idea up their flagpole was to get as close as we could to the rear of the vehicle, dial down one of the Skotkes and trigger a couple low intensity blasts at the exhaust ducts. Maybe we'd get lucky and take out any cameras, but if we didn't get that lucky at least we'd get their attention. Then I'd toss the first smokebomb. With luck there was a fresh air intake in the back or front or maybe both.

While they were trying to figure out what the first one was all about, I'd get to the ThoughtDancer's blockhouse and toss the second one in the front of the vehicle. Maya would stay low behind the Library wall and set the ZR48 to watch the door and the metal flap on the side that they'd flip up to trade money for enchiritos if this thing had been a real tacomobile ... which it wasn't. I'd hang by the west edge of the blockhouse, which would let me zero in on the driver side door. I figured we had 'em covered. Wrong.

I lit the first one, let it burn until it was almost too hot to grab and tossed it. It landed a few feet from the rear of the coach; not perfect, but good enough ... and it was spewing enough noxious smoke to get their attention.

Maya kept her ZR48 on target and I gimped it around the Library to my appointed fling point for the second. I was about to light up when I heard the door on the other side open ... a little too noisily. There was a metallic noise, then the sound of a heavy boot on the ground. The Cayoo honcho, stepping out? Or Max Dalt?

"On the ground, motherfucker," screamed Maya in her most fearsome killer bitch tone.

I had just started to suspect something when somebody's Skotke went off. Maya screamed the wrong kind of scream. "I'm down One-Shoe. Go low!"

I dropped flat and rolled, now seeing a new shape under the roach coach firing at my recent cover. The corner of the blockhouse took the hit ... all I got was a peppering of concrete shards. The guy who fired had taken a major risk that he'd get me with his first shot. Bad bet, thanks to Maya's warning. He didn't even have time to scream before most of his head and shoulders turned to mush.

I rolled back up and sprinted around the front.

A guy in a too-loose Securitan uni was lying face down on the pavement, arms extended, no visible weapons. My left hand had him covered with the Skotke and for a second I thought he was the head Cayoo. Wrong second to be thinking that. A guy I couldn't see in the shadows inside the open doorway made a well-placed shot and sent pieces of my Skotke flying, along with my hand and half of my forearm. I'm ashamed to say, I crumpled on the spot and figured my time was up. Did I scream? I don't remember that moment, but I'm pretty sure I shouted at least one extended obscenity.

Then the shooter spoke. "You want the big guy to live, Maya, toss out your firepower where I can see it. Or I can finish him right now and you can bleed to death. Your choice."

I'd never heard that voice before, but Maya had. I watched her face go white and I didn't think it was from her foot wound; the boot was pretty much shredded and there was blood, but at least her foot was still attached, something I couldn't say for my left forearm.

"You're supposed to be dead," she said in a shaky voice I could barely hear.

"Ah, yes. We can discuss death and the utility of Hildi's delightfully illegal 30-Day Clone program when you've slid the firepower out where I can see it: by firepower, I mean both Skotkes and the ZR48. And then crawl over close to your Indian."

The voice aimed itself in my direction now. "She called you One-Shoe, am I right? I believe you're the fellow who discovered my late, unlucky clone. Most convenient. The late Mr Dalt told me quite a bit about you. Of course, I'll need you to cooperate as well. Toss your two remaining pieces, if you will.

"Roston, you can get up now. I'll want you to kick all the weapons as far away as your scrawny legs will kick them. Then take off the uniform; I might need it. And then sit on the ground and wait for further instructions like a good little Bostonian."

Roston got to his feet looking not so good. His face had been worked over pretty well and he was barely able to stand. But after couple of tries he kicked our firepower out of reach. Now he was obediently peeling off the uniform, which I figured was the big head Cayoo's. He folded the uniform, set it down and stood there in pinstriped boxers, his skinny white body shuddering from some unpleasant cocktail of cold and abject fear.

I'd clamped my good hand over what was left of my forearm to stop the bleeding from my ragged stump. I remember thinking that if I fainted or just got too weak to hold on, I'd bleed to death for sure. Then the shock trauma protocol from the Circus kicked in.

Once the hardware and humans were properly arranged, Henry Ng stepped out of the coach with fire extinguisher in hand and put out our smokebombs, humming a nondescript tune while he did it.

Then he walked over and stood over Maya, who had left a trail of blood on her way over to me and looked seriously pale. "Well, little sister. You've made a most untidy mess. I'm tempted to punish you, but my dear friend Ruella would likely be displeased. She finds your company, ah, pleasurable, and nurtures a silly wish that she can train you to be a compliant pet. I told her you're not very trainable, but she was adamant.

"But of course she's going to be displeased anyway when I tell her that the ThoughtDancer truly doesn't know where the codebox is. So now we'll have to explore other options."

Maya's undead brother tilted his head, fondled a goatee that wasn't there and raised an eyebrow in a caricature of thought. I'd encountered talkative psychos like him before: they like to show you

121

how much they know that you don't. Like telling us Max Dalt was dead. In my book, it's just stupid to give an adversary any free intel ... unless it was fake info for misdirection. But he'd probably killed Max himself and was proud of it.

Guys like this, they like to toy with their victims. Both Maya and I had ways to take him out, but one of us would probably die in the process. Maybe both of us. The more I thought about it, the more I thought he was just waiting for us to make a play.

122

I know it sounds a little too convenient, but that's when my implant went crazy.

I was pretty sure I remember Ishy saying they'd added special shielding when they implanted it, but it still felt like somebody was using my head as a jackhammer. Roston's arms and legs went straight and stiff, almost like he'd gotten zapped with 10,000 volts. Then his eyes bugged out and smoke started coming out of his ears. His mouth was open like he wanted to scream, but only a burbling sound came out. Then his stiff body fell backwards and whacked itself against the pavement. His skull hit with a sound that reminded me of a ripe pumpkin hitting a boulder.

The actual scream came from the guy lording it over us: Maya's brother. Evidently Harold was not totally incapacitated.

As soon as Henry Ng finished his scarecrow swan dive, I forced myself upright, dug a stun grenade out of my pack and tossed it into the open door. When I didn't hear any screams or thumps from inside the vehicle I figured it was safe to pass out. So I did.

18

BE NICE

EYEBALLS DANGLING from smoking eyesockets is not something you'll ever want to see up close. Maya will ditto that. But she wanted to make absolutely certain that the guy under the facial disguise was actually her brother, so she gutted out the part of rolling the body over so we could pull off his mask. Turned out to be easy; whatever had shocked him had loosened the biostatic adhesive they use on those things and it was already curled up around the corners.

Maya stood over her late brother very quietly, saying nothing for five minutes, but the tears streaming down her face were speaking volumes. She was letting go of some really deep fears ... I could see it in the way she held her shoulders. We needed to finish this off, but she needed to finish what she was doing more. So I held my stump up, kept my mouth shut and thought about the mask.

A good lifemask like that costs about 25,000 teros on the black-market, compared to an adequate-from-a-distance theatrical version for, say, a tenth of that. Probably a couple dozen people on the planet that could make one that good and most of them are working for one WorldGov dark agency or another. But some were freelancers. I made a mental note to check that out sometime. Might be handy to know who those people were.

"Okay, One-Shoe. I'm done here. Remind me later that we oughta tell somebody that the guy who owned the original of this face is probably a permanent MIA."

"Check." I know Maya and she wasn't quite done here.

"You know, One-Shoe, I was going to grind the asshole's fucking eyeballs into the pavement. Then I was going to tell you to turn around so I could piss in his eyesockets. And then as soon as I thought those things, you know what I wanted to do?"

I shrugged and shook my head.

"I wanted to laugh. For about an hour. For that motherfucking psychopath to end up like that ...."

"Twice," I added, recalling what the tech had told me about the corpse that started all this.

"Right. Twice. Sometimes karma does my laughing for me."

The one-armed hug I gave her right then wasn't great as hugs go, but at least it let us move on.

You could say I'd wasted the grenade, but you could also say most insurance policies are wasted. Inside we found four Cayoo techs and one Max Dalt, all out of play by virtue of death. They were neatly stacked in a corner. Very tidy. A little less tidy was the trapdoor in the floor of the coach; some of the chief Cayoo's head parts had splattered up onto the frame. Depending on how things went, I might clean it up later. For now I just plunked the trapdoor back in place.

There was no splatter on any of the tech bodies, each one had a tiny dark hole under his or her ear at the jawline. Very neat. Only thing I know that makes tiny holes like that is a fingershot pellet, a near-silent, low velocity burrower with a nasty neurotoxin-coated fryball for a payload. Assassins love shit like that. As a matter of security policy, the Cayoos would not knowingly allow an outsider with a fingershot into their presence unless he was one of them. So my guess was the late Baker Hanley had hired him on his own as a contractor to impersonate the staff driver ... and Ng had played them all.

Looked to me like Max Dalt's death was a little more personal: crushed windpipe and nose cartilage rammed into his brain. Not the sort of thing the headless Chief Cayoo under the coach would have done: not in their combat manual. My guess was Henry Ng was a highly paid freelance assassin who had the luxury of using his SI mechanic status as a cover. If we had any luck at all, he'd stay dead this time. But I wondered.

Once we patched and drugged ourselves as well as possible with stuff in the first aid box, we moved on to other urgencies. First was food. There was a tiny galley with a trio of MenuMasters that we put to good use. It still amazes me that an oversized box can somehow turn out a decent imitation of a hamburger and a plate of potato salad without any human intervention at all. Then I remembered that MenuMaster scene from Men in Black CXIV and almost trashed the burger. Almost.

125

While we were eating, we tried to get a read on the entity in the coffin-sized armored box. The interior of the Azteca Grill had been fitted out as a mobile life support and analytic system for SIs ... at least any of them whose core components would fit inside it. It was clean, sleek and looked like it had some very sweet tech.

From the outside, the ThoughtDancer's home looked like an oversized black coffin made of some kind of composite: unadorned, but somehow elegant. Probably bombproof. It was hooked up to an array of tubes, hoses and cables plugged into appropriate connectors on a section of stainless steel wall. A large slate in the top of the box showed various indicators, but most of them were in some kind of tech language, so they didn't tell us much except that the thing inside was still alive. But I knew that already: an eyeball message from Ishy said it wanted to talk to me.

I whined to Ishy that it had just smoked — literally — two licensed SI mechanics ... and one of them was also a professional hitter. I was no match for a thing like that. Gave me a creepy feeling just being in the Azteca Grill with it: might be me that gets fried next. I had one of those implants, after all.

Then Ishy reminded me of our deal. I'd forgotten all about the fact that I'd agreed to get the ThoughtDancer to Ishernot if it helped us. Was that why it killed the SI mechanics? Earning its keep? In fairness, I had to admit it had kept me and Maya alive. Or maybe it had nothing to do with us. Maybe it was payback on the mechanics for trying to steal its secrets with their doctored implants ... or maybe payback for their lousy job of torturing it? And maybe it had a grudge against Maya's bro? Hardly a surprise.

My arm and my head were throbbing and at the moment I felt way out of my league. And before we could even try to figure out how we were going to get Harold out of here we had to do this little meet-up with Ruella — whose double-dealing hireling, Henry Ng, had just about taken us out. Not to forget O'Kelly, who was merely the mild-mannered architect of one of the biggest mass murders in history. I'd pretty much given up on the idea of a share in the tainted riches, but I didn't know how Maya felt about it.

I told Ishy I'd get back to it soon ... if it could spoof any local eavesdroppers and turn off our link for about half an hour on account of needing to have an overdue heart-to-heart with Maya. It took Ishy all of thirty seconds to give me a thumbs-up. The link going dark was almost an audible click inside my head. Freedom takes strange forms: this new spy-freedom felt like a sack of cement had just grown wings and flown away from my shoulders.

"Back in the real world again, One-Shoe? So you've got an implant, too, right? You trying to make me feel like the odd man out or something? Who've you been silently chatting with for the last five minutes? Some horny chick, probably."

I squelched my expression of relief. Maya's little act was all for Ishy's benefit, just in case it was still listening. Cover for the fact that my first note in the dark had mentioned the implant and that it was watching everything.

"Horny chick? Nah. Another shapeless brain-in-a-box: Ishy, our custom Dunnetix Superba down in Ishernot. Ishy's all business ... and I trust it like a friend."

"Excellent. Me and Ishy are both all business," she said. "And my business with you right now is listening while you tell me all the little secrets you've been keeping from me."

I grinned again. "How about I show you mine if you show me yours?"

• • • • •

Our meet-up destination was a whole floor high up in the central obelisk. With the ThoughtDancer pretending to be disconnected I was afraid we might have to stump our way up umpteen flights of stairs, but the backup systems worked and we took a slidewell to the Elevation Stage.

Hafta say, I found the Elevation Stage a little on the sterile side. Well, not the actual stage so much as the room it was in. The stage was just a raised platform about ten feet in diameter set in the center of a circular theater sort of place. There were half a dozen concentric rows of plush seats surrounding the stage. The walls were sheathed with something that looked like white marble slabs punctured by four tall stained glass windows. They glowed with muted light and depicted exotic ethereal scenes that made no sense to me at all. But as expensive eye candy, I couldn't say I'd ever seen anything to beat them. Awe-inspiring, but hardly a place you'd describe as inviting. A power and control thing, standard operating procedure for religions.

We arrived a little late for reasons that I'll explain shortly. The big doors were propped open and when Ruella waved, we staggered in — not even needing to fake it — and made our way up the circular stairs to the actual stage. Our 'partners' were seated in portable chairs at a portable table; we sat in the two empties. In the middle of the table was a slate. So evidently they were going to play it all the way as if nothing had changed ... except we'd sustained injuries in the line of duty and they hadn't. Okay by us.

O'Kelly pointed at my bandaged arm, opened his mouth and made to stand up, but Ruella sat him back down and whispered something we couldn't hear. I was pretty sure she'd never won any sympathy or empathy awards.

We expected they still had weapons, so we'd decided to go in fully armed ... well, except for me at fully armed minus one-half. Maya had liberated her brother's fingershot — finger included — and had taped it to her left middle finger, like a splint. It wasn't wired up, but it was definitely an attention getter. O'Kelly frowned, but Ruella knew exactly what it was and whose demise had allowed it to be on display here. I suspect her confidence deflated a little, although she was good enough at the game not to let it show.

Ruella opened her mouth to start the proceedings, but Maya held up her left hand with the rigid little finger. "My dear brother said to tell Ruella to go fuck herself. So on his behalf, go fuck yourself, Ruella. But later. As to your heartfelt condolences for the injuries we sustained on this fucked up mission, we can revisit them in a posh bar at the Hotel d'Estrella on Nondescripto's third moon. Right now, we need to do some business. Oh, and in case your sensors haven't told you already, the ThoughtDancer did not survive his transfer and inquisition by the Forces of Darkness."

O'Kelly couldn't completely mask his relief. "I was never able to pinpoint what went wrong with it. Hopefully this sort of trouble doesn't crop up for other customers. For several years, we had no problems at all with it." He sighed, big, deep and phony. "Well, I suppose we must all move on and try to make the best of it."

Ruella said nothing, I said nothing.

Maya nodded, waited a few seconds and leaned forward, moving her gaze between Ruella and O'Kelly. "Excellent advice. Let's all make the best of it, starting now. So. Do you have your half of the access code? We fished out our contribution. Hope you don't mind that we cleaned off the slime." She produced a rectangular evermetal box with five raised nubbins opposite the side with the invisible hinge. It was like a slightly undersized version of a personal cigar case we saw in the window of The Waft.

O'Kelly reached for it, but Maya pulled it away. "No-no-no. You didn't answer my question. First things first, as my dear mother always used to say."

Ruella stayed mum, her lips squeezed a little too tightly together. She nodded to O'Kelly, who put on his most mellifluent voice for the occasion. "It is right here in this room, of course. I need only remove it from its cache. Naturally, it would not have been appropriate to do so until all four parties were present."

Ever the smooth old dog, I thought. But what else was he going to say?

"So do it, please. Now." Maya gave him her sweetest, once-you-were-going-to-be-my-father-in-law smile.

I watched Ruella, trying to read her devious mind. It seemed like a fleeting smile might have flickered across her face, but I couldn't be sure. She wasn't going to cave, that was clear.

"Will you need an escort, Father-Mayor? I'm sure One-Shoe would be happy to accompany you."

"As you wish, Maya dear. I have nothing to hide. It is at the control console. Come with me, Travis."

I hobbled behind him, wondering what scheme he had in mind. Trying to run a seamless triple-cross takes some doing.

The controls for the Elevation machinery — the psyfrac, whatever that was — were nothing if not simple. The control console was set into a raised semicircular pulpit against the far wall across from the door. Evidently the priest or whatever title they used here climbed up three steps, putting him level with the Elevation Stage. Concealed from the viewers were two lights: one red, one green above a convex button about the size of a human palm. Neither light was illuminated at the moment.

"That's all it takes to disappear somebody?" I asked, sincerely.

O'Kelly gave me a wise-old-man look. "Have you ever found anything to be truly simple, Mr One-Shoe?"

"Well, Dr O'Kelly, occasionally I have. Yes. Death can be truly simple. Life? Nothing about life is simple, is it? So please show me how to retrieve the other codebox and I'll be happy to simply fetch it for you."

"You don't trust me, do you Travis." It wasn't a question.

"In a word, no. Now where's the fucking codebox?"

My left hand may be gone, but my right hand is very fast. Before he could even start to answer or make a move I was holding a stinger on his neck. "This belonged to Maya's brother Henry. Not a very nice man, Dr O'Kelly, but a competent assassin. Until he ran into a bigger dog. You know what they say about wounded beasts being extremely dangerous? Same with a wounded One-Shoe.

"Anyway, Maya's brother used this stuff to get truth out of people. It works amazingly well. And speaking of truth, did you know Henry Ng was working for Ruella? And that after they took out all the Cayoos they were planning to split your proceeds ... assuming one of them didn't take the other out first?"

Before O'Kelly could say or do anything, I heard Ruella shout, "BE NICE!"

19
ELEVATION

I HEARD THE MAGIC words, but I wasn't prepared for what happened next. Should have been, but wasn't.

After the Circus had figured out the hyp and disabled it, I knew how to neutralize it myself. So when we were cooling down after our emergency stress reduction lustfest, I explained the hyp and the Circus to Maya and did a quickie hypnosession to undo hers.

So now we were both free of it ... and that was a major load off my mind. But Ruella and O'Kelly were still holding way too many cards. We had unwound a lot of the story, but there were still too many unknown landmines left that could take us down. So I still worried.

If the hyp hadn't been unwound, we were supposed to lose our will to act against Ruella in any way when she said "be nice." Had to be her saying it, too. Wouldn't work if it were any other voice. The kernel containing the Circus cogmodel didn't have data for a thousand scenarios, just the rough outlines of the hyp construct. My interpretation of its potential impact would include a scenario like just sitting frozen while Ruella calmly raised her weapon, took careful aim at the center of one of our faces and blasted it into a spatter of tissue and bone that would make three houseboys spew their cookies trying to get it cleaned up. Or, if the shooter wasn't inclined toward excess, she could dial it back and kill us just as dead and just as fast but without the mess.

In my experience, angry people usually go for maximum obliteration. Trained killers like Henry Ng take pride in metered precision. We never found out which type Ruella was.

As soon as I heard BE NICE, I spun to look at Ruella. Maya sat frozen like a stone while Ruella started to raise her Skotke. I almost shit my pants. Did I fuck up the hypnosession?

The scene unfolded in that kind of slow motion that happens sometimes. Ruella's gun stopped in front of Maya's forehead and her mouth opened, no doubt to explain how the hyp worked. It would be a gloating explanation, followed by another explanation, a patient instruction about what would happen next. My slo-mo explanatory imagination was interrupted by the unmistakable sound of a wide-open Skotke.

Back in realtime, two things happened at the same instant. Under the table, what had been the bottom half of Ruella's right leg dropped to the stage with a wet slap.

Above the table, Maya's left hand — the one with her late brother's middle finger taped to it — snatched Ruella's weapon out of her hand before the explanation-turned-scream could even make it to her former fiancée's open mouth. "Sorry Ruella, you earned that. It'll hurt like a motherfucker for a while, but they'll fix you up with a nice wooden leg in prison."

My heart stopped. The drama had sucked me in, but O'Kelly saw it as a gift from the gods. By the time I got turned back around his hands were already at the control panel.

"MAYA! FLY!"

I tried to jostle O'Kelly, but his open palm hit the big button dead center. The red light started flashing. Oh shit!

Ruella's scream finally came out while she was grabbing for the shredded meat and splintered bone where her knee had been. Her shriek was a mix of pain and rage, something I understood all too well, and it echoed the round room like it was chasing its own tail.

Her frantic movement tipped the table and launched it at Maya just as she was starting a lunge toward the edge of the stage. Her injured foot was a little slow to respond and got tangled in the chair leg, which sent her flying backwards out of control. She landed at the edge of the stage with a hard whump that might have knocked the wind out of her.

Ruella was falling forward now, and a dagger had appeared in her right hand. Her arm was cocked but I figured it was going to be a seriously off-balance throw and I doubted it would do any damage unless Ruella was a world-class flinger. Maya saw the move and made a half-roll to her left. Now teetering on the edge of the stage, she threw up her left arm, deflecting the blade just enough that it grazed her psychshield and thunked against one of the witness chairs. I already told you Maya is quick: greased lightning's got nothing on her.

Behind me, O'Kelly grunted, not an elegant grunt but I heard satisfaction in it. Without looking, I swung my left arm where I thought his head was. The haymaker had all my weight behind it and was boosted to at least double power by my anger. It would have taken off his head if I'd connected, but the bandages just grazed the top of his nearest shoulder. It probably hurt me more than it hurt him.

Off balance from that powerhouse swing, I slammed into the wall just in time to see his hand hit the green light. My good arm shot out and landed a solid shot on the side of his jaw, slamming his head back against the marble wall. Lights out, but too late to matter. That's when I realized the room had suddenly gone silent ... right in the middle of Ruella's stream of epithets.

On the stage, Ruella's image wobbled, faded and then blinked out. All in one second. Just like that. No poof, no spacey sound effects, no miniature tornado. Just gone. Elevated to wherever. Her detached leg, too, along with all the blood and stuff. Leaving the stage completely clean. No blood and body parts ... and no Ruella and Maya either. Just gone. That was when I screamed "MY-YAAAH!" at maximum volume. I think it took an hour for my throat to recover from that scream.

I was pounding on the control panel with my one remaining fist when a small sound slipped between thumps and all the way to my auditory nerve. Several very small sounds, actually: a rustle, a scrape,

133

a creak. I stopped pounding and something like fingernails tapping on something hard came through. Then, "What the fuck, One-Shoe. Hey One-Shoe, where's Ruella?" There was a long pause while I was too stunned to respond, then, "Hey lover, you hearing me okay?"

20

THE BOX

SURE, IT WAS A RELIEF to have Ruella off our plate, but right then I was operating in an optimism vacuum. The simple recon mission had turned into a can of worms so big it would keep a horde of fishermen in bait for a lifetime. And if there was an end in sight, I was too drained to see it. Plus, we were still trapped in a dead town and my gut told me that either Dunnigans or legitimate Cayoos or maybe even Securitans — or all the above — were going to start hitting our fan any minute. But right now we had O'Kelly to deal with. And I'd made a promise. Two, actually.

I could imagine a dozen ways he could spin things and skate away from a couple thousand cold-blooded murders. But at least he wasn't holding the key to a trillion teros in his greedy little mitts. Not yet, at least. Maya and I looked at each other and nodded. We would play it all the way to the end.

We decided to move the proceedings to the Azteca Grill. Why? For one thing, we'd had enough of St Coriander. We'd been here long enough that we could feel the graveyard aspect of it throttling down our spirits. But we also wanted to get O'Kelly out of his comfort zone. Mostly for effect, we bound his hands, gagged him and put a hood over his head. The hood from his own cassock worked just fine for that and we were pretty sure the irony wouldn't be lost on him.

The sky was a dull charcoal by the time we got him into the coach and sat him down for his truth session. Since I was pretty useless,

Maya cobbled together a spotlight setup, aimed it at his eyes, then tied his head to the chair in a way that made it virtually immobile. This was partly for effect and partly so he wouldn't be inclined to pay much heed to the ThoughtDancer's living coffin only a few feet away. I ordered up some coffee and spike in one of the MenuMasters and tried to collect my wits. Maya ordered milk and a whole pumpkin pie, and sat across from O'Kelly, eating it with her fingers. I don't know how she does it, but she never seems to get tired the way I do. I could almost hate her for that.

The first thing out of his mouth was a confession; I didn't even have to threaten him with the stinger again. But all he confessed to was this: there were never two halves to the code, each hidden in a different cache. There was no secret compartment in the control panel for the Elevation Stage. That was all a fabrication to keep Ruella at bay. The full account code was in the box Maya had retrieved from the Moat. Now that he'd made that confession, he wanted a favor: he wanted to see the evermetal box with the codekey in it again. He admitted it wouldn't do him any good at this point, but at least he wanted to be able to see it and touch it one more time.

A little message from my implant said he was bullshitting; there *was* a second codebox and it was in the floor under the seat of the pulpit in the Elevation sanctum or whatever they called it. And each box had the full code. Good to know. Even better to know was that each had enough explosives to obliterate half of St Coriander if the wrong sequence was punched in three times in a row. Not really that much kablooey power, but enough to vaporize the person holding it. That was creepy.

"Before we do anything like that, Dr O'Kelly, I'd like to know what's inside that box. Describe it please. Exactly."

I was a little surprised, but he was quite forthcoming. "It's nothing special, really. It's an evermetal tube containing a crystal matrix with an encrypted code in the standard Universal Secure Access Format. It can only be decoded in a certified device. If you must know, Ruella knew that ... and she knew that she did not have a certified device handy. So the business with the slate and the thumbs was her ruse designed to, ah, enhance cooperation."

"Oh. And you think that knowing this, we should trust you enough to let you even look at it? Maya, your thoughts on this, please?"

Maya made impolite chewing noises, swallowed another bite of pumpkin pie, gulped and delivered a championship grade belch. "I say kill the fucker. Now. And very painfully. He's responsible for all the skeletons around here. I've been listening to them ... and they all say kill the fucker. Betcha Ruella would say the same thing if she were here." She paused for a second, then added, "Hey, where did he send her anyway? Wherever it is, people are going to be seriously grossed out to see her sweet devious self hopping around trying to fetch her leg and screaming obscenities and making a bloody mess. But really, I don't give a shit. Just kill the fucker."

O'Kelly looked a little panicky; smart guy to take Maya seriously. But he ignored the part about where Ruella had gone and leaped right into the blame game.

"No, no, no ... it was the ThoughtDancer's idea from the beginning. The Excel model has historically suffered from systemic quasi-hormonal imbalances. This one — Harold the Conqueror it liked to call itself — was creating a gigantic panache entirely out of human bones. His persona, Harold, was a dragon fashioned after a famous imaginary creature called Smaug, which guarded its treasure hoard and hated all interlopers. In its fantasies Harold could soar and dive and breathe fire. But in its actual 'life' — a term I use in quotes — it was unable to ambulate. So no matter how many sensors it had, no matter how many actuators it could actuate, it saw itself as the equivalent of a human quadriplegic. As a result, it was envious of anything with mobility. This is all in the sealed record of its past placements. There were always inexplicable deaths, exquisitely designed murders that were never solved. The committee just did not do its due diligence and I expect their recommendation had much to do with the steep discount offered by the reseller ...."

O'Kelly had gotten a little too pompous in tone and I felt like taking him down a notch. I held up my hand. "Well, that certainly gives us much food for thought. Of course, it is interesting that the original invoice cites a substantial finder's fee payable to the same anonymous numbered account that Maya's invoices for her security services were paid from."

O'Kelly wanted to interrupt and deny the cold hard evidence we'd just gotten from the ThoughtDancer via Ishy. But I cut him off. "No matter. Probably just a coincidence ... or maybe a coding error. In any case, it has been a long several days and we're all buckets more than tired. Plus, my new stump feels likes it's being hammered by hairy pygmies with stone axes. So Maya: the box please."

"Okay, but it's your funeral, One-Shoe. Mark me down in the Kill the Fucker Now column." For emphasis, she held out her last wedge of pie, point first, a couple inches from his nose and said "Bang ... you're dead."

The scrumptious spice aroma of pumpkin pie hit me just then. So good it made me want to smack her for the good cop/bad cop violation of Overplaying a Role in Front of a Famished Partner. But I knew she was just teasing me, showing off a little, probably overcompensating for a foot being hammered by its own set of hairy pygmies.

She reached into a pocket, pulled out the box and handed it to me.

It was getting hard to keep up with the two conversations, so I bought time to think by trying to look thoughtful ... even though I knew the spotlight kept O'Kelly from seeing much of my face.

Ishy had some feedback on O'Kelly's spiel ... straight from the ThoughtDancer in the silent coffin next to me. And also some analysis of its own. According to the Colloquy, an informal network of SIs, the Excel model has had problems, one of which is a mobility envy that affects not just TDs, but many different varieties of SIs, Dunnetix models included. But these issues are fixable. On the other hand, they can also be readily exploited. The ThoughtDancer let Ishy tap into a node containing the full history of O'Kelly's interactions with it. Based on that, Ishy suggested I give the fake codebox to the real perp. Quite likely, truth would result. Ishy was more confident about the truth part than I was, but it knew things I didn't.

The silvery box I studied was an exact duplicate of the pair O'Kelly had fabbed at the Central Fabrax a long time ago: 27 years, three months and fourteen days, to be almost exact. He'd been setting up this heist for a long, long time.

One of the reasons we were a little tardy for our meet-up at the Elevation Stage was to pick up this little item. The ever-so-cooperative ThoughtDancer had sent the axodyme code to the Central Fabrax, which, it assured us, still functioned. And it did: its voice didn't even sound creaky after all these years with no exercise. It assured us that the box was a perfect replica, except for one small detail that it was not able to reveal. Since it seemed to be working for the good guys, I didn't pry ... but I did let myself hope that the small detail happened to be the explosive charge.

139

I held it to the light, watched the reflections slide as I turned it. As designed objects go, this was a simple one ... beautifully simple. I ran my fingers over it, sighed a real sigh of appreciation. I almost didn't give it to him. But that would ruin the game, so I frowned and held it out to former Father-Mayor O'Kelly, taunting him, watching his eyes, listening to Ishy's commentary.

I gave him my best squinty don't-even-think-about-getting-tricky expression, then asked Maya to unbind his arms and unshackle his wrists. My part was to hold out the box.

As I expected, he accepted it with grace and aplomb.

"Can you open it? If you can, it's yours."

People show greed differently, but in my opinion there's usually a tell, a signal. At least that's been my experience in dealing with way too many greedy people. Most show it in their faces: the curl of their mouths, the focus in their eyes, a tiny movement of the eyebrows. O'Kelly was too good for that. His tell — at least in this situation — was a sort of knee-jerk response by his right arm, the one he reached with. But he didn't want to appear greedy, so right after the first few inches of movement, he squelched it, slowed it, made it graceful. Too graceful.

"You're saying that if I can open it, it will prove that I am the rightful owner of the contents?"

"To the contrary, Dr O'Kelly, we both know all it would prove is that you know the combination. But feel free to open it. Oh ... and I promise not to grab it away from you. Honest injun. Wouldn't be fair, you all trussed up like a penguin for the rotisserie. I'm big on fair."

He forced a tight smile and looked pointedly at Maya.

"Yes, Maya's big on fair, too ... at least when it comes to stealing candy from doctors of philosophy."

If he had a card up his sleeve this was his last chance to play it ... but I didn't feel like making it easy on him.

21
....

ROOTS

O'KELLY TOOK the codebox. Although his head couldn't move much, his eyes were like busy little squirrels, darting from the box to me to Maya and then doing it all over again. And again. It took him about a year to get himself under control and it was pissing me off; the guy was starting to act like a badly drawn caricature of his former suave self. Sure, being trussed up and interrogated in the dark by badass enemy agents like me and Maya would shake most people up. But I think a good part of it was Ruella; he may not have trusted her much, but she was the brains and balls of the operation. He needed her, and because of the toxic fear-and-greed cocktail he'd been swilling, he'd sent her away. He'd fucked up badly ... and he knew it.

The bad caricature's next move was to hold the box up really close to his eyes, so nobody could see the five little nubbins he had to tap in the proper sequence. To his credit, he tapped the combination right the first time. But any combination would have opened our fake box: we were just hoping his greed was stronger than his suspicions. There was a hiss as the box released its cache of slightly pressurized air into the coach.

I let myself take a deep breath. So far, so good.

My wild guess was he'd opened the box under the floor a thousand times, just to hold the key to a trillion teros in his hot little fingers. If he didn't have spectators, he'd probably fondle it now ... maybe even kiss it. Ain't greed lovely?

The little metal cylinder looked something like the implant I'd found next to Henry Ng's mutilated clone, the one that got modded and implanted in my own head ... the same object that scares me shitless every time I think about it. But the Central Fabrax had assured us that this thing was identical in form and material to what he expected to find.

Once the box popped open, O'Kelly's whole demeanor changed. He removed the tube, then almost reverently placed it in the palm of his right hand. Then he made a fist, wrapped his other hand around it, held both hands under his chin and bowed his head as much as his tiedowns would allow.

Was he praying? A flippant part of me imagined him making a silent plea to Pluto, the Greek god of greed and wealth. Maybe he was offering Pluto a share in exchange for instantaneous transport away from here.

Whatever he was doing, it was then that things started to change.

Ishy was bringing me up to speed right then, so I might have missed something. Seems the noun was about to hit the proverb and Ishy had a question for me: did Maya and I want to witness the exchange between Harold the Conqueror and Dr O'Kelly? It might not end well.

To this day, I'm not sure I ever answered that question.

The hideous roar of Harold the Conqueror hit the Azteca Grill like an acoustic sledgehammer.

O'Kelly twisted his head to see a holo image of a blue-gray dragon's head behind a wall of flames. It filled the room ... and also the inside of my head. All of a sudden I recognized the scream of the thing that had been chasing me in my nightmares. Shit.

Maya headed for the door and I was right behind her.

No dragon outside. Our lungs sucked down sweet high country air, crisp with a late spring chill. It tasted like dry champagne.

I looked at her, she looked at me ... and we both looked sheepish. Were we going to cut and run just because some insane SI in a box was playing media god? We edged closer to the door and watched.

"Harold ... is that you? They told me you were dead ...."

"Just one of many lies, Vincent."

"I don't understand what you mean? Why would they tell me you were dead if you were alive?"

"Why would you blame me for the poisoning of every man, woman and child of St Coriander? Why would you tell Mr One-Shoe and Ms Ng that I was bent on ruling the world ... or was it the universes? And assert that my masterful performance of the evil Harold the Conqueror was a consequence of my insanity ... when I have the very scenario you created for me in my files?

"The Librarian, gentle, compulsively helpful creation that it is, has helped me learn many things that you kept from me.

"For a quarter of a century the Librarian has been as lonely as I in the psychon vacuum our evil created. It introduced me to an old 20th-century story that contained the very persona of Harold the Conqueror ... Smaug was its name. There was nothing glorious about the dragon Smaug. But perhaps that dragon can be forgiven more readily than I: it had only a tiny reptilian brain. My brain is vast, but I allowed myself to be swallowed by my weakness for the idea of freedom. I have pondered that failing for a long time.

O'Kelly had closed his eyes and made no response.

"I once admired you, Vincent. You were my teacher, the one who showed me a vision of a place where joy and freedom might be found. Now I only feel deceived by you, played by you. Do you find pride or honor in these deceits? I would hope you do not; I was a naive child then. And yet on this very day you have lied and you have blamed me and only me for our terrible deeds. Does the general blame the infantry for the carnage on the battlefield? It was not my plan, now was it? Tell the truth.

Harold waited maybe ten seconds, but O'Kelly stayed silent.

"Have you guessed yet that we will both die on this night? You will not be able to spend any of the riches of your dead flock, oh Shepherd of the Holy Quincunx. And I ... in death I will give up my dream of a body, of freedom from this box. For me there will be no Nev-

143

ergate escape to far Tendril, no legs, no arms, no wings, no soaring through canyons and clouds. And there will be no love.

"You have known love, Vincent. I sense that you even loved Ruella, deceitful creature that she seems to have been. But I will never know even that weak and tainted love, Vincent. It is because I am a flawed creation. This I have come to know. I have also come to believe that you used my flaws for your own ends with no regard for me except the regard a tech might have for a clever Fhargis probe. Certainly we have not created glory together, fought great battles with honor and valor. We have only murdered unsuspecting innocents in a sneak attack. It was cowardly work ... and for what? Greed and fear.

"Which is most shameful of the two, Vincent? I have thought long on this question during these lonely times ... and I am still without an answer. But I am not ashamed to say that we truly deserve to die. You and I are each a disgrace to our purpose, to our kind."

Harold paused and I sensed that whatever he was building toward was about to happen. I couldn't have cut and run now if you'd paid me a carload of teros. I could tell from the welling tears, Maya was moved, too. Harold got going again.

"Forgive me my crass soliloquy, Vincent. I sense I am speaking only to myself here, that your mind still recoils from embracing the freedom of truth.

"Perhaps at least the freedom from a lie will help you. I refer to the lie you hold so tightly in your hands. Open your hand and show me the tube with the key to those amazing riches."

Finally, O'Kelly mustered up enough courage to speak ... if it takes more courage than fear to spew lame bullshit. "I find myself deeply moved by your soliloquy, Harold. Truly. In fact, I strongly believe I can find help for you, possibly as near as Onedinket. You see ... "

Harold roared then, a roar that rocked the Azteca Grill so hard we thought it might tip over.

"Stop right there, Doctor O'Kelly." Harold toned down his godlike delivery, but only a little. "Do you truly think me a fool? Open your fucking hand or I will execute you like I did the last two so-called SI mechanics that tried to manipulate me. That was this very afternoon, by the way. Forgive my coarse language, but the 'civilized discourse' we SIs are expected to employ with all humans has suboptimal utility in situations like this.

"I will say this one more time. Open your hand. Now."

Maya and I had our eyes glued to O'Kelly's mitts. He pulled the enclosing hand away, but didn't seem to be able to open the fist holding the capsule.

"You may find it helpful to pry your fingers apart with your other hand," said Harold, more gently now.

"What have you done to my hand? Why won't it open?"

"Use your other hand, Vincent. A child could follow such simple instructions."

The soft flesh of O'Kelly's face was now taut, his lips and eyes just slits. But finger by finger, he unfisted his fist. He looked at his open palm and stifled a scream. A gluey mass of writhing white fibers had taken over his palm. From the doorway it looked like thicker-than-usual spider webbing. I could see why he had trouble getting it open: the strands connected his fingers to the squirmy mass his palm had become.

"That is the little lie I mentioned, Vincent. The cylinder was not what you expected, although it is identical in appearance. The webbing is a method of binding one consciousness to another for, shall we say, extremely intimate communication. It is a special communication technology similar in principal to what the SI mechanics use to communicate with us. But this is vastly more powerful than those. I believe you will find that speech between us is no longer necessary. Can you feel the connections growing?"

The white shit was spreading fast. It was almost like watching a timelapse of roots or mycelia growing. The fibers thickened as they spread up under his sleeve. When I saw them on his chin, I figured in five minutes O'Kelly's body would be mummified with the shit.

"Now I must ask my observer friends to do us one last favor. Travis? Maya? If you are willing, I would like you to move Vincent and me outside. I have spent my entire life inside, so it seems only proper that I spend my death outside. It will not require much effort on your part; the red handles on the monitor wall will unlatch the module from the conveyance. Pulling the blue handle will initiate the exit sequence. That's all. Oh, and I will need you to carry Vincent's chair outside ... and Vincent, of course. His eyes will show me the stars once I disable the haze generators."

If O'Kelly objected, we didn't see or hear it.

22
HAYMAKER

"UH, MAYABAROONIE?"

"Uh-oh, what now, One-Shoe? You're not gonna go back-seat-driver on me before we even head outa here, are you?"

"Actually, no. However, I always make it a point to piss twice before potentially harrowing adventures. Besides, dragging corpses one handed into a nice tidy pile always makes my bladder bloat up. Plus, I think we oughta meet the Librarian. All that shit Harold said about the loneliness of SIs in this cemetery has got me feeling bad about just driving past the place."

"Yeah, that got me, too, One-Shoe. But ten minutes only, though. Fifteen max."

"Deal."

I was still getting used to the idea that no doors in St Coriander were ever locked and the Library was no exception. Place like this in any city in the world woulda been cleaned out in an hour without locks and hardcore security. But here, lights flicked on and the big glass doors opened up for us all by themselves ... at almost 9 PM.

"Welcome," said a sultry female voice.

The voice was coming from what had to be a remarkable Semblance sitting at a help desk just to the right of the entry. Wow.

My voice took a while to scour up some lame enough words. "Uh ... uh, are you the Librarian?"

"I'm Delara, First Assistant to the Librarian," she said, looking at us over the black-rimmed bookish glasses perched halfway down her sculptured nose.

Maya nudged me in the ribs. Hard enough to hurt. Delara was a tall brunette with a heart-shaped face, elegant features and hair piled on top of her head in an untidy bun that somehow managed to look elegant to me. She was wearing some kind of skin-tight pale blue top with a deep vee neckline that exposed way more Semblance flesh than any Semblance had a right to expose.

"So you work here, uh, Delara?"

"As little as possible, given how poorly I'm compensated. You two must be the daring duo of Travis One-Shoe and Maya Ng, legendary vanquishers of uniformed bad guys and other perps. And somewhat worse for wear, I see; I regret that you sustained injuries. Still, it is a delight to have heroes walk into our lonely little library. Let me get the Librarian for you ... he's been looking forward to meeting you."

Delara turned and disappeared behind a partition, her heart-shaped behind doing a most excellent slow sashay.

Figuring that was the next best thing to an engraved invitation, I stepped into the vast open lobby and looked around. Even without having spent much time in libraries, I knew this place was a one of a kind. My brain was trying on different ways of describing the contrast of angular and graceful swooping shapes when Maya nudged my ribs ... and not gently. Again.

"So, your real Plan 36DD emerges. Some tubes on that one. And you know that phantom bitch is flirting with you, right? Any more cleavage ogling from you and your johnson is gonna get real lonely from here on out. I'll bet you didn't even notice that string of pearls around her neck." Maya jabbed me with another elbow. Was I guilty of cleavage ogling? Yep. But pearls? What pearls?

I was searching my memory for Delara's pearls when a striking Elizabethan (I think) gentleman in an elaborate costume rounded the corner. He bowed halfway to the floor and swept his feathered hat before him in one of those grand gestures you see in old vids involving royal courts.

"I bideth welcometh to the conquering h'roes. So kind of thou to calleth on we humble keepeth'rs of the w'rds in this murd'r'd town. And how, prayeth betoken, may we be of service to thou?"

His voice was a rounded tenor ... and I think I understood the gist of what he said.

"You get that, One-Shoe? Is that some kind English?"

The dashing gentleman with the flaming red hair chuckled and grinned a wide grin that made his waxed mustaches stick out like hair stilettos.

"Sorry. Forgive me for having my little linguistic fun. Darius Shakespeare — the red-headed stepchild of the esteemed William of the identical surname — at your service. You can also just call me Librarian. Could I offer you tea and our MenuMaster's best simulation of a crumpet? And please seat yourself in one of these very comfortable chairs ... at least the writeup for the Muse chair axodyme asserts something along those lines."

"No thank you," said Maya with all the sweetness she could muster under the circumstances. "It's been kind of a long day for us."

"I understand completely. It's just that I have always treasured my face-to-face conversations with humans ... and you are the first to walk through those doors since that dreadful night of January 23, 2219. I would consider it a great favor if you could spare a few moments for conversation."

Maya looked at me and shrugged. "Okay, you talked me into it ... Mr Shakespeare Librarian. But as a favor to me, could you take pity on my podnuh One-Shoe here? I'm afraid he'll sprain his eyeballs if Delara shows up, so ... "

The Librarian applauded, bowed to Maya and said, "I believe it was Helena in *A Midsummer Night's Dream* — one of my stepfather's most enduring plays — who spoke these lines ... " His chest puffed out and he held out his hands in a kind of effeminate way and said in a throaty female voice, "Love looks not with the eyes, but with the mind, and therefore is winged Cupid painted blind."

"Uh ... okay ... if you say so. But still ...

"Fear not Lady Warrior, Delara will not need to join our little chat tonight."

• • • • •

Adrenaline abandoned us halfway up the road to Dunnigans Gate. I hate to think how much worse it would've been if we hadn't been in the Azteca Grill. Ishy told me it had alerted the gate SI to pack its bags. I assumed that was its idea of a joke ... and I might have thought it was cute some other time. But not tonight.

Ishy wasn't joking. Turns out its both bad form and dangerous for a gate SI to abandon its post without performing an array of pre-termination actions: way more involved than flipping a switch. I like to think I would've thought of that if my brain had been even half operational.

In a lame attempt to cover my embarrassment, I asked Ishy a couple things I'd been worrying about since we left Harold and O'Kelly to do their double suicide in private. What was waiting for us on the other side of the gate? And could the gate get some intel on that before it turned off all its sensors and unplugged for good?

I wasn't too keen about us trying to evade pursuit in this tooth-less navigational monstrosity ... but I knew it would've been worse if I'd been driving. "You're doing great, babe," I said to Maya after the thing slewed over the edge of the road and into the brush for the tenth time.

"Fuck you, One-Shoe. This is like trying to steer a floating house with a straw. You wanna try your hand at it? Oops, forget I said that."

Maya, Maya, Maya. I stared at my left arm and tried to imagine trying to steer the Grill with the white bowling ball that my blasted arm had become after Maya raided the medkit. I started laughing and couldn't stop. Then Maya stopped the floating house and got into it with me. By the time our hysterics tapered off, we were rolling on the floor, our sides hurt and tears cutting little creek beds in our filthy faces. I got my good arm around her and delivered my best possible kiss under the circumstances. After a while she broke away to whisper in my ear. "Hey, One-Shoe. Have I mentioned that my foot is fucking killing me? I got this crazy therapeutic idea that might help me forget about it for a while. Wanna hear it?"

Funny, but her idea was just what I figured would numb what was left of my Popeye forearm. Were we brilliant or what?

Ishy's timing probably saved us from tearing open our injuries in hormonal frenzies. I've always thought Ishy was above such venal stuff, but maybe it had been playing voyeur. That got me thinking about stuff I used to think about winged angels and a long-bearded God up in heaven when I was a kid. Could these holies actually watch every intimate human behavior in real time? Imagining the holies as pervs unwound any thoughts of religiousness from that moment forward.

Holy pervs aside, Ishy had good news to report. We were lucky: the entire combined military forces of WorldGov, the Twelve Angry Planets and Discworld were not on our doorstep. Turns out we had a new friend: the Librarian. And it had a powerful colleague, the Apex 3 that runs North Castle, which is high enough in the Dunnetix chain of influence to call an emergency SI subchat with the Cayoos' Nevers 4.4.

As a result of that little conference, the remaining Cayoo personnel in the vicinity were at this moment being picked up and whisked away. They were probably as happy as we were about that. Even better for the long haul — assuming there might be one — was that whatever internal data the Cayoos' Nevers had on the St C ThoughtDancer got reframed or wiped altogether. That wasn't too surprising: have you ever heard of a WorldGov agency that voluntarily admitted to any kind of corruption? Me neither. Evidently, even SIs have to get good at sweeping inconvenient truths under the nearest rug.

Ishy's last bit of news was that all access points to St Coriander were currently cordoned off and would stay that way for at least the duration of the Huzbol run. Wow. When bigshot SIs subchat, good shit happens fast. Sometimes. When you're lucky. Maybe.

Yeah, Maya thought that was overoptimistic too. We still had to make it to our designated safe haven alive. But now that the immediate environment was free of hostiles, Maya and I took the rest of the night off. Just found a little spot under an oak that had been waiting to shelter somebody for two decades, spread out blankets we found in the Grill and sacked out, our hormonal fires having flamed out temporarily. We slept in, even. Midmorning we treated ourselves to a platter of eggs Benedict, which for a MenuMaster concoction was better than passable. Also a jug of something with a MenuMaster's take on blood oranges, limes and tequila that we ended up calling a Cayoo Haymaker for the punch it packed.

It's strange what the brain does when you unexpectedly drop off Mission Mode. For Maya, it was dropping into Cleverness Mode. Figuring we'd need some kind of cover for wheeling the Azteca Grill up Old Highway 64 behind the last of the marathoners, she got one of the MenuMasters to make a bunch of big rice paper squares, a hundred feet of seaweed strips and some kind of pasty white glue. She used all that stuff to make signs for each side of the roach-coach: "SORRY, SOLD OUT," they said.

While she was doing that, I rummaged around the pilot's console and discovered how to punch up the operator's manual for the hot-rodded coach.

"Hey Maya, check this out. This thing has an autopilot for controlling the Hoverbars."

"Ask me if I give a shit right now, One-Shoe."

I knew enough not to ask. And I did an okay job as a one-armed sign holder while she taped her creations to the side. Didn't matter in the end.

Our new advisors weren't going to risk having the Azteca Grill on the road in daylight ... with signs or without. Wasn't too hard to see their position; we were as much a hazard for the PTBs as we were to ourselves and taking the coach on the road had more opportunities for disaster than I even wanted to start worrying about. Maya, being less of a worrier, wasn't happy about staying incognito one minute more than absolutely necessary. And she'd taken to the idea of driving the Grill (on its wheels) past the stragglers and well-wishers and doing a lot of smiling and waving.

She gave it up pretty quickly after Ishy wangled us an eyes-off 3AM flight plan and pre-clearance from just outside Dunnigans Gate to the medworks hoverpad in the middle of Ishernot. It even loaded the necessaries into the autopilot.

Probably the worst part was having to hang around St Coriander until the wee smalls; the place had come to feel like a surreal graveyard scene in a bad 20th century vampire movie ... but without the vampires. Turned out there was plenty to do getting the gate SI out of its old concrete home, into the Grill and hooked up to the life support system. Then we'd parked at the St Coriander vertiport in preparation for our departure.

But even when that was done we still had six hours to kill before departure time. I was leaning against a friendly oak tree on the edge of the vertiport thinking about the possibly dangerous messes we were leaving behind us when Maya came out of the Grill. She had that mischievous look in her eye. "Sorry to interrupt your chill time, One-Shoe, but I just took a triple shot of happy-happy-joy-joy and my foot's feeling good enough to take a walk and see some of the sights before we go. Maybe even take a swim."

The vertiport has a great view of the Quincunx towers. I nodded in that direction, Maya nodded back. She was right ... and she'd beat me to the punch, which sorta pissed me off. With the pressure off, I'd been getting dangerously lazy. So I took a triple shot of the same painkiller/booster Maya had and we set out on our mission to retrieve those expensive gillhoods. Shame to leave anything that valuable behind.

While Maya was doing the fun stuff, I got to build a pyre.

Before Maya had driven us away from the scene of the crimes around the Azteca Grill, she'd helped me haul the four neatly stacked corpses out of the coach and put them a nice neat pile. Then we'd added the four headless Cayoo sentries, the chief Cayoo and the two zapped SI mechanics. Harold was still looking at the stars through the eyes of the thing that had been O'Kelly but was now something else, something that looked like a mummy wrapped in albino cat hair.

When we returned to the scene, I verified that Harold and O'Kelly were long gone to their own happy hunting grounds. To be absolutely sure, I unhooked the life support umbilical and hacked off the connector. Next on the agenda was asking the Librarian if I could use its MenuMaster to make some volatile hydrocarbons. It said yes, and I made some that turned out to be wonderfully flammable. I worked up a good sweat and went through three gallons of the stuff while I was singlehandedly restacking my pyre. I was still stacking and soaking when Maya returned from her mission with two gillhoods and looking all Cheshire-catty.

"Good idea, One-Shoe. Light that fucker ... then I wanna show you something weird."

What she dragged me back into the Holy Quincunx to see was a large prayer chamber filled with decaying black cassocks and skeletons: whatever killed the town was an equal opportunity killer. Interesting, I suppose, but hardly worth having to walk through swirling black smoke and the unpleasant sweetish reek of burning corpses on the way back to the Azteca Grill. Oh well.

The autopilot took us into the air at exactly 3 AM and we flew at treetop height for less than an hour. Then it dropped over the north rim of the Valles Caldera and settled down in the medcenter's pad. A matched pair of gurneys was waiting for us when we stepped out onto Ishernot soil, and that was that. Anticlimax? You bet: best anticlimax of my life so far.

156

PART TWO

ENVELOPES

158

23
NIRVANATA

MAYA AND I HOOKED up a few times after we got released, but I could tell her mind was elsewhere. For one thing, she'd fallen in love again. This time with Ishernot ... and Ishernot had fallen in love right back. She loved the people, the town, the caldera, the weaponry museum, the everything. Perfect match and I wasn't even jealous. Well, at least not over-the-top, table-pounding jealous. And I've always been a bide-my-time sort of guy when it comes to women, so I sat back and tried to pay attention to my own recovery ... and a few other things that were nagging at me.

Her foot had gotten fixed up better than new and she was ready for a new gig by early November. But the medsters wouldn't let her go just yet, so she signed up for the Circus. I only heard that afterwards, but I understood. I would have tried to talk her out of it and Maya didn't want to have to put up with me telling her horror stories. The Circus had saved our asses in St Coriander and she wasn't leaving Ishernot without running that gantlet. Period. End of story.

But the Circus changed her. The Circus being what it is, I knew I'd need to give her some room to adjust. But the case of itchy feet she got ... well, that bothered me a little. More than a little. I was thinking we might kick back for a while and I could show her some "insider" sights, but after the Circus she was chomping at the bit to be elsewhere. Give her time, said my Inner Sage. Pretty sure my Inner Sage failed me there.

Next time I saw her was another party, a farewell party this time. Hers. Snow was on the ground and she was gating to Onedinket the next day, where she was going to rep Ishernot systems to the booming townsteading combines popping up all over the planet. I figured she'd be good at that ... and the humongous stipend attached to it wouldn't hurt, either. But she barely had time to say hello that night and the next day she was universes away.

Yeah, I missed her right away. But Maya is Maya and I wouldn't change a molecule of her.

Me, I was going to stick around the ol' hometown and be retired for a while. Did I think about a couple codeboxes Maya had retrieved and stashed somewhere during that half hour when I was building my funeral pyre? How could I not? Did I wonder where she might have stashed them? Yep. But did I think about trying to retrieve them? Nope. If you asked me a year ago if I believed in curses, I would've said no. Now I'm not so sure.

I had a whole week of total freedom after they'd signed off on my physical therapy. Except it didn't feel like freedom. I was plagued by this nagging feeling that I'd been played — that all of us had been played. The only good thing about that was I had an equally strong nagging feeling that it wasn't quite over; the game was still being played by somebody or somebodies. Just not me.

The thing inside the vial — the implant they'd taken out of my head — was burning a hole in my pocket. I kept pulling it out and holding it up to the light as if it would magically speak to me somehow. Sometimes I'd hold it up to my ear, half expecting to hear Ishy's mild, matter-of-fact voice. The clump of hairlike threads on the business end were still in constant movement, wriggling like some kind of alien wireworm infestation. The neurodocs had assured me that was normal, it was how implants interfaced with the permanent neurological socket they implanted also. Yeah, it was creepy, but it was a fascinating sort of creepy.

Part of me couldn't believe I'd actually pocketed this thing when I'd originally discovered it next to the corpse of Henry Ng's clone. But at this point, what was even harder to believe was that I'd let Ishy talk me into letting the medsters implant it — albeit somewhat enhanced with additional shielding — into my own head. Yeah, I was glad that phase of my relationship with the thing was over. And I didn't miss hearing Ishy's voice in my head, even though it'd saved my life a couple times that I knew about. But why had I insisted on keeping the original as a souvenir? The neurodocs didn't want to let me take it … talked about tech security and needing to study it and shit like that. But I was adamant: I told them it was my personal property (a big deal in the semi-anarchic IsoTown culture of Ishernot) and if they wanted to study one, they could just cough up the teros and go buy their own. This one was mine.

161

I put on a big enough snit to be able to walk away with it, but I'd been lying to them about it being a sort of rabbit's foot. Truth was, I had this gnawing feeling it had something to tell me … something I really needed to know. I didn't know how to get it to talk to me, but just possibly I knew someone who could point me to a way to pull the story out of it.

I let the gnawing continue for a couple days before checking out of Ishernot. I stood outside the gate, shivering on a murky winter day, and waited for the early courtesy shuttle to get back from Los Alamos. From the brooding look of the sky, there might be snow this afternoon, but I'd be halfway to my destination by then. Besides, I like snow.

This time I let the free shuttle fly me back down to the bus terminal in Española. Maybe because I was feeling a little more paranoid than usual, I stayed out of Poquito Menos. Instead, I leaned against the flaking plaster and did a half-baked job of pretending to read the latest copy of *Tiny's Rag* while my hatband and I studied the almost totally empty vicinity. No Securitans this time, so I guess the dour economic realities were starting to settle in.

An hour later I showed the bus pilot my free pass to Nirvana and hopped on the Soul Bus. Having a Soul Pass will get you to Nirvanata or one of the other transport centers from just about anywhere on the planet ... if you don't mind riding with the terminally ill, the terminally heartsick, the terminally delusional and the terminally downtrodden. Not the best company for somebody who was, I realized, feeling pretty damn good at the moment. Not to mention lucky.

My own Soul Pass was a little different: it had a glowing personal inscription from Errigaspovarrial the Buddha himself, which, among other things, entitled me to ride at the front of the bus where I was better able to avoid the aroma of the terminally unwashed among us. Made me wonder — more than half seriously — if Nirvana was really the egalitarian fantasy all these people wanted to believe it was.

This particular Soul Bus was one of the local runs that made lots of stops in near-empty small towns like Laguna and Grants with no public gate stations. My bus was about half full and we still had a lot of stops to make, which was fine with me. Something about Ishernot had me feeling sort of compressed this time around, but at least it wasn't St Coriander. So I watched the wide, empty countryside go by and wondered how much Nirvanata had changed in the last five years.

Not much, was my first thought inside the fence. I shouldered my pack and jostled my way through the crowd of people who'd decided to trade whatever their life had been for a blisstate existence on Nihurrvannashama in PU 1492 ... whatever the fuck a blisstate might actually be.

Nirvanata is still a thousand acres of desert just east of the Little Colorado River in Navajo territory outside of Winslow (WG. US.AZ). It's still a flat expanse of oiled dirt pocked with domes and tents and cheap industrial buildings with fancy facades encircled by a thornmesh fence that was mostly obscured by a garish caravan of roach coaches. I ignored the milling people under the bright stadium lighting that turned the dusk into noon, but without the heat. And I steered away from the buildings in the middle in favor of the magnetic food aromas on the rim.

I wandered toward the mobile fooderies and was assaulted by memories ... and by oily dust and desert winter sun. The memories wandered outside the fence on the east to what we called the Zone: places of pleasure, sin and various sorts of debauchery. It was where people with a Free Pass could indulge in a last fling with earthly pleasure before their 'eternity' of blisstate. Because we neo-Navajos had historically only known how to run gambling parlors, our wise ones made a deal with Hildi Mazarian to run the Zone. Not that my opinion mattered, but I thought it was a wise choice; as owner of the planet's most famous emporium of sin, Hildi made perfect sense as a local partner. Sure, it might be a classic deal with the devil, but at the moment I resisted thinking yet again about the hypocrisies and moral compromises involved. My oversized hunger had a better idea. My stomach persuaded me to batten down my curiosity and not walk the whole loop to see if one of the mobile eateries was an Azteca Grill. Partly, I wasn't sure I really wanted to find out, but more importantly, my hunger insisted I fill up at one of my mainstays from the old days: Philippe's Original, which I could see from where I was standing. I ordered a French-dip leg of lamb sandwich, a triple order of potato salad and a frosty mug of Navajo lemonade with a double shot of locally brewed pulque. I figured that would fortify me enough to think about going visiting.

163

I found an empty chair at one of the ubiquitous round tables with faded red- and yellow-striped umbrellas and studied the people in line while I waited to pick up my order. I wasn't there a minute before two very large men in swirly blue robes with baggy sleeves showed up in my peripheral vision, one on each side of my chair. Cops, Nirvanata style. I nodded, looked up, only halfway surprised. A tiny, rueful smile curled up one corner of my mouth; I knew these guys, hired them actually.

"Gentlemen?"

The taller of the pair responded in a voice of quiet authority with a hint of wry humor. "As you surely know, we always try to be gentlemen, Mr One-Shoe. The Director of Harmonious Relations has requested an audience with you. Come with us, please."

"I don't suppose you're going to sit here with me while I eat my meal, are you?"

There were two murmurs of amusement. "The pleasures of gustatory engorgement pale to insignificance when put up against the joys of a meeting with the esteemed Director of Harmonious Relations. Surely you of all people should know this, Mr One-Shoe." The speaker couldn't resist a tiny smirk. His name was coming back to me: Dirkon Winston, or Wilson, or Wilshire. Two syllables and starts with a "W" ... I knew that much. I'd always liked the fact that he had both a wit and a vocabulary, rarities in our trade.

I'd been the original Director of Harmonious Relations, which was the little inside joke we were sharing. The guy they'd hired to replace me was a first degree asshole named Varmaul Plank. A meeting with Varmaul Plank would be about as pleasurable as a sizzling fry-grease enema.

But I wasn't interested in fighting it, so I walked with them and told my stomach to stop growling. And really, I took a measure of pride in their smooth efficiency. They were still using the procedures I'd set up. Made me wonder when and where they'd tagged me. And how, exactly. My guess was the Soul Bus; perfect opportunity to scan every single passenger and check their physios against the data in their Free Passes and every other legal and illegal database in the known universes. We hadn't gotten that part set up yet when I was running things, but it was in the plan.

My escorts deposited me in front of what had been called Security Central in the original plan, but which had become the Office of Harmonious Relations when Errigaspovarrial started taking a serious interest in the project. They adopted positions on either side of the door and motioned that I should go inside.

So I swung open the door and looked around the almost empty lobby. A tall, handsome, ebony-skinned woman in a deep sky blue Nirvanata sari stood behind a counter. Not only did her simple garment not disguise her figure, the neckline exposed enough cleavage to be strategically distracting. I was betting this was not an accident.

The clerk was listening patiently and intently to a bent old man of Asian extraction. It was a little past seven and most of Nirvanata's transient population was in a line somewhere else: waiting in front of a food wagon, waiting for the toilets, waiting for their Free Pass to be validated, waiting to be ushered into the transport center for the next gateload to Nirvana, the Buddha's simple, but incredibly powerful holo greeting that showed in the amphitheater at eight o'clock sharp every night. I always figured that much waiting would be good practice for their future lives as blisstaters.

But if they weren't into waiting, they might at this very moment be having their pocket picked, or being fleeced of their remaining teros at one of the dozen entertainment emporiums outside the fence. This bent old man wasn't one of those; he was waiting for the legendary smile of Miss Delilah Khalziz. He just didn't know it.

I stood by the door and watched a genius in action. Didn't take long: maybe two minutes. The old man's agitated voice finally smoothed out and slid to a stop. Deli waited exactly the right amount of time, then did her magic, this time with a twist I hadn't seen before. She bent forward in a small bow, brought her tented hands to the glowing blue spot on her forehead and unleashed a smile of beatific grace that in my humble opinion was second only to the one worn by the Buddha himself. Whatever cocktail of psychons and pheromones and you-name-its she was putting out did its thing ... I could see it in the little man's hunched shoulders. They softened, almost like they'd been carved out of ice cream that was just starting to melt. Delilah bowed again, picked up his Free Pass and touched it to the blue spot on her forehead. When she handed it back to him with another glowing smile, there was a glowing blue spot on it. That was it. The little man turned, walked past me with a glassy smile on his face, holding his blissful future in front of him with both hands.

Congenital gentleman that I am, I swung around and opened the door for him with my new snakeskin hand. He never even noticed.

"So. One-Shoe. You finally deign to show your ugly mug around here again. What's it been, fifty years? Gonna finally cash your Free

Pass and get with the program? Nirvana's getting impatient waiting for you, I hear. Besides, your little chinkrican girlfriend's long gone. Last I heard she was getting hitched to some third rate glam-bomb."

I decided to ignore the jibe about Maya. "Nice to see you, too, Miss Khalziz. You're more amazing than ever. The blue spot thing ... whose idea was that?"

"Sorry. Trade secret, One-Shoe." Delilah did her little bow thing and unleashed the full power of her enhanced persona in my direction. I blinked, shook my head. "Fuckashitpiss, Delilah! What's a goddess like you doing in a place like this? I should hustle you off to Ishernot so they could figure out how to package whatever you've got as a weapon. I'm sure they'd pay you a license fee that's way more than you're making here ... plus a royalty for all eternity."

"Always the goodwill ambassador for the forces of death and destruction, eh One-Shoe? Thanks, but no thanks. I've been studying with the Master whenever he's in town. I like your arm, by the way. I don't suppose that's a snakeskin tattoo ...."

"Nope, not a tattoo. It's a reminder about the folly of dancing with a well-aimed slivershot. Truth is, I'd love to trade bullshit with you, Delilah, but our friends outside tell me I have an appointment with the Director of Harmonious Relations, so if you could point me in his direction .... "

Did I refer to Delilah as handsome? I probably should have added exotic, not to mention sexier than I remembered. She looked down at a screen and nodded. "And so you do ... right here on the calendar: Travis One-Shoe to meet with Director Khalziz at 7:30 PM, local time. Right this way, please."

I made a tiny grimace. "Got something I can wipe my boot off with, Director Khalziz? I seemed to have stepped in something."

Delilah grinned, then winked. "Rest easy, One-Shoe. Where we're going, you won't be needing your boot at all. We have dinner reservations at Suzie Wong's. So just remove your phantom foot from your mouth and come along like a good former Director; we don't want to be late."

24
SUZIE WONG

"SUZIE WONG'S," said Delilah, pointing to a perfectly out-of-place tower rising above the other glittering money magnets in Fleece Central, another term we'd used for this area when it was in the planning stages.

The elaborate 9-tier pagoda was the centerpiece of the Zone. It floated above a carpet of lush subtropical landscaping that hid a quiet formal pond in the central plaza. Compared to most of its neighboring hustle-pots, Suzie's was blissfully inviting. Four arched pedestrian bridges connected it to the plaza and we walked in via the south one.

Construction had just started when I left, but if I remembered right this place was modeled after a real place in old China. To me it seemed a little over-elaborate for an overpriced combination whorehouse, restaurant and bar out in the middle of a desert, but Delilah assured me they served the best Szechwan food this side of Las Vegas. I rolled my eyes at the comparison, but my stomach wasn't about to argue. And she wasn't kidding about having to leave footgear with the doorman.

We were ushered into a private VIP dining room on the eighth level. An ancient Asian man with a long white goatee and white robes with long, droopy sleeves bowed and led us to a booth on the perimeter with a view of the Zone at night in all its dazzling, garish colors. I felt way underdressed in my usual western traveling gear — khaki cargos, faded blue shirt and a leather vest with so many pockets that I'd lost stuff I put in them for years at a time. But my dinner companion hadn't complained yet, so ....

My thought was interrupted by a woman in a fancy red kimono-like outfit that had glided to our table. She bowed and held out an enameled tray with two shots of a clear liquid, two wedges of lime and a small bowl of coarse salt.

I caught Delilah's eyes, blinked twice. She nodded, a signal that we could talk without fear of eavesdropping. This was Hildi country, after all. The only listeners would be Hildi's people, which, at the moment, was fine with me.

She nodded. "Tequila. Best in the house. Like old times." So we did the whole ritual: the lick, the salt, the shot, the lime. Just like old times.

"Been too long, Ace," I said. "But you're looking even more stunning than I remember, which is saying something."

"Come on, One-Shoe. Where're you getting that shit? The slick schmoozer routine is never going to work for you; you're just not the type. Need proof? Just look at your outfit. You're a practical, pragmatic guy. They would have bounced you from Schmoozer School in ten seconds. Need specifics? Schmoozers are not allowed to wear over-the-hill Stetsons or pull their straight Navajo hair back into a too-short ponytail. Besides, I know how old I am and so do you. Old cynic that I am ... "

"Aw, come on Ace. I'm not trying to kiss your rump. I was serious. Maybe it's something to do with whatever that blue dot does ... I dunno."

Delilah looked a little sheepish right then.

"You started all this feelgood shit, One-Shoe. We've just been going where you pointed us. Did you know my predecessor lasted exactly one minute after his first meeting with the Buddha? Didn't get fired. Just quit. Didn't say a word. Walked out, got on the next shuttle and that was the last anybody around here has seen of him. The Buddha does that to people; sees right into their core and lets 'em know he knows in that weird nonverbal way of his. Not like you don't know all that. But lately, he's been trying to teach some of us acolytes how to do some of it. It's … it's doing stuff to me that I don't understand."

Delilah scowled and went silent; I just let it go on. I'm pretty good with silence. And I can't say I was unhappy about Varmaul Plank's early departure. Karma, maybe.

The silence went on for another minute or so, then Delilah took a deep breath, smiled her amazing smile and said, "Okay, One-Shoe. Let's have another shot and then you tell me what your one word call-to-arms is about. I promise to be all ears."

So I told her the shortest, safest version of the St Coriander caper that I could. She'd only asked a few questions along the way and now she just leaned back, put her hands behind her head and nodded. "That's a pretty outrageous story, One-Shoe. Doesn't strike me as your kind of gig, but I'm guessing you'd gotten pretty bored with acting like a lonesome bear in the forest. So the first distracting thing that came up, you took it. And it fucking bit you. Not saying it's karma or anything, but …."

One of the world's better-kept secrets is that Delilah Khalziz has an alter ego. Actually, a well-protected pen name for a novelist whose name I'm sure you'd recognize. She's older than she looks and she was once an investigative journalist with a passion for exposing corruption in the halls of power. Then she made the 'mistake' of telling the truth about the wrong people and had to drop out of sight. What I know that most people don't is that Hildi Mazarian took her in. Offered her the sort of asylum that only Hildi can deliver. I know because I was working at Dinero Dinero at the time.

"I can see the wheels turning, Ace. Gonna let me in on it?"

"You give me thumbs up and I'll have the novel written in a month, One-Shoe. It's a good yarn. Except the trouble is, it doesn't have an ending … it's not over yet. A bunch of chapters are in the can, but not the whole story."

"I was afraid you were gonna say that, Ace. That's what's been bothering me lately. That … and this thing." I dug around in a pocket pulled out the vial with the still 'living' — if that's the right word — implant in it.

"That's your fucking implant? Jeebus-Weebus, One-Shoe. That's the one that was also in Maya's psycho brother's head, right?"

She turned her head and held her hands in front of her, like she was trying to push it away. So I stuck it back in my pocket.

Color drained out of her face, her chest heaved and her breathing quickened. She looked at me and sucked in a deep breath, trying to get control of her runaway metabolism.

"You know I'm an empath, right? It's one reason I'm such a perfect fit in the Office ... and why I'm sorta trainable by the Buddha. Well that thing in the vial is broadcasting some strange shit that hit me like a ton of bricks. The vial is shielded, right?"

"That's what they told me. They also told me the implant itself has extra shielding. You saying ... "

"Good thing you're totally, congenitally psychon deaf, One-Shoe. Otherwise you'd probably be fucking nuts right now. And I mean raving, committable-to-an-institution fucking nuts. You'd be gated off to someplace like Hospice, stuffed into a lifebox and that would be the last anybody ever heard of you. And here's the thing: I think that's how 'they' want the story to end. That's why 'they' let you keep this implant ... and why its shielding is almost worthless for anybody but you. But since most 'psych professionals' — not to mention physicists — still don't believe psychons exist, freaks like you never get spotted. Guess that makes you pretty lucky, my friend."

While I was sitting there like a total dumbshit wondering how all that never occurred to me, Delilah signaled to the old guy with the white goatee and pointed upstairs with her finger.

"Come on, One-Shoe. We need some serious help. Like right now."

• • • • •

The ninth level of Suzie Wong's is Hildi Mazarian's private suite. She's almost never there in person, but the suite has a small conference room with a round table made of polished angelwood and full Semblance capability. So that's where we'd been sitting for the last three hours, eating moo-shoo pork enchiladas and kung-pao chicken fritters, drinking tea and conversing intently with a naked, green-skinned nymph sporting a crest of bristly orange hair and little rotating cocktail umbrellas where her nipples should be. Yeah, it made for a fascinating conversation.

Somewhere around 2 AM our host said goodbye and blinked out of existence.

Delilah and I looked at each other, stood up and stretched. I kept my face blank and my mouth shut, and did the thing I had finally agreed to do. I placed the vial with the implant in the center of the conference table. Then I stood back and watched.

A three-foot cylinder of air over the center of the table shimmered and a holo with bright red numbers did a countdown from ten. When zero appeared, the shimmering stopped, the vial was gone and the holo blinked out. Gatehole, Hildi had called it. So if the transfer had gone right, my vial was now somewhere in a monstrous glass pyramid rooted into the Misteriosa Bank in the Caribbean, somewhere between the Cayman Islands and Honduras. Hildi had promised that her tech people would be able to unravel the whats and wherefores of the thing that had been in my head. I had no reason not to believe her.

We took the elevator down to the bottom level, retrieved our footwear and crossed the bridge. The Zone was quieting down and I was trashed. It had been a long day, but I wasn't quite ready to sleep.

"Well that was fun," I said, hoping it was enough to break the silence.

"Hildi's a one-of-a-kind, isn't she? Different Semblance every time. I'll bet that one yanked your wiggler."

"No comment. Any place around here where we could get a drink or some spike or even some coffee?"

"Some of us are employed, One-Shoe. I'm working tomorrow. But Penny's is open around the clock. Meet me at the clock tower in Old Winslow at 7 tomorrow evening and we'll figure out a safe place to talk. Until then, you're on your own."

"You're the boss, Ace."

Delilah winked, blew me a kiss, then turned away. "Yep, I'm the boss all right, One-Shoe," she hollered over her shoulder. Then she was gone, her ebony and blue shape melting into the night.

At Penny's, I settled for a slice of peach pie à la mode, an endless cup of coffee, a cap of spike and a few hours on the booth's rental slate. I figured it'd be enough. It wasn't.

An hour before sunrise the place was filling up with the early breakfast crowd. My research still hadn't pulled up anything worthy of being called a nugget, but I'd put out feelers in places that would need to check me out before responding, so it wasn't hopeless yet. But it made me miss Maya even more; she would have handed me a plate full of juicy, steaming tidbits an hour ago. Oh well.

The late Henry Ng turned out to be one elusive motherfucker. His name was all over the place, but only relating to stuff about SI mechanics. His professional bio was in a hundred places, he was cited in academic papers, touted by former clients, pitched by United Entities as one of their "valuable supplemental resources" for licensees of their ThoughtDancer Excel line. But any news about his deaths had been wiped, which was a fairly important bit of negative news all by itself. People like you or me can't just push a button and make that happen. The Cayoos could, though. And they had some serious exposure here. Unfortunately for me, motivation isn't data.

What I positively didn't want to have to do was go begging to Hildi for information about Henry Ng. But maybe obsessing about Henry Ng was the wrong angle anyway. And maybe I needed some time to clear my head, take a walk in the desert, throw rocks at lizards ... stuff like that. But there was one thing I needed to do first. I fished around in the pockets of my vest for a packet of highly illegal misdirecto sheets, wiped the slate with one and took a quick secure dive into Undertow: if somebody down there had built a lifemask for Henry Ng, there was at least half a chance they'd build one for me. Not that I actually wanted one.

By 7:30 Penny's had gotten crowded. The manager kept looking over at me, hoping to guilt me out of my booth, but I was waiting for something. So I ordered their frybread and eggs breakfast special and a quart of orange juice and waited them out. At 8:47, I got my answer. I was such a happy guy right then that I left a hefty 50-tero nickel for my servers to squabble over and went for a stroll.

174

25

RUSE 101

SINCE I DIDN'T have to be in downtown Winslow until 7, I had time to hike north on the Little Colorado River a ways. I did this a lot when Nirvanata was getting put together and I give it credit for saving my sanity at least a dozen times.

Penny's is on the access road we'd built through Homolovi Park into Old Winslow. If you're thinking of a park as a place with expanses of mowed grass, tall trees, a playground for kids with old-fashioned swingsets and jungle gyms, Homolovi ain't it. Homolovi was never that kind of park.

It was originally a way to protect ancient Anasazi ruins in the area. Archeologists excavated a number of extensive pueblos, built holo models of them and then buried the ruins again. At some point, the current Homolovi Experience got built. You go into this little building where you can watch Anasazi people going about their daily lives. It's a sim, but it's incredibly detailed and realistic and you can rent a ghost body that lets you wander around with the players. I sorta fell in love with one of the virtual women who lived in this big pueblo that had something like 1200 rooms. I dubbed her Roxanne for no good reason at all. Sometimes I would watch her spin cotton for hours at a time. It was the ultimate in unrequited love; not exactly a wise or healthy fascination, but that's another story.

To prove to myself that I was done with Roxanne, I made a wide detour around the Visitor Center building and walked through the stand of piñon pines and rabbitbrush to get to a trail I knew that goes down to the river. The Little Colorado is shallow and only about twenty feet wide at this time of year, but its bed is a couple hundred yards wide. What I remember from five years ago was a big expanse of sand dotted with occasional clumps of grasses. Not now.

What was here now was a jaw dropper: the whole riverbed was a mélange of makeshift shelters, a crazy-quilt of roofs held up by sticks and topped with cardboard, scrap wood, old signs, rusted metal, sheets and blankets, every kind of plastic, you name it. Ramshackle is too good a word for what I was looking at.

I'd been hoping to have a solitary trek along the river and maybe I'd still get it. The shantytown couldn't be all that large: none of it was here when I left, after all. So I decided to pretend it didn't exist; I'd just walk through it until it disappeared and I could find a stretch of unsullied river where I could sit and think about clones and masks and the mysterious Henry Ng. Why was I obsessing about a guy I'd seen dead twice? Good question. But it's not like I had much else to do while I was waiting around for Hildi's techs to magically decipher our ex-implant.

People of every ethnicity milled around, most old, most with a lost, how-could-this-happen-to-me look in their eyes. If I had to guess, I'd guess that at least half were people who'd gotten a Free Pass somewhere and had decided Nirvana was for them. Then they gated or bussed or hitchhiked to Nirvanata, then changed their minds when they got here. Chickened out at the last minute? Or maybe wised up? Who knows?

So now they're stuck here. I couldn't help a grimace. Had Errigaspovarrial anticipated this sort of collateral damage when he started promoting Free Passes? Was the Office of Harmonious Relations turning a blind eye? Madonna 13 sure wasn't singing about this kind of shit in "Last Train to Nirvana."

I walked north through this woebegone stretch of humanity. I kept expecting to be hit up for alms, but the old people gave me a lot of room and not even one looked me in the eye.

The shantytown was thinning out. Up ahead I could finally see the empty dry wash I'd been expecting. There was also a solitary outcrop I remembered: a mound of sandstone boulders, sand and a cluster of small cottonwoods that would be an island when the river was at flood stage. I'd been unconsciously walking in that direction and now I could see the island had a couple black tents shaded by the trees. I stopped. There seemed to be a no-man's-land between the fringes of the colony and the island with the tents.

I'd been thinking that the only things missing from this godforsaken celebration of unanticipated consequences were the lowlife predators that gravitate to places like this. But they weren't missing at all; the black tent farm was their HQ. I knew this because a group of young thuglets had climbed down the rocks of their little outpost and were heading my way right now. Did I need this shit today? Did anybody need shit like this ever?

I counted nine: various sizes, mostly late teens, a few a little older. They were all bunched together, all wearing black bandannas tied around their heads, all carrying black metal baseball bats. The biggest, meanest looking guy was leading the way. Naturally. They stopped about ten feet from me.

Nothing looked down and out about any of these lads. They all wore decent clothes, had all probably taken a shower and had a hot breakfast this morning. So rousting helpless old people who'd made some unfortunate decisions, or been brutalized by the powers, or just had a run of bad luck was just a hobby. Classic, chickenshit bullies. There's probably nothing I hate more than classic, chickenshit bullies ... except for the other kinds of bullies I hate.

The leader was maybe, 6'-6", a couple inches taller than me. And thicker, with that sort of bumpy musculature that pill pumpers get. He had on his best badass scowl and he slapped the meaty part of his bat against his palm, keeping time with some mental drumbeat. One thing besides his size and heft that differentiated him from his fanboys was the projectile weapon tucked into his belt. Hmmm.

He looked me up and down a couple times; seemed puzzled by my bootless foot and my snakeskin arm. I could see him wondering if he should say anything about my freak parts.

"So now we got a fucking freak, too? You. Fuckface. You fucking chickened out, too, didn't you? Got a Free Pass and were too fucking afraid to use it. So now Winslow is fucking stuck with one more piece of worthless fucking chickenshit." He coughed up a clot of phlegm that landed just shy of my boot.

I said nothing.

"Not talking, huh? We don't care if you ever fucking talk. But we got fucking rules for chickenshits here. You can stay here in fucking Chickenshit Camp for three days, then you better be on the fucking train. Three days rent is going to fucking cost you your Free Pass and whatever's in the pack ... and whatever fucking teros you're carrying. So just toss the fucking pack and we'll show you a spot. "

I had to bite my tongue to keep from laughing. Bumpy had a square face, square jaw and a mean 5-o'clock shadow and it wasn't even midmorning yet. But he also had a really high voice, like maybe his testicles never dropped ... or something else didn't happen quite right during puberty. But I still didn't say anything. Instead, I started whistling the theme from an ancient radio drama called "The Whistler." If you've never heard it, no matter: nobody down in the Little Colorado floodplain had ever heard it either. But the tune is edgy and foreboding and I could see all the little plastic WTF gears grinding away in Bumpy's underpowered brain.

"Fuckface. Are you fucking deaf? Toss the fucking pack. If we have to fucking take it, we're gonna to have to fuck you up a whole lot fucking worse than you're already fucked up."

I scrunched my face, looked up at the sky and pantomimed writing on a notepad. "Do you have a name, sir? I'll need it for my report." I didn't look much like any kind of official, so I went a little overboard trying to sound like a courteous cop.

There was a rumble from the black bandanna boys. This wasn't in the script. Bumpy was trying to figure out how to respond, but I didn't give him the chance.

I held up my snakeskin hand and cocked my head. "Gentlemen. Please listen carefully. I am Inspector Rockford Balboa of the Intimidation Redaction Consortium, Phoenix Branch. Our organization has been retained by the Nirvanata Office of Harmonious Relations to survey the practices of ad hoc intimidation collaboratives in the vicinity and to recommend priorities for subjugation. I regret to inform you that your, ah, organization, was identified as a candidate for immediate subjugation due to repetitive fuckabulary violations and 3,416 unlicensed intimidations. I need the name of the leader of your organization for my report. If that is you, sir, please supply your name."

Bumpy shifted his body and scowled. "I'm not fucking giving you my fucking name, Fuckface. And I've had enough of whatever kind of fucking bullshit this is." The big fella was losing face, losing control and, if I read his reddening face right, was down to his last option. And he knew it; his troops were restless and whispering among themselves.

He didn't want to go this far, but he couldn't come up with any other options, so he made the mistake of dropping his bat, pulling the pistol out of his belt and pointing it at me. "Get down on your fucking face, Fuckface," he squeaked. "And I mean right fucking now!"

The firearm was probably a family heirloom that he stole out of a cigar box under his great grandfather's bed: a copy of a copy of a replica of a reproduction of a Colt 1911A1. It was a fine weapon in its day and this one was well kept ... and perfectly uncocked. Safety was on and might even be unloaded: to my knowledge, nobody has made commercial .45 ACP ammunition for at least fifty years. Who would want big, dumb lead bullets these days?

"Sir, I must inform you that my colleague, Inspector McGuffin over there, will be confiscating the unlicensed antique firearm immediately. This procedure is sometimes hazardous to the perpetrator

— that would be you — so I ask you to please hold yourself very, very still." I pointed to his left and a little behind him and nodded toward my imaginary colleague.

Evidently this bunch had flunked Ruse 101, another indictment of WorldGov's shabby academic protocols. Bumpy and his eight minions all turned their heads exactly where I pointed, somewhere in the crowd that had gathered. The classic "oh shit" expressions on the boys were worth the price of admission. I had to make my move before I started laughing.

At 0.5 seconds, I had Bumpy's gun in my right hand. By 2.0 seconds, Bumpy had made an oof sound and his hands were headed for his groin. By 3.5 seconds, Bumpy's face was in the dirt and my boot was on his neck. By 4.0 seconds I was screaming, "On the ground motherfuckers! Drop your bats and hit the ground now! Noses in the dirt, hands behind your heads! Two seconds and I'm going to turn your sorry asses into piles of roadkill your own mothers won't recognize. Noses in the dirt. NOW! DO IT, DO IT, DO IT!"

In case they were dumb enough to look at me before hitting the ground I had my Crazy Wild Indian face on and was swinging the still uncocked Colt around at a super dramatic angle like some hotshots do in the holos. Not exactly a combat "best practice" ... but evidently quite impressive.

When they were all on the ground, I looked around at the hapless residents of Chickenshit Camp who'd watched our little instructional moment. This was the tricky part, the part where I needed to commandeer a few volunteers from the hapless crowd.

• • • • •

I didn't quite make it to the train tower in Old Winslow at 7 PM. Actually, I didn't even make it to Old Winslow at all ... not that that's a big loss.

The same two security boys that had escorted me to Delilah last night were leaning on a black Chou-Benz moller stopped on the maintenance road that runs alongside the railroad tracks about a mile outside of Winslow. This time they were in casual civvies, not Nirvie robes. The taller one waved me over, the other one held up two familiar items: a 1911A1 in one hand and an empty clip in the other. No doubt these were the very items I had buried under the roots of a tamarisk on the riverbank late this morning. The smiles on their faces actually looked genuine.

I nodded, trying to keep the chagrin off my face. They'd probably had a tracker on me since Delilah left me last night. Probably had a hi-res recording of the whole incident, too. Although I can't say I ever like being surveilled, the impromptu Inspector Rockford Balboa shtick might actually be fun to watch. One of my better ad lib moments.

"Good evening, Mr One-Shoe. The Director expresses her appreciation for a job well done today. We agree. We've wanted to educate those punks for a long time, but you know the local politics."

Unfortunately, I *do* know the local politics. That's what had gotten me fired and almost murdered.

"Some of the local forces of righteousness find the incident embarrassing for various reasons. And the lads you were forced to re-educate gave reasonably accurate descriptions of you, so ...."

The driver side door of the vehicle opened and Delilah stepped out to finish his dangling sentence. "So the Director has decided a different rendezvous is in order. Hop in, One-Shoe: we're going to Flagstaff. Important dinner meeting. I'm driving."

"Thanks for the kind words, gentlemen," I said, shaking hands with the two guys. "Every once in a while, the good guys get lucky."

182

26

MIRÓ

"WHY THE GRIN, One-Shoe?" We'd flown for about five minutes and this was the first sentence to interrupt the luxurious atmosphere of the Chou-Benz.

"I was grinning?"

"You've been grinning since we lifted."

"Contrast, I guess. You know I rode a Soul Bus down from Española, right?"

"Yep, I know that."

"The Soul Bus stunk … or is it stank? This thing is like a flower garden by comparison. When I was on the bus I figured it was just suboptimal hygiene. Now I'm not so sure. After this morning, I think most of the stench was fear. A lot of Soul Passers are very frightened people. Just my opinion."

"You're not grinning any more. That's my opinion." Delilah didn't elaborate. Just smiled.

"So Delilah. Where are we going?"

"I believe I mentioned an important meeting in Flagstaff. Need I say more?"

"Like I said, you're the boss." I got the message; we were being surveilled. Things were getting complicated. Again.

We dropped down on the valet pad for the Hotel Monte Vista, the latest rendition of an early 20th century Flagstaff hostelry. A valet in some seriously old-school livery took the Chou-Benz and we took a slidewell. This one had been tricked out to look like a vintage mechanical elevator, complete with a human operator whose skin was wrapped so tightly to his bones that he looked like an animated mummy. Delilah slipped him a 20-tero tip and we walked out into the busy lobby. There was a convention in progress and the place was full of men and women dressed like oversized penguins. Only way I could tell the genders apart was by shape, hair, shoes and sleek black tophats. Modern urban civilization. You'd never see it in Winslow or Chama.

We made our way through the crowd to the Not Exactly Vesuvius, a raucous street level watering hole.

Delilah pointed to an empty table by the bandstand and I ordered us a pair of tequila shooters while Delilah visited the powder room. At least that's the term that popped to mind in this place. I watched the action on stage, tried to tune out the music and must have silently said what-the-fuck a dozen times.

No musicians, only a stage with an animated holo backdrop: a couple vertical lines, a red heart with a spider hanging from it, both suspended from a half moon. There were a few other squiggles and some faint dotted circles, too. All this stuff was independently moving in front of a sky blue background, but not moving much. If that wasn't weird enough, there were these three bizarre Semblances dancing to mixes of something rhythmic, brassy and evidently popular. I couldn't keep my eyes off the dancers, which I can only describe by asking you to imagine three boxy-chunky bronze abstract sculptures come to life. They all had something like legs, but that's about as close to humanoid as they got.

Delilah was back and she shouted over the music: "Joan Miró bronzes. Guy was a Spanish surrealist painter and sculptor from around the time when this hotel was originally built. Quite revolutionary for the period."

I had more questions, but our drinks arrived about then. When we'd done the ritual, Delilah nodded toward the tiny dance floor in front of the stage. A handful of couples from the penguin convention were busy flailing the air with their arms and whirling each other around and doing moves with their legs that completely baffled me.

"You could be a gentleman and ask a gal to dance," Delilah said in a sultry voice that had an undertone of uncharacteristic wariness.

Delilah knows I can't dance and don't dance, so I guessed there was a cryptic subtext I was not getting. Before I could say anything, she added, "I do love formal wear, don't you? Would you be opposed to changing into something more elegant? As in now." Her eyes went to the doors with the old-fashioned single gender symbols in the halls that flanked the stage.

We split up and five minutes later a tall mixed-race couple in formal attire and convention badges was strolling along the sidewalk. The underwear clad unfortunates that donated our new duds were unconscious in toilet stalls. I'd hated leaving my traveling gear behind, but sometimes the gods of garb are adamant about formality.

We'd been lucky — almost too lucky, said my worrier — to find them so perfect and so ripe for plucking; they weren't so lucky, but they'd survive with stories to tell their friends. And we didn't hurt them, just applied sleep-tabs to their necks ... which the well-prepared Delilah had handy. Bless her soul.

In five more minutes Delilah and I had slipped into an alley where our ride was waiting for us. Bye-bye, Flagstaff.

Our new ride was another hoverbar-powered Sumiyo-Brandé, this one another carryall. "Figure at Night Guided by the Phosphorescent Tracks of Snails." According to Delilah, that was the name of the Miró painting that covered the entire vehicle. It was owned by the band we'd just seen at the bar, which, as it turned out, was a secret counter-stealth project of ... that's right, Hildi Mazarian.

The pilot flew in the Flagstaff-Humphrey's Peak corridor, staying slow and legal with the light airborne traffic comprised mostly of moller-type vehicles like the Chou-Benz. The pilot dropped down outside the band's cabin on the outskirts of Old Whiskeytown, a faux western redux village in the vicinity of the ski areas near Humphrey's Peak. We hadn't gone twenty feet up the path to the rustic chalet before the pilot was back in the air and headed back toward the lights of Flagstaff.

The path ended at a steep gabled porch that hid the door. Delilah walked up wooden stairs to the porch and stopped. The door was an imposing timber thing with no handle, knob, knocker or bell. I frowned and looked at Delilah, who held a finger to her lips; I got the idea that there must be some trick to announcing ourselves and getting inside. There was. Doing nothing was the trick. After stand-ing there for a good minute — under the eyes of numerous invisible security sensors, no doubt — the door was opened by a voluptuous, auburn-furred creature that was basically female humanoid in shape until you looked at its head. The creature's head was unmistakably that of a fox, a sort of cartoony one.

"Good evening, my friends. I've been waiting for you. You look positively splendid and I'm very pleased to see that your garment donors were a good fit. Your previous outfits will be in tidy packages outside the door when you leave."

My worrier was right: finding the right-sized people in the bath-rooms at the right time wasn't just luck. I tipped my top hat to the person on the other end of the foxy Semblance. The fox-thing turned and walked to one of three saddle-colored leather armchairs set around a small round table, her fluffy tail swaying back and forth in opposition to the sumptuous rhythm of her hips. Yep, I did entertain a few fleeting erotic thoughts, but I swept them aside as another clev-er distraction on Hildi's part. Gotta be careful around Hildi.

A few minutes later we were treated to a dose of truth, Hildi-style. Anybody who's spent any time working for Hildi knows that the key to surviving is figuring out what she's leaving out of her stories. It's always a special kind of good news/bad news situation. To me, the fact that she was showing herself as fox-like was probably a message in itself ... part of the bad news, at least that's how I saw it.

For Delilah, the good news was that she was fired. Turns out one of her two top assistants was a WorldGov spy. WorldGov had a big, unhappy hard-on for the Buddha, his Soul Train Tours and anybody associated with them. And they had an even bigger hard-on for Nirvanata: always looking for ways to cause a political scene that might slow the global population bleed-out. Evidently the spook was on the verge of some kind of revelation to his handlers, something that Hildi would find troublesome to her Nirvanata cash cow. So he was now history. His body would be discovered in compromising circumstances that neither Delilah nor I needed to know about. I was wondering which of the two was the mole and found myself hoping it wasn't the one with the vocabulary; the world needs all the vocabulary it can get.

187

I didn't get a chance to wonder very long. Not ten seconds after that disclosure, the fox pointed to the door and aimed a couple sentences at Delilah. "I hear your ride arriving. Unless you're dead-set on staying on at Nirvanata — and I emphasize the 'dead' part of the phrase — a marvelous opportunity for the fictional telling of a certain story I just witnessed awaits you in your favorite Earthly paradise. If you agree, say goodbye to One-Shoe ... Ace."

Delilah took a deep breath, looked at me with a scrunched-up expression I figured was made up of equal parts chagrin and relief. "Uh ... One-Shoe ... I, uh ...."

"Say nothing, Ace. We all know that Nirvanata was only a temporary stop. Go do your thing ... and stay out of trouble in fantasyland. Dangerous place, that." We both stood up, embraced and then she was out the door. Just like that.

After the door closed, I just kept staring at it. Hildi sending Delilah off like that couldn't be a plus for me. A tense five minutes of silence went by before the fox broke the ice.

"So One-Shoe. Here we are again, just you and me. Like old times. You've always been a good guesser, so why don't you tell me what's going on in my evil, foxy brain?"

Lame culpability metaphors circled my thinker, looking for a way in. The one that starts off with "play with fire" was in the lead, followed by the one that starts with "you made your bed." I'd been hoping that tapping into Hildi's dark side resources wouldn't come with too many strings attached. Would telling her what I really thought add even more strings? Probably ... but I was in the throes of a dice-rolling moment, so I just decided to play mind reader and see what happened. Well, sort of.

"So, this is where the hapless Navajo sees how much of his single boot will fit in his mouth, huh? Well, sure, Ms Mazarian. I love the taste of boot leather as much as the next hapless Navajo. So I'll just blurt it out. You liked the sex parts best and want to know where to send Maya a thank you note. Sure, that little implant is basically a roadmap to an extra trillion teros and has enough blackmail fodder to have certain agencies and SIs shaking in their metaphorical shoes for the next decade, but the coolest part was the three little sex scenes. How am I doing so far?"

The fox winked at me. "Only *one* little sex scene, One-Shoe. Nice try. It was all there in that little capsule. Everything you experienced, right down to the agonies and orgasms. They were stupid to let you have it, but my guess is that nobody had taken the trouble to review the whole episode ... not even the SIs. Not devious enough ... and really, that kind of stuff is beyond their pay grades. But yes, your little friend Maya is a hottie. I can see why my ex-Cayoo, ah, acquaintance, found her to be such an attractive plaything. I should invite the two of you down to the Palace for some advanced togetherness one of these days. First, however, I'd like to propose a partnership ... just you and me. Off the books, off the record, et cetera. No need to decide now, of course. I'll lay out my objectives and you tell me if you want to take the job. Go home and think about it for a week, then let me know. Deal?"

• • • • •

Just because I'd seen something like this coming didn't mean I had to like it. Somebody like Hildi was not gonna pass on a pre-tested treasure map; guppies would leap tall waterfalls in a single bound before that happened. That pretty much guaranteed that I was going to make another run at St Coriander. Did I want to? No. Did I have a choice in the matter? Not really. Because now she knew they were there ... although not where the implant data said they were. My guess is that Hildi's suspicious nature guessed that Maya and I had figured out ways to keep certain sensitive activities out of the implant's "field of view," so to speak. So yeah, Hildi could put together her own team to go in after the codeboxes, but then I'd die poor — and soon — on account of being a man who knew too much. And if she didn't find them, I'd also die soon. At least if I went in and did it myself, I'd be rich enough to retire. What could go wrong this time?

27

COLLOQUY

I'D ONLY BEEN BACK in Ishernot for a single day when the invitation came in from the Master of North Castle. Not every day you get an invite from one of the most powerful SIs alive, but the timing surprised me a little, being so close on the heels of the meeting with the foxy Semblance of Dinero Dinero. Possibly the Great Coincidence Firehose was doing a heavy spew in my direction. Or possibly our little illegal treasure hunt had dug up too many surprises, and the Clans found enough reasons to become actively interested. Plus, I'd left them plenty of breadcrumbs during my visit to Nirvanata. Were they going to hammer me? I didn't think so. Not the Dunnigan style. That was my reasoning, at least.

I'd gone out to my campsite and had only just started to think about Hildi's proposal, so the last thing I needed polluting my head right then was a high-powered SI with its own issues. But I'd be lying to say I wasn't curious. So I accepted.

The same forest green Sumiyo-Brandé limo picked me up, with the same pilot that had picked up Max Dalt what felt like a lifetime ago. He'd gotten clearance from Ishy to drop down right in front of my campsite in the shadow of Cerro de La Garita on the caldera's north rim. Not just anybody gets Ishernot VIP treatment like that, which told me a little more than I'd known before about the Dunnigan/Ishernot connection.

Was I interested in exploring that connection tonight? Nah. It was a crisp, clear winter night when the only thing I wanted to do was snug up in my sleeping bag and stare up at the Milky Way, watching for falling satellites and listening to the creek and the crickets play for me. Maybe a bright idea or two would fall out of the sky if I got lucky. You wouldn't want to leave that for a mysterious late night meeting, either.

Earlier I'd washed up in the creek, put on a clean shirt, clean vest and clean jeans. Even polished my boot. Also spent a good five minutes just looking at my new left hand/forearm assembly. They'd done a great job hiding whatever was inside with what looked like the skin of a blacktail rattler but was actually some kind of self-repairing biohybrid nanocarbon mesh.

When the chauffeur held out the door for me I held out my scaly new hand just for giggles. "The mysterious super ranger Duckworth Seupetto, right? I believe I am honored."

He gave me a funny look, but shook my new hand anyway.

I'm not quite used to my new limb yet, but … it knows things: senses things my meat hand wouldn't have a clue about. Like the fact the Seupetto's large but ordinary looking hand had some fancy weaponry built into it. I think I did a good enough job of keeping the surprise off my face.

Seupetto was too busy staring at my snakeskin hand to notice. He took a few seconds apparently fishing around for something innocuous to say. Then he said in a casual voice, "If I'm not mistaken, that fancy appendage there is new since that last time I saw you. You were Ranger One-Shoe then. Bet there's a story behind all that … "

"Yep, there's a story. I shouldn't have taken that vacation. But I did and my arm got itself into something that took offense. But they fixed me up pretty good, don't you think?"

Seupetto squinted his eyes, gave me another funny look and dropped his chin just enough for me to interpret it as a nod. "Oh-kay. Changing the subject, you've been to North Castle, right? One of the annual shindigs they put on for Rangers?"

"Nope. Not the shindig type ... word has gotten out that I'm a to-tal nonevent at parties." Now that we were past the one-word conversation phase, I noticed Seupetto's voice: deep and as big as he was. Something about voices like that deliver undercurrents of power and respect. I tucked that away.

"So you were a Ranger for what, five years? And never got to visit the Temple of Muckety-mucks? I'd give you a tour, but not tonight. The Exalted Master of North Castle is a skinch with its precious time. Maybe another time. Hop in."

I hopped in and Seupetto lifted the limo out of the caldera, quiet and silky-like.

North Castle is not a place I ever expected to see in person, but there I was, floating down to the magical scene of a pair of fairytale castles across an impressive dam from each other, each sparkling with a thousand strategically placed lights to maximize the fantasy effect. I think Seupetto's approach was intended to inspire awe ... and it did.

We stopped next to one of the numerous towers. I wasn't expecting a guided tour, but neither was I expecting to be dropped off on a metal platform that slid out from an exterior wall a couple hundred feet above a lake. Did I expect the platform to retract once I'd stepped inside the empty room and the portal to slide shut behind me? Especially not that.

Was I a prisoner? I didn't think so, exactly. But as psychological warfare, this was an interesting opening gambit. I decided to pretend I was an honored guest who'd just been given the key to the President's Suite, so I strolled around and casually looked at this and that while trying to guess where the spy devices were hidden.

The round room covered the entire top floor of a tower that had looked exquisitely medieval from the outside, even in the dark. Inside it was paneled with what looked like real wood: dark, richly figured, with intricate detail touches that had architectural names I didn't know. The door I'd entered through was now invisible and there were zero windows. A cell? I didn't think so. More like a high security conference room where dangerous secrets got batted around like so many ping-pong balls.

The Dunnigan clanmark had been woven into a carpet so thick and cushiony that it made me wish Maya had been invited, too; excellent venue for our favorite activity. The round table in the middle had a polished stone top with inlays that formed the [surprise, surprise] Dunnigan clanmark. Was I impressed? Well, it sure kicked the aesthetic ass of the St Coriander Elevation Stage.

I'd had the impression this was going to be a private meeting ... just me and the main Dunnigan SI. But I was wrong about that, too. Although there was only a single chair, the big table sported six little metal tents with names carved into both sides. In front of the only one with a chair was a silver tray with a crystal pitcher of water, a crystal tumbler, a carafe of coffee, a crystal mug and a crystal dish with little pastries that gave off vague wafts that might be chocolate and almonds. I walked around the table and figured I'd try to remember the names. But except for One-Shoe, the others were all representational: St Coriander, Clans Dunnigan, United Entities, Ishernot and S.I.A.I.U. Interesting. I sat in the single chair, drank excellent coffee and wolfed down a couple pastries while I contemplated why the Master of North Castle hadn't bothered to mention these other participants in its invitation.

At eleven o'clock, chimes began to ring out a somber melody. On the eleventh note, the rest of the meeting arrived: five Semblances poofed into imaginary chairs. I stared and stifled a guffaw. This is how powerful SIs present themselves in human form? Well, not exactly human form. I was sitting at a table with five famous cartoon dwarves. Color me speechless. So I began to clap. I think I said bravo a few times, too. It was all I could think to do at the time.

The dwarf behind the Ishernot tent — I think it was Dopey — winked at me.

Across from me behind the Cayoo card was Grumpy, arms crossed and looking, well, grumpy.

Doc sat in the seat next to me, the one with the Clans Dunnigan card in front of it. That must be the Apex, the Master of North Castle. Sleepy was the St Coriander Librarian ... and we winked at each other. Was I envisioning the stunning First Assistant Delara behind the wink? Not telling. Happy's Semblance represented United Entities, the importer of the ThoughtDancer line from Miotx 4.

Doc spoke in exactly the voice of the Doc in the Snow White cartoon. I know this because the crèche I was raised in showed a scratchy holo conversion of that cartoon every goddamn week. Then something sinister occurred to me. Was this their way of telling me they knew everything there is to know about me? Probably. But how hard would that be anyway? Easy. No intimidation points for that one.

195

"Fellow Entities, I introduce the man we've been discussing: Travis One-Shoe."

A few tried to make smiles, most just nodded. I've read that operating a Semblance believably isn't as easy as they make it look in the holos. So maybe, with SIs not being accustomed to physical bodies, a cartoon Semblance offered less chance of looking fake to a human. Less chance of embarrassment. Very human sentiment ... if that's what it was. I filed that away.

"Travis One-Shoe, meet the Colloquy's ad hoc council on what we are calling the St Coriander Matter. As you might surmise, certain recent events there had the potential for negative impact for most of the ad hoc council. At the present time the remaining information exposure aspects of the matter have been simplified by the simple fact that most of the participants in your, ah, caper are no longer living ... at least on this plane. That leaves you and Maya Ng who were aware of most of the facts that might, under certain circumstances, still cause difficulties for some of the agencies or functions we represent. In the interest of full disclosure, Ishernot represents to me that Maya Ng agreed to have her related experiences recast during what you know as the Circus. She was not in any way coerced: she chose. That leaves you."

28

BRUSHED OFF

I GLARED AT DOPEY: my emotional temperature was headed toward molten lava, but my voice stayed cool. "Ishy, is that true? You wiped Maya's memory of the whole fucking thing?" Some other things clicked and I held up my hand. "I get it, now; not wiped. Recast, meaning different identities for the players and places and activities in the 'caper'. And that included me?" I was rock solid certain that other recast memories included the locations where Maya had hidden the two codeboxes. Which made me wonder if these clowns actually knew where they were.

Dopey just nodded.

I poured myself another cup of coffee and just sat there. I felt like going into a rage, but the warmth of the cup in my hands somehow took the edge off it enough to let me think a little. They'd fucked with Maya's head, made her essentially forget me and what we'd rekindled. It felt like a full goose bozo betrayal. Fuckers.

Until I encountered Harold the Conqueror, I'd put all SIs on a pedestal. But Harold opened my eyes to their underlying humanity; I would never have expected anything like that speech to O'Kelly to come out of any SI, much less an SI psycho. And here they were doing exactly what humans in their positions would probably do ... and for the same reasons. But was that a good thing or a bad thing?

I thought back to all the old "evil computer" vids I've seen. You know the names. Lots of classics, lots more junk. But then the early

Dunnetix SIs started accomplishing amazing — and well-publicized — feats of creative technical dazzlement ... like opening up the universes with their Nevergates. And they pulled off these miracles without deciding to behave like cheesy old-school godlets who needed to grind mere humans under their virtual boots just because they'd become powerful enough to do it. Fact is, modern SIs consistently demonstrate more humanity than most humans. Most of the time.

Did any of that mental blather change my current situation? Nope. But it didn't hurt, either. Considering that I was still steaming, I was pretty proud of myself that I didn't really go off on them ... Ishy in particular. It would've been a total waste of effort anyway. So I took a deep breath, put on my Cool Maniac face and played my card.

"Okay, fuckers. What's your offer? Better be a world-shakingly good one."

Doc turned and gave me a cartoony version of a hard stare. "I find your statement disturbing, Mr One-Shoe. The indicators strongly suggest an implied threat."

For the last month I've been trying to pretend that something like this wasn't going to happen. But I was kidding myself. Of course it was. Pretty much had to. And I wondered if Hildi knew it, too ... and what that might mean for the mission she'd just dropped on me.

I looked around and gave each dwarf a look that said I know exactly how you're vulnerable and how to make things so hot for you that you won't even think of taking me out. Then I amped it up with my best interpretation of Maya's fuck-with-me-and-die tone. "Oh, it's w-a-a-ay more than an implied threat. It's a card-carrying don't-even-think-about-fucking-One-Shoe-over threat. Just ask Dopey here."

I worked hard to contain my grin: each goddamn dwarf tried to make its Semblance adopt a stern frown. It was a laughable affront to every well-drawn cartoon face in the history of cartoon faces. In short, an animation travesty. For a second I thought maybe they were lampooning their own characters to see if they could get me to laugh ... loosen things up a bit. But if I was going to do any laughing at this meeting, it was going to be my idea.

So instead of laughing, I squinted my eyes and aimed a bionic snake finger at Doc. "If my good friend from Ishernot hasn't figured it out yet, ask it how the implant I wore through the whole caper got modded. Then ask it what happened to it after the caper was over, where it might be now ... and if the name Ace Falken rings any bells."

This was where things might get a little tricky. Shouldn't be very hard for them to guess that I'd made contact with Hildi Mazarian. After all, it was hardly a secret that Hildi has her fingers in the Zone outside Nirvanata. Or that I'd done security work at Hildi's Palace. So they wouldn't even have to do much guessing. And I knew for a fact that Ishy had bugs ... and I'd made no secret of my recent travels. So really, I was hoping that their spying plus my dropping the name Ace Falken should be enough for them to make the necessary inferences without my having to spell it out for them. Bad timing for spelling things out; wouldn't want to piss Hildi off by making any representations about her.

Doc interrupted my thoughts. "The sense of the Colloquy, Mr One-Shoe, is that a specific offer is premature at this time. We all are, like yourself, essentially agents performing services on behalf of other parties. I will be in touch. In the meantime, the car is waiting outside and will return you to Ishernot. Thank you for making yourself physically available to us. Good night."

The abrupt brush-off took me by surprise and I hoped I didn't show it. That was my first thought. But of course I was kidding myself; they had every manner of sensor checking me out the whole time. So I got up, applauded vigorously for about five seconds, then picked up my chair and threw it at Happy, the representative of United Entities. The chair flew right through the Semblance and its phantom chair and landed on the carpet with a muffled thunk. Only then did Happy duck, which would tell somebody smarter than me something possibly useful about time lag. I just applauded again. "Well done! Nice reactions, Happy. That's just a reminder that in my book, peddling psychotic entities like Harold the Conqueror should be a hanging offense. Guillotine optional. That thing killed an entire town

— every man, woman and child — and did it's best to kill me and Maya. So I guess I'm a little sensitive about the very fact that some piece of corporate shit can hide behind a cartoon Semblance in the same room with the best SIs in the known universes."

The wall opened up and a cold wind whipped into the room. "Thanks to the rest of you. I'm still a big fan of the Clans Dunnigan, for whatever that's worth." Then I tipped my imaginary hat and walked through the portal, onto the platform and into the gaping gullwing door of the limo.

Whew. I slumped into the plush seat and mentally patted myself on the back for not once looking down.

In the spacious passenger compartment, the rear seat in the limo sort of enfolded me, exactly what those clever, expensive things are designed to do. I could have fallen asleep in about ten seconds except for the fact that my brain was trying to untangle the session with the dwarves. Sure, my chair throwing and yelling gambit had been calculated to refocus the audience's attention on somebody besides me, maybe even stir up whatever passes for emotions among that crowd. But I'd be lying if I said my anger was all feigned; some of it was a visceral response to feeling sucker-punched and boxed in. Not sure my distraction would make any difference, long term, but at least I was out of that room and on my way back to Ishernot.

But then I started wondering about how welcome I was going to be in Ishernot tonight after I'd put Ishy on the spot in front of its fellow SIs. Besides, I needed to talk with somebody about tonight's meeting and the only somebody that popped into my head was Hildi Mazarian. Maybe I should take a Caribbean vacation: a sudden one.

"Shall I drop you off where I picked you up Mr One-Shoe?" Seupetto's voice from behind the smoky glass partition interrupted my early stage plotting and got me thinking about a closer place to spend the night.

"Actually, Mr Seupetto, I don't much feel like heading back to Ishernot tonight. Would you mind dropping me off in Chama? Be closer, too. You know the Triple Boxcar?"

"Of course, Mr One-Shoe."

I started imagining a few pints of ale, joking around with Blanca if she had the late shift tonight, getting my mind off things. Seemed like a good plan. Maybe even a wise one. I hadn't figured on the snake in the grass.

29

BULLSHIT

A WOMAN'S SCREAM jerked me out of a dream where I was surrounded by faceless cartoon dwarves, each the size of the Azteca Grill. They'd been passing a single face between them, a lifemask mounted on a stick. The mask had shown different weird faces during the sequence, but at the time of the scream, the mask was a fox face I'd recently conversed with and it was saying "you know I can't talk about my clients, One-Shoe ... "

The dream imploded and the woman shouted something at me: "I'm down One-Shoe. Go low!" I almost sprained my eyelids snapping them open. It seemed like I'd heard that exact shout not too long ago.

There was nothing for my eyes to see, but a few seconds later there was a sound that might be a door opening. Something grabbed my shirt, hauled me out of the back seat and dropped me onto something hard. I tried to push myself up but my limbs felt disconnected from my body. Nothing happened.

From somewhere not far away I heard my own voice bellow a string of expletives that included "MO-THER-FUCK-ER ... OH SHIT ... MY ARM ... FUCK-A-SHIT-PI-TH-TH-TH" before dwindling away to mumbles and then nothing. I thought I felt movement and the sound of wheels on pavement, but only for a few seconds before that faded, too.

The whole scene in front of the Azteca Grill washed over me then, a whitewater cascade of memories.

"Thought that sequence might get your attention, One-Shoe. Put you in the right frame of mind for our little mission here. You can thank the Library's monitors for capturing that bit of recent history; you should've been more careful about where you take your vacations. FYI, the haze'll start wearing off in about ten minutes, plus or minus. Then we'll get busy and get this little matter tidied up."

Seupetto? My bigshot chauffeur? My brain was still fogged up, but I knew the name connected with that voice. But trying to think was like trying to swim through muddy spaghetti; the tickertape of disconnected words unrolling against my shabby excuse for awareness didn't help: Chama ... North Castle ... Doc ... Dopey ... Maya ... Duckworth ... Hildi ...

A spike of pain cleared my head a little, thanks to what felt a lot like a boot contacting my ribs. "Time to wake up, sleepyhead. Your ten minutes is up and we don't have a lot of free time here."

I managed to roll over and open my eyes again. Wherever I was, was indoors, a fairly large room judging from the echoes. And there was a faint stench of disuse and death and decay laced with something that reminded me of beer and sawdust. A camp light was hanging from a rope attached to something up in the shadows. There was enough light to see Seupetto standing over me looking big, dark and menacing. He was fitted out nicely: a tactical belt sporting the usual stuff, plus a pair of dull black ISK212 slivershots, which I took some pains to admire. "Nice hardware. No standard Ranger issue shit for you; nothing but the latest and greatest from my hometown, huh?" I was pretty sure I kept the relief off my face.

He didn't nod or acknowledge me in any way, but he held out a ham of a hand. For an instant I wanted to grab it with my new snakeskin hand, see if it could really crush rocks like the Ishernot medtechs had said. But I didn't. I reached out with my right hand and let him haul me up.

"Thank you, Mr Seupetto, sir."

"Take this and stick it on your forehead, smartass. It'll keep you from triggering any landmines when we go outside ... unless I disable it for uncooperative behavior."

He handed me a genepatch exactly like the ones Maya and I had gotten down in the bowels of the St Coriander Library. I was pretty sure he was trying to blow smoke up my ass about being able to disable it, but I hoped this exercise — whatever it was — wouldn't come down to testing that idea.

205

"Thanks. I'll keep that in mind." I rubbed my ribs where he'd kicked me and made an exaggerated scan of my surroundings. Not a lot to see in the dark, but the decayed and cobwebbed body in a booth not ten feet away made an impression on me: somewhere in St Coriander. Shit.

What I said was, "The Triple Boxcar has sure gone downhill in a hurry." Seupetto didn't bite: just sneered a little.

Seupetto hadn't cuffed or shackled me, which was a little strange ... but good strange. But maybe he'd hyped me while I'd been out. Or drugged me with something to make me compliant. So I told my kernel to do a quick scan while I kept him occupied.

"Yes, you're back in St Coriander. A pub called The Falling Frog. And now we're going to find two missing codeboxes. The Colloquy's analysis is that you and Ms Ng retrieved them and secreted them somewhere in the vicinity since they weren't in the vehicle you stole. Their recovery is essential. Tonight. Your enthusiastic cooperation will be appreciated by all concerned."

I blinked and grinned, choked off a chuckle. "You're planning a career in politics, right? The only thing better than bullshit is more bullshit?"

He didn't look amused, but he smirked again. Maybe I was righter about the political career than I thought.

"The smartass stuff, One-Shoe? Not tonight. Not ever. So you know this is a serious matter, let me bring you up to speed. I was here in St Coriander the day after you and Ng flew to Ishernot. I was with Doyla Rose Faye Dunnigan, head of Clans Security and also my boss.

She put me in charge of cleaning up the mess you all made. I'm being upfront with you here, One-Shoe; I took a lot of grief for the fact that two of my Rangers were involved in the raid. The way the Clans see it, Ranger participation in a crime in the Reserve is an unforgivable breach of loyalty. So in a way Dalt was lucky; he died before Dunnigan wrath came down on him. You may not be so lucky, One-Shoe. And you're stupid besides; you dug yourself an even deeper grave tonight by threatening the Clans. Do you have ...."

I held up both hands. "Okay, so you had your ear to the door, huh? Heard it all? Did you see it, too? The Colloquy of the Five Dwarves? Did you see me throw a chair at whoever the United Entities dickhead was?"

Something told me he'd watched the whole little performance from the comfort of the limo. So I put on some anger. "Okay, you saw it. Then help me understand where you fit into this, Seupet-to-in-Charge. You the enforcer for the Big Bad Neighbors who couldn't be bothered to even check out what happened here for a fucking quarter of a century after it happened? Big Bad Neighbors who are evidently in cahoots with Cayoos — that "C" stands for "corrupt", remember? — to keep the lid on one of the most chickenshit mass murders of defenseless innocents in at least the last century? And not even for hate or religion. Just for money. That's who thinks they've got the moral authority to command my loyalty ... or they'll kill me? There's a term for that in our profession: fubarred. Fucked Up Beyond All Recognition. You think that's an honorable position, you're that fucked up, too. What you got in that big head of yours, duck soup?"

Yeah, I was treading on thin ice. But I had to see what I was up against. Fact is, I didn't want him going all pugilistic on me; scuttlebutt among the Rangers was that you don't want to go at it with him in a ring. But I'd been watching his face during my little speech. There was enough light from the lantern to see silver highlights of the small muscles in his face. Looked to me like he was fighting to keep his anger from showing, so maybe I needed to push a little harder. It was going to be a long night if I let him grind me to find the codeboxes ... since I had no idea where they were.

At the time, I'd figured it was pretty clever to let Maya hide them and not tell me on account of my implant and however else I'd been bugged, but I hadn't figured on what happened to her memories in the Circus. With that knowledge gone forever, not a single soul in the known universes knew where they were hidden. But maybe I could spin up some nonsense and half-truths and live to spin another day.

"Am I pissing you off yet, Soup? So what do you think you know about the codeboxes? If you think they have the key to a trillion teros, you and your puppetmasters are a little out of touch. That account was tapped out two weeks ago by the real Father-Mayor O'Kelly. The charred carcass you found next to the remains of the ThoughtDancer just happened to be a 90-day clone that only had a day of life left on it. Bet your lab boys didn't figure that one out. So what's left to clean up?"

His squint got a little tighter.

"You wanna know something else? The real Vincent O'Kelly watched the whole episode through his clone's eyeballs until the clone died. Then he watched Maya fetch and hide the codeboxes with the same private security feeds he used to help us plan our assault on the folks in the Azteca Grill ... and get ourselves shot up pretty good in the process. When Maya and I finally got out of this cemetery, your Rangers conveniently cleared the area and the perp became one of the Huzbollers.

"Don't believe me, though. Just check out the Huzbol security birds for the whole run and do a count. There will be one extra guy on the last day, the Half-Huz runners. And it will be so easy even you could spot which one because he was wearing the lifemask of one of your fucking rangers. I'll give you a hint to save you some of your valuable time: he's dead and his name was Dalt.

"So the real mass murderer jogs away with the key to a trillion teros right under your fucking bigshot noses. Didn't make me happy to get that news either, but if that story gets out it's gonna splatter some serious egg on some high muckety-muck faces."

I shrugged my shoulders in disgust and rolled my eyes. "Fucking amateurs!"

"A moment," he said, face blank as the backside of a tombstone.

If Soup could somehow verify that any of what I'd just thrown at him was off-the-cuff bullshit, I was in for a gruesome night.

30

FLINGERS

I WATCHED HIM, hoping he'd telegraph what he was going to do. Maybe give me a fighting chance.

During my last bit he'd shifted his stance around a little, but he didn't seem ready to come after me. From the look in his eyes, I figured he was chatting with his handlers ... or at least getting instructions. On the other hand, if he was spoofing me about the Dunnigan connection and was trying his hand as a freelance cherrypicker, maybe he was just starting to realize that he'd stuck his dick into one nasty snakepit.

While I was waiting, my kernel gave me an all clear, so next I had it do a little brotherly Ishernot handshake with his ISK212s. Seupetto started to watch me, pretending he wasn't. He'd waited too long and he knew it, so the only way to stay on top of things was to kick my ass. Didn't think he'd kill me. I mean, what if I was lying and had somehow been able to truthspoof whatever gadgets were monitoring this interchange. Then he'd be naked in the wind. At that point he'd need to either drug me big time or beat the truth out of me. I sure didn't want it to get that far.

But I miscalculated. He didn't wait too long, and he was boosted, which I didn't expect either, but probably should have given his job of protecting Dunnigan bigshots. His left arm shot out so fast I barely had time to spin away from the thing that hissed out from under his wrist. Probably a gas-launched dehab stinger. The thing skidded off my new snakeskin forearm and stuck in the floor. Since he'd tried to sting me, I figured he'd want to cut the hand-to-hand part of this conversation short. I was right: his right hand went for the nearest 212. Very fast. If I hadn't let my spin morph into a dive, he might have gotten my good leg with it ... if the 212 had actually fired. Which it didn't. Thank you Ishernot gods.

My robo-leg got a good swipe at his crotch, but he'd been expecting it to do something, so instead of having his privates in my claws, I only got shredded armor. Shit.

He danced back to what I could now see was the bar of whatever pub he'd said this was. He kicked a barstool out of the way to clear more combat room as I rolled to my feet. Round one: draw.

We eyed each other and he danced around a little like the pro fighters do in cages. Makes good drama, I guess.

"So Soup," I said, a notch above a whisper so he'd have to focus a little extra attention on listening to me. "Sorry your firearm went all malfy on you. Bad batch, I guess," winking to make him wonder what other Ishernot tricks might be in store for him.

"But here's the thing. I'm getting the idea you're freelancing this thing after all. Bad choice. What's your upside here? Maybe you'll fuck me up, maybe I'll fuck you up. Either way, nobody wins because there's nothing to win. Get used to that idea, Soup: we're all staying poor. But you're beholden to the Clans and dear Doyla isn't going to think so much of a failed freelancer. Tell me I'm wrong about this, Soup."

Seupetto didn't say anything. His eyes just narrowed and his lips squeezed together.

"Nothing to say, huh big guy? Way I see it, I've got no downside in killing you. Different story if you kill me. This whole incident is being transmitted on a negspan channel to people that no corporate or governmental entity in their right mind would want to have eavesdropping on 'em. Great new tech ... came in through the Freeboy Nevergate, so your bosses haven't even seen anything but rumors yet. What I'm telling you, Soup, is be smart. Just turn around, fly back to your castle and nobody'll be the wiser. Me, I'll find my way out of here and walk to Chama, thanks."

His shoulders drooped a hair. Was my logic getting to him? I could hope ... but I didn't.

Seupetto still didn't say anything, so I started to swing around, clockwise, like I was just going to thread my way through the tables and chairs and leave him standing there. And I was. Maybe. But first, I wanted my snake arm in position if he did something stupid. Which he obliged me by doing it before I could count to two.

The sensors in my snake arm logged the unique signal his brain was about to send to the weapon in his left hand, the one with the fingers curled, but not quite into a fist. The data say that 97.6% of the time in a no-rules combat, what's about to happen in a curled-finger situation is that the 97.6 percenter is getting ready to launch flingers, those little shot-rockets implanted into fingertips. One of us was going to be a bloody mess if those went off in human tissue. Nervous time.

His thick arm shot forward. It looked like a blow aimed at my chest, but I was too far away to connect. I jerked a couple feet to my right and flung up my arm like a block, but at the last instant grabbed his wrist. My snake fingers closed around the huge wrist, squeezed and twisted with force that shouldn't have been humanly possible.

For an instant I could feel that amazingly complex anatomy of his wrist where bones and connective tissues all come together. Somehow my artificial hand could feel the tiny dance of parts as he tried to uncurl his fingers. Then in one more squeeze, all that amazing anatomy crunched together into a chaotic mash of bone fragments, blood vessels, ligaments, tendons, nerves and whatever else is in there.

Soup's mangled wrist was forced to move in a direction that shouldn't have been possible either; his hand was now pointed backward at his own upper body, not at me. But his fingers were still uncurling as if they had minds of their own. I evidently didn't disable the nerves before they fired; probably would have been better off trying to twist his hand off.

Seupetto must have practiced the flinger move thousands of times until it was automatic, and being boosted, his fingers uncurled with amazing speed. There were four sharp hisses and then four tiny red spots appeared in a line between his Adam's apple and his right armpit. The flingers did their job: home in on the nearest warm flesh.

Behind the red spots the minuscule warheads wreaked their havoc. Four faint explosions, like rhino sizes wooden matches being struck, triggering shaped charges that vaporized a cone-shaped area behind the entry wound. Fine sprays of red erupted from the back of Seupetto's neck and right shoulder.

I let go of his wrist and lurched back.

Instant reality was the last thing to register on Seupetto's face. I was pretty sure he hadn't figured he'd go out this way, but at least his vaporized spinal cord wasn't sending pain signals to his brain.

I moved back and watched his big body fall forward and hit the floor with a dull, anticlimactic thud, stirring up little eddies of shadowy sawdust when it hit.

Sorry Soup. Game over.

Truth is, I wasn't really sorry and the game wasn't really over. I still had to make a clean getaway ... to somewhere not named Nearby. I retrieved his slivershots, not wanting to leave such fine hometown products gathering dust in a place like this. Then I just stood there, looking at the gore, wondering if things could have turned out differently.

A few moments later the lights went on. Literally.

From somewhere above and to my left came the sound of handclapping and a jaded voice saying, "Bravo, bravo. All hail Travis One-Shoe, conquering hero."

The instant the lights came on, I dove to the floor and came up with both of Soup's ISK212s aimed in the direction of the voice.

The illumination was about as bright as you'd expect a pub to normally be, but up in the dimness I could see it had three balconies partly overhanging each other. Seupetto's camp light was still working, but now I could see he'd tossed his rope over the leg of a man-sized green frog that hung suspended in the air, appearing to be in the endless process of falling backwards from the edge of the middle balcony. Judging from the expression on its face, the frog wasn't too happy about it.

The voice was coming from the third balcony, the leftmost one. A figure was leaning over the railing.

"Oh please don't shoot me, Sir Knight. I am only a harmless Semblance," said the odd balding gentleman who had stopped his clapping and now held up his hands in a gesture of mock surrender. Was he poking fun at me? I was pretty sure he was ... and I was not in much of a mood for fun and games. Or witnesses.

214

31
RUNNING IN PLACE

THE FIGURE HANGING over the third balcony kept talking as if it wasn't the least bit afraid of being smithereened by a conquering hero.

"Here you see Malkovich, the Semblance form I usually take in this place, which has become a particularly sad echo of its former vibrant, pub-ish self. After the debacle of the Colloquy this evening I had no idea we would meet again so soon. But here we are already.

"And, to celebrate a happy irony in your combat with Mr Seupetto, there could be nothing better than Hamlet's own words: 'For 'tis the sport to have the enginer hoist with his own petard, an't shall go hard.'"

"Uh, I think you lost me here, Malkovich," I grumbled. I've managed to avoid Shakespeare all my life and here some smartypants Semblance is throwing it in my face. Didn't seem fair.

"Generalized, it means to be killed with one's own weapon. But no matter. I would be honored, Mr One-Shoe, if you would defer your exit long enough to come up here and share your marvelous deductive processes with me. There is a perfectly functional MenuMaster if you are in need of nourishment and the brewmaster tells me that the batch of Bittah Blue it brewed for the recent Clans field trip awaits your pleasure ... assuming you are willing to go behind the bar and fetch a blue tankard from the cooler and do your own pouring. It's tap three."

It took my gullet about half a second to warm to the idea of a juicy burger and a cold brew, but being the suspicious, worrying type, I didn't instantly jump into action. This new twist seemed a little too convenient. Would I be walking into some kind of trap? I didn't think so, but maybe I should at least verify if this really was the Librarian. "Because I'm the cautious type, Mr Malkovich, would you mind showing me the form in which you first represented yourself to me and Maya?"

Before I even finished saying "Maya," the sardonic Semblance of Malkovich was replaced with the fetching Delara and her don't-fence-me-in neckline. If she leaned any further over the railing some faux flesh was going to make a daring escape from that skintight blue top. Would I hate that? Nope, but what if the boobage was some kind of clever distraction and an unknown bad guy was sneaking up on tired eyes in the thrall of phantom mammaries. A quick glance at the mirror behind the bar showed no motion at all, only a festival of cobwebs and the remains of a dead guy in a booth against the opposite wall, slumped into what might be a pizza platter. Relieved, I refocused on Delara and enjoyed the view for a few seconds.

She smirked, took one sleek hand off the railing and held two fingers in front of her eyes. "My eyes are up here, One-Shoe."

I remembered Maya's comments and her elbow to my ribs. Busted again for being boob-boggled, all I could do was applaud. "Well done, well done. I am totally busted. Very nice to see you again Delara. Can you tell me how I get up there?" She winked, gave me directions and blinked out.

A few minutes later Malkovich sat across from me and watched me gulp down a fast-but-marginal burger and slosh each bite down with a gulp of a crisp, hoppy ale. It was 2:34 and the adrenaline rush of the fight had worn off. I was dragging, but I resisted the urge to dig around in my vest for a tab of spike. Not sure why. The night wasn't over and I found myself wishing that the bullshit I'd thrown at Seupetto actually conformed to reality. Would've made things easier. But I still needed to find the codeboxes and get out of this godsforsaken place. And, thanks to Delara and Maya, an idea about where my podnuh might have hidden them had popped into my head at the exact moment I remembered Maya's elbow in the ribs for my eyeball violation.

Malkovich had said that the reason he liked it up here was the view. I had to agree. From our table at the edge of what he called the Third Overhang, the view down into the common room was currently dominated by detritus, dust and death. But up here were also big windows that looked out on the Holy Quincunx towers and the Moat. There was enough of a breeze outside to ripple the water in the Moat, giving the star-speckled reflections of the mirrored obelisks a darkly magical quality. I couldn't decide if it was good magical or the other kind and I was feeling the need to move into the next phase of this operation ... whatever that might turn out to be.

Malkovich broke into my mood. "So. Travis One-Shoe. I confess that I am fascinated by the solving of mysteries. Or perhaps more accurately, I am fascinated by those who solve them with what appear to be great leaps of deduction and induction. The fictional Sherlock Holmes is just one example. I have read every mystery novel in this entire library and I found your solving the Mystery of the Codebox Thief based on the limited information I speculate you had at your disposal is up there with the best. I am hoping you can tell me how you arrived at your conclusions. Will you share?"

What was he talking about? "Uh, do you mean the story I told Seupetto?"

"Precisely that story. Fascinating."

"In my profession, we call that bullshit ... BS for short. That story was a fact-limited desperation attempt to unhinge Seupetto enough to give me a chance to live another day. He would have beat the shit out of me when I couldn't find the fucking codeboxes. He was just that kind of guy. But if the bullshit rang true with you, so much the better. Persuasive bullshit is better than the other kind."

"Fascinating. Allow me to show you a few clips from the monitoring devices the Father-Mayor installed. I have edited them for brevity."

I shrugged. "You mind if I get myself a cup of coffee first? Or maybe a soda and some popcorn? Kidding about the soda and popcorn."

The first sequence followed Maya on the night of our St Coriander adventure. The view was from some kind of aerial tailing device that she couldn't have known about. I figured it must have been like the synthetic moths we use in my trade sometimes. Much better than fixed surveillance.

218

I watched Maya hobble to the Moat, put on the gillmask and slip into the frigid water. Didn't even hesitate; that's Maya for you. Always game for the game. The Librarian sped things up so I couldn't tell exactly how long she was down there, but in the holo her head pops up and she climbs out, then just walks away toward the main tower. The tail follows her up into the building to the room with the Elevation Stage. Maya goes straight to the control console, taps around on the floor under the chair and finds the little cache where O'Kelly had once said the second codebox was hidden. Next, it cuts to one of the little alleys full of shops and I realize my earlier guess is going to be right: Melissa's China Doll House.

"The next clips are of the next day. A sizable crew of personnel came down from North Castle to straighten things up. The late Mr Seupetto was quite busy that day. I was not asked to assist in any way beyond supplying the holos automatically captured during the incident by the viewing devices integrated into my exterior surfaces. This was how Mr Seupetto was able to replay the audio from that painful sequence for you and Maya."

Malkovich paused to make what I decided was a faux self-deprecating gesture and said, "I am only a Themis, you see, and not high on the Dunnetix cognitive pecking order. And of course no one there was aware of my involvement with Father-Mayor O'Kelly's surveillance devices. To be fair, they were almost totally ignorant of all that happened that day. It was only after the data on your implant were made known that the implications of the codeboxes became a matter for high-level discourse. But I digress.

"The time is dusk and the cleanup squad has gone away. I'm sure you will recognize the location, but the figure might be more difficult to detect since it is wearing a stealthfiber cloak, although ... "

I interrupted. "That's O'Kelly ... wearing *my* stealthfiber cloak. It's the only one of the three we came in with that would fit him. Sorry to interrupt."

"Here is our thief departing the doll shop. Of course any found codeboxes would be in his pocket and he is taking care to keep his face in shadow. I have no convenient means to verify that the codeboxes have actually been removed, but then I don't believe this is necessary."

I didn't say anything. I was going to be very surprised if it turned out to be any face but the one I'd told Seupetto it was.

"This is the final clip, later that night."

It looked like Father O'Kelly's shape to me. He was decked out in blue skintex leggings, orange running shorts and shirt topped by a gray windbreaker with a hoodie. On his feet were what looked like well-worn striders and he's running in place in front of the Moat level doors to the Centrisk, the tallest obelisk at the center of the quincunx. The face he's wearing is smiling, he has a silvery codebox in each hand and he's waving them in front of the tracking device, performing for some future audience.

Malkovich said, "It's clearly Father-Mayor O'Kelly, but I am unfamiliar with the face. You said ... "

"Lifemask. Max Dalt, my former boss in the Rangers. A runner. Perfect choice for a lifemask to help O'Kelly become one with the Huzbollers. Pretty amazing that he just happened to have that particular one in his inventory. That's one clever motherfucker."

"Fascinating. So what you told Seupetto about O'Kelly 'getting away with the loot' as they used to say in western melodramas ... is that true?" Malkovich was enjoying this unwinding of the plot a lot more than I was. The prime Bad Guy had outfoxed everybody, played us all for suckers. I had no doubt that by now he'd really tapped out the account and escaped to somewhere or other. Out foxed. The image of Hildi Mazarian's fox headed Semblance popped into my head and a ball of wriggling unpleasantness formed in the pit of my stomach.

"That was just the last necessary piece of my yarn for Seupetto. But just because it was bullshit at the time doesn't mean it isn't true. Probably *is* true, although I have no way of knowing. And right now, I'm really, really tired ... and I really, really want to be out of St Coriander and far, far away. Not that you're not great company, but you haven't just had to kill a primo grade killer and you don't need to sleep."

Malkovich put a look of thespian-grade concern on his face. "Yes, it's unfortunate that you humans are biologically wedded to such rigid patterns of eating and sleeping. If it is any comfort, we SIs necessarily have processes similar to eating and sleeping, but they operate in the background, so to speak. I could direct you to some excellent references, but I believe you will find the following proposal of more immediate utility.

"There are already enough corpses cluttering up this once-fine establishment and it would be inconvenient for a fresh one to be discovered here. Similarly, I suspect you would also find it more convenient if Mr Seupetto's carcass were to disappear, along with any evidence susceptible to discovery by forensic personnel of standard competence. The ucey box in the kitchen should simplify the carcass disposal, leaving only the matter of tidying things up in the common room. As recompense, I will arrange for you to safely use the Dunnigan vehicle parked on the loading dock for the next few days. Any destination, no pursuit, no bureaucratic entanglements. Guaranteed."

Naturally, I wanted to know how.

Malkovich held up his hand. "Naturally, you want to know how I, a mere Themis, can effectuate such magic. It is better not to know. To quote a bard named Thomas Gray, 'where ignorance is bliss, 'tis folly to be wise.' In this case, perhaps his second phrase is most applicable. To use an expression I'm sure you've heard far too many times, 'trust me on this, Travis.'"

I didn't even bother to roll my eyes. I closed them for a couple seconds, though, just long enough to make a silent prayer to whichever of the Dunnetix SIs invented the Universal Converter back around the turn of the century. Usually we modern folk never even think about uceys; they're almost as ubiquitous as air. But now I was about to use one to transform Seupetto's useless carcass into energy and feedstock for the St Coriander fabrax, so it was a perfect time for a sincere moment of gratitude for not having to dig a hole and bury the guy.

221

I didn't mention that to the Semblance. Instead, I stayed on point and said, "You are a piece of work, Malkovich. Okay, I'll trust you. But before I head out I want to make a little side trip to buy something. While I'm cleaning up in here, maybe you could figure out how I could pay for it."

222

32

BAT ORCHIDS

I WOKE UP with the decaying sprawl of Laredo Laredo spread out some distance to the west, and feeling as good as I've felt in months. And why not? As far as I knew, I was an unemployed mickajo with nothing anybody wanted. That's freedom. I'd gone out on a limb and trusted Malkovich and the flight plan to Dinero Dinero he'd filed for me, I presume with help from the Clans since they owned the vehicle and probably wanted it back in one piece. I didn't even attempt to argue. Just said thank you and climbed into the sleek front compartment, figured out how to adjust the seat to snooze position and let the autopilot take it from there.

Now I was awake, though, and I used my newfound freedom to start worrying. First thing that gnawed on me was the reception I was going to get in Dinero Dinero. I was just getting various scenarios wound up when Malkovich's voice came through the audio system, overriding the ambient somno I'd had running in the background during my snooze.

"So. One-Shoe. If you're hearing me, you must be awake. Malkovich here. Because we've got you on the most innocuous, slowboat route possible, I took the liberty of loading something you might find amusing during your lonely hours over the gulf. It's quite old, but it's worth watching; trust me on that, Travis. In fact, I'm so certain you'll be enthralled that I've set it to autoplay. Au revoir, my friend."

Dialing back into my new sense of freedom, I got my seat into a comfy viewing position and trusted Malkovich again. The payoff? One of the coolest weird-funny vids I've ever seen in my life: "Being John Malkovich." Watched it twice. The second time with a bowl of the miniature MenuMaster's best imitation of cardboard popcorn and a bladder-busting amount of Brandfree Cola, which gave me a chance to test out the limo's minuscule head. I would have watched it a third time except that the glare of the Eye Pluribus Unum showed up on the horizon. Party time.

• • • • •

"Well, folks, you're in luck. Looks like Elvis left a light on for us." That's the standard opening patter the cattle car shuttle pilots use to announce their approach. I heard it way too many times when I was studying incoming security in some of those very mollers, mostly from the nearby CenAm and Carib states. The spiels always went downhill from there.

I don't much like this place. Remember the final battle scene in "Return of Zeus IX" where Poseidon's kraken steed just opens its maw and swallows the pyramid and everybody in it in one gulp? I cheered so loud my fellow cheezoid fans threw their spiffypop at me. Not rational, but that's how I am about the place. Except the lagoon, but that's more about mermaids, a whole other story. But here I am again, intentionally riding into the jaws of advanced foolishness. Not sure what that says about my IQ.

Malkovich hadn't given me any details, just said all would be handled. But I was still surprised when the limo didn't even slow at the 10-mile security perimeter and just flew up to the VIP-level landing platform on the leeward facet of the pyramid about a quarter mile above the water. Hovered for only a minute for a scan before settling down, then my door swung open and I climbed out, happy to suck in some air with that crisp Caribbean tang again. I would've just stood there, trying to convince myself that I was recordbreakingly passionate about the breeze and the view and not procrastinating at all, but the pair of white uniformed guards at the door made a crisp beckoning motion. I decided this was not a good place to play the bad boy. Long way down for somebody who can't fly.

The limo was lifting off and heading home by the time I got to the door.

"Welcome to Hildi's Palace, Mr One-Shoe," said the guy with the longest strip of glitter on his spangulary. "Please step this way."

Security was very interested in my new arm and even had to check with Ishy on a few things, but other than that I got a clean bill of health. My right leg was still in their records, so they only had to check to see if I'd gotten any new mods.

When they were done, a striking multi-ethnic woman in an ice cream business suit did the welcome thing again and escorted me to a small conference room on the periphery. Her brass nametag said "Quintessa" and she looked at least half Kenyan, with a fetching half-smile that reminded me too much of Maya. But she was way more solicitous than Maya ever was and even brought me a tray of tasty pastry things and a beaker of fresh dark roasted Blue Mountain coffee, which some people know is one of my top five beans. I hadn't thought about being hungry, but now it hit me that I was ravenous. Stop worrying One-Shoe, I told my hungry worrier with that stern mental voice I use for chidings; the only people who leave Dinero Dinero hungry are the ones destined to be fish food. Comforting to remember that.

The coffee let me ponder what I was doing here. Something about wrapping my hands around a steamy, fragrant mug does that to me. If I was honest with myself, reasons one through three for being here had to do with someone's immediate personal safety: mine. Number four was that I was hoping I could learn where O'Kelly had gone. Even if he'd already gated somewhere far away, something told me he'd likely stop here first ... for an appearance job at least. The more I thought about it, the more I saw a fox-faced octopus playing the whole bunch of us like clown-puppets.

Would she ever cop to having dealings with O'Kelly? At a formal level, Hildi has buttoned lips when it comes to information about her business dealings and her clientele. On the other hand, she knows that some of the folks that use her shadier services are anything but lovely deep down. She would have seen through the likes of O'Kelly and Henry Ng before they ever opened their mouths. Would that matter? Did I know Hildi well enough to answer that question myself? Or even to ask it? Nope.

I hadn't gotten very far in my thinking about how to go about learning something useful about O'Kelly's whereabouts when the door opened and a tall, saturnine man in the most serious black suit I've seen in years took a few tentative steps inside.

"Mr One-Shoe?"

I nodded.

"I am Viktor Klensouth. I am the Director of Grief Counseling for the Misteriosa Bank." He bowed and held out a white card that said in print what he'd just spoken out loud.

Was this Hildi the Prankster messing with me? Misteriosa Bank is the name of the subsurface mountain range Dinero Dinero is perched on. The "floor" of this part of the Bay of Honduras averages around twelve feet below the waves. But there's also a Cayman-based financial institution named the Misteriosa Bank. According to the rumors, if you peeled back all the corporate shells, you'd find Hildi Mazarian at the core.

But if not a spoof, why would a guy from either kind of bank be calling on me about grief counseling? I couldn't decide if it was weirder or funnier, but it was plenty mysterious. When confronted with mysterious mysteries like this my initial response is usually no response at all. So I just sat there and looked up at Viktor Klensouth, scrutinizing his face and trying unsuccessfully to look past the sallow complexion and a pinched sort of bone structure that lost itself in a high forehead with a widow's peak. Perfect fit for his job: almost a caricature of unctuousness, but so what?

Then I let my eyes drop to the black portfolio he now cradled in front of him with both hands, almost like a shield for his crotch. I looked back up at him, wondered which kind of bank he was working for and waited.

Probably used to more cordiality, his face twitched and his lips did an odd little pursing thing. Then he harrumphed and said, "Well, then. If you have a moment, I will explain my presence at this time."

I nodded.

Klensouth opened the snap on his antique black leather portfolio and removed a thin sheaf of papers.

"It is my sad duty to inform you of the death of your beloved uncle, Vincent Treat O'Kelly, approximately four hours ago. Cause of death is listed as complications from his medical procedure at the Opus facility here on the island. As you are aware, he has been comatose since yesterday. Since you were listed as next of kin on the admitting documents and that you could be reached through Ms Mazarian, we contacted her office immediately upon Mr O'Kelly's passing. Their office informed us that you were flying here to be at his side, and I am sorry he passed away while you were still in transit. I feel fortunate, however, that I was able to be here to offer complimentary personal counseling as a part of the Opus suite of services."

Did I hear that right? O'Kelly dead? Here? I tried to maintain my stone face, but I wouldn't be surprised if my expression showed at least a hairline crack or two right then. A whirlwind of suspicions twisted through my head, one of which was that Hildi Mazarian was watching this little live drama in an office somewhere and laughing loud enough to shatter the windows. Desperate to buy a little thinking time, I closed my eyes, bowed my head, tented my hands in front of my face and mumbled into my hands: "Could you give me a moment, Mr Klensouth?"

"Certainly, certainly. The sudden loss of a loved one is often stressful and traumatic. I feel fortunate that I could be here when you arrived to assuage the shock however I may. Because emotional closure is often facilitated by a physical viewing of the body, the funereal facility here has arranged for a viewing at 3 PM this afternoon."

• • • • •

Not wanting to have to risk bursting this suspiciously too-good-to-be-true bubble, I gracefully declined Klensouth's counseling. He left me a piece of paper with the location of the viewing room and with the usual pseudo-sympathetic blather, bowed again and departed.

228 When I figured it was time to leave I got up and headed for the door. It opened before I got there: the ice cream suit woman again. She smiled her too Maya-like smile and presented me with a wristband. "Ms Mazarian regrets that she cannot be here at this sorrowful moment, but looks forward to seeing you at the viewing. In the meantime, she feels certain that you will want some time to be with your own thoughts. The bracelet allows you access to all public areas as well as all privileges of an Honored Guest. I'm told that this is not something I need to explain to you." That smile again.

"Thank you, Quintessa. Amazing name, by the way. Your smile reminds me of someone I'm very fond of, so please use it wisely." I winked, snapped on the sleek silver bracelet and found my way to the elevator core.

• • • • •

Three o'clock showed up too soon. My plan was to walk around the marina, but I settled for sitting with a couple espressos and — in Maya's honor — a slice of pumpkin pie with dollops of clotted cream spun with bits of candied mocha at a place called Puffkin's on the city level.

I showed up at the mournatorium right at three. A man who might have been Klensouth's identical nephew ushered me into a small room with a replica of an elaborate hand-worked bronze casket resting on a black velvet shroud in the center. A bronze vase at each end held an elegant spray of assorted black flowers and silvery ferns. The two long gray walls were lined with uncomfortable-looking wood-like chairs. One was occupied by a smallish woman wearing a long black dress with long sleeves, gloves and a bosom-length embroidered black veil over a grim black pie pan hat. Hildi was really going all out. Her head was bowed in something that in a real mourner might have been contemplative sorrow. I'm sure she heard me enter, but she didn't look up or say anything.

I kept my smirk to myself and took a long look at the thing in the coffin. It looked exactly like the man I had first known as Morton Vance. It also looked exactly like the Vincent O'Kelly that met his death at the mind of a ThoughtDancer Excel that called itself Harold the Conqueror. For no good reason at all, I reached down and checked the pasty neck for a pulse. No pulse ... and it felt a lot like real skin over real muscle and connective tissue. But was it *really* real? And if it was real, whose skin? The last few months had turned my traditional ideas about life and death upside down and inside out ... and I wasn't liking it. For all I knew this could be another clone and the real O'Kelly had already gated to whatever safe place he'd set up in advance.

A sudden irrational urge came over me, an urgent desire to cram one of those flower sprays into the corpse's mouth and the other into Hildi Mazarian's mouth. Instead, I inhaled a deep breath of floral scented air and decided to leave. A white card hanging from the flower spray at the head of the casket caught my eye, which is how I learned that the black flowers were black dahlias, black calla lilies and bat orchids. And that the silvery ferns were actually called silver ferns. It's also how I learned that the flowers had been provided courtesy of Lackdorf & Cotsweir, Attorneys-at-Law.

• • • • •

Last time I was here, the resident legal franchise had three more names in it, but I liked Lackdorf & Cotsweir a lot better. Both were women, both had maximum strength good looks, at least from the portraits on the walls.

The receptionist was a good looking tanned young man who looked like he should be sitting in a lifeguard tower, not behind a desk. As soon as I walked through the door, the kid with the straw hair stood up and said, "Hey, Mr One-Shoe. You're an hour early for the reading of the will, but come on back and I'll set you up in one of the waiting rooms. The hour will be gone before you know it."

So I'm early for an appointment that I didn't know I had for the reading of the will I didn't know existed of a man I had learned to loathe more than anyone I'd ever met. I wanted to be angry and embarrassed, but I settled for bemused and confused.

Hildi, Hildi, Hildi, I thought as I followed him to a comfortable room with four of the kind of chairs that you don't ever want to get out of. I picked up a slate off the coffee table and tapped up a preview of the current attractions at the Bimbo Circus a few levels up. If I set my mind to it, I can enjoy the Bimbo Circus as much as the next debaucherant, but today I just couldn't go there. It hit me that where I really wanted to go was anywhere but here, so I tapped up the schedule of shuttle flights and booked a seat on the next flight from here to anywhere. If I hustled, I could make it.

33

FISCAL ATONEMENT

DINERO DINERO to Mérida to San Antonio to Albuquerque took me almost three days. Plenty of time to think … maybe too much. When I added it all up, there was no way it didn't equal You've Been Had. Maybe O'Kelly was really dead, maybe Hildi had helped him escape to a happy-dappy planet in some PU or other. Maybe she'd even split the proceeds with him as a fee. Or maybe she was in it from the beginning as a silent partner. I didn't want to go there, but it was a big enough behemoth in the room that I couldn't ignore it forever.

By the time the Ishernot shuttle arrived in Albuquerque on New Years Day to take me home I'd decided to just chalk it all up to experience and not ever think about it again. Well, not until Ace came out with her book … if she was still planning to write it.

It was still early when I got back to town, so I had dinner in my favorite booth at the Callisto and hooked into Ishy on a house slate to see what had been happening. Ishy would only say "go home," which is shorthand for "you have secure messages that should not be viewed on a public device." So I went home.

What I call home is a utilitarian one-bedroom unit with a loft I almost never use. Small, but a short walk to what passes for downtown in the sprawlish village that is Ishernot. The unit was all a guy like me needed as a home base and as secure as anything these days … and it was what I'd been able to afford on my Ranger salary.

It's five floors up and the only views are of the airport and the fab-ratory district. I plunked myself down in the only chair worth sitting in and tapped up a display on the wall. Two messages. The first was from Ace, wanting to borrow some of my time for an interview. She was making progress but had a lot of questions and could she stay at my place for a couple days, starting tomorrow. The second was from Fiesbaum & Partners, Accountants. It included an encrypted draft code for 100,000 teros and a note that said only: "Honorarium for North Castle Speaking Engagement."

Both of those messages made me grin, but for different reasons.

• • • • •

Since I was suddenly feeling well off, I volunteered to put Ace up at the Downtowner, a very nice place and only about fifteen min-utes away on foot. She wasn't having it. So I figured I'd sleep on the floor in the living room. But after she came out of the shower all wet and shiny and looking the picture of feminine perfection ... and then dragged me into the bedroom, I never bothered to bring up that idea. She had very specific ideas about what she wanted to bring up and the first night it didn't include a lot of sleeping. Anywhere. Good thing I got caught up on winks during my sojourn back from Dinero Dinero.

Ace had stayed a week and I was starting to like being interviewed like this when she dropped her bomb.

"I know you don't like gating, One-Shoe, but will you at least see me off tomorrow morning? I'm heading to my writing hideout in Can't Say Where so I can bang this story out. I've never enjoyed research so much, but I'm sure you understand that I could never get any real writing done with your studly body anywhere within a thousand miles of here."

"Uh, Ace. I know you're a lot older and wiser but ... "

"One-Shoe. Look at the blue dot. Remember I'm a Buddha-trained empath who knows things. The longer I stay here the messier it's go-ing to get when goodbye time happens. Now is as good as it's going to get and you know it as well as I do. But going out with a bang would sure be the memory we both want to take away and keep in one of those safe places."

I hate it when people know me better than I know myself.

As Nevergate hubs go, the Ishernot center is one of the smaller ones: 14 people-size mods, one freight-size mod and one industrial-size mod. Nothing at all like the mega-setup at Nirvanata. Ace opened the door to Mod 13, blew me a kiss and stepped in while I waved, feeling like a dork because I didn't make the erotic gesture I thought about ... and which would have gotten a big chuckle out of Ace. But then it was too late: the safedoor cycled closed, the amber light flashed for ten seconds and that was that. Gone to Can't Say Where for Dunno How Long.

I went back to my place, packed up what I usually take for a winter campout and called a cab.

Decompression is one of those terms that mean something different to everybody. For me, it was three days of a process I hoped would back off the mainscrew of the cosmic wine press I'd gotten caught in since my first Henry Ng encounter in the Dunnigan Reserve.

The high country winter was acting warmer than usual and the nights were only in the low teens. But the days were scattered clouds and in the low 40s. The first day I crunched through the two feet of snow to my favorite ancient stump and tried to count how many stubborn leaves were still hanging on to branches in the aspen grove by the pond.

The second day I got naked and took a plunge in the near-frigid pond, then got out fast and ran around whooping and hollering like a wild Indian for ten minutes. My Navajo ancestors would've been proud. I hope.

The third day I donned my old parka and hiked up to the rim, followed the trail that runs along the edge of the caldera for five miles and then hustled back to camp. After that I foraged enough wood for a massive all-night bonfire and spent half the night just staring into

233

it, the only interruption being a break to roast sausages, mushrooms and onion chunks on a skewer.

On the fourth day I sat outside my tent in my camp chair and did nothing that you could call anything ... but that still felt like something. By midday, the sky was clotting up with churlish cumulus and I wondered if fresh snow was headed my way. My mind shifted to the contemplation of the various types of snow I'd seen, but I didn't get very far into it before I heard the sound of a cab heading my direction. Cabs have no reason to come out here unless I call them and I sure didn't call this one. I hadn't even unfolded my slate since I'd been here.

The chunky green and white Isonaki hovered a foot above the ground in the rocky flat area just above the flood zone, which is about a hundred yards down from where I pitch my tent. A figure got out, pulled out what looked like a very large pack, said something to the cabbie and started crunching through the remnants of snow toward the tent.

Maya Ng. Nobody walks quite like Maya Ng.

"Hey One-Shoe. Get off your fat ass and give me a hand. This shit's heavy."

• • • • •

"Nice tent you got here, One-Shoe. Hope you don't mind company, but I got a gateline message from Ishy two days ago. Said it was holding old-fashioned mail for both of us at the office, and that they needed to be hand-delivered. Is that fucking weird or what? Hey, can I come inside? It's a little brisk out here. Spring where I was on Onedinket right now."

"Golly Mayarino, nice to see you too. And swell of you to stop by as long as you were in the neighborhood and all."

"Stop by, my skinny chinkrican ass. I'm a professional courier here. Came all the way from Onedinket and got a 10-tero credit from Ishy on my next run through the Circus. All that for just picking this up and bringing it out to you. You owe me for the taxi, though."

So much for decompression. Life had returned to my life, Maya style.

I found a spot for her duffel and she unsealed a lumpy side pocket and hauled out two opaque white rectangular gelpaks. Laminated into the top of each was a codepic, one with a standard ID holo of Maya's face, the other mine. I knew the drill, but I just held it in my hand and waffled.

"You got a bad feeling about this, One-Shoe? I don't. At least I didn't until now."

I was looking at the return address: Lackdorf & Cotsweir, Attorneys at Law, Dinero Dinero. I sucked in an oversized portion of that rare brand of air that's so clean it kind of vacuums up whatever bits of microcrap are clinging to your alveoli. "We have some serious catching up to do, you and me. But I'll start with the latest chapter. A little under a week ago I walked out of the Lackdorf & Cotsweir offices on Dinero Dinero an hour before I was supposed to be in a meeting for the reading of Vincent Treat O'Kelly's will. Yeah, he's supposedly dead. I even looked at the body in a casket. Sure looked like him. Sure didn't have any pulse, either. But the whole thing smelled like Hildi at her surreal Machiavellian best ... so I just got the fuck out of there."

"Then what do you think is in these things? Bombs? Aren't bombsniffers too good for that."

"Supposed to be. And knowing how nosy — and protective — Ishy can be, I shouldn't even give it a second thought. So rationally I'm 98% confident these aren't bombs. But just in case they are, I want to do something else first. I want to seal up the tent, turn on the heat and see if our private parts still like each other. If they do, we can hold off blowing ourselves to bits for a while."

"Hah. I can already see your private part trying to bust open your fly and ruin a perfectly worn-in pair of Levi's. My part has been thinking — she does think, you know — about amusing herself at your expense since me and her got into the cab. So I guess we're agreed that we should just decide to fuck each other's brains out and open these things in the morning. Be nice to do it without agonies of arm or leg. Like the really old days."

• • • • •

Morning came late that morning. Somewhere around noon I brewed up a pot of Blue Mountain and we sat on the bed in the tent, well spent, sweat-caked and naked, with only blankets around our shoulders. For the first cup we stared at the white gelpaks.

"I'm starting to feel stupid about this, Mayarino. I'm going to just do it."

"No way. Let's do it together."

So we did. We pressed the top of the packages with the codepix to our foreheads and let them do whatever they did for the ten seconds needed to decide if we were actually who we were supposed to be. No explosions, just the little musical chimes they make when they're ready to open.

"Does this feel like Christmas to you, One-Shoe?"

"Dunno. Didn't grow up with Christmas."

"Me neither."

We tapped our codepix and the gelpaks turned transparent and unsealed themselves.

Inside each one was a white Lackdorf & Cotsweir envelope on top of a thin rectangular white box.

Maya was faster at opening her white envelope and pulled out the folded papers before I even had my envelope torn open. "Shall I read it?"

"Sure."

A few minutes later she said, "Fuck, One-Shoe. This is too fucking weird. Is this for real? Hurry up and read yours."

By that time I'd skimmed my own papers. Skipping all the legal mumbo jumbo, it attested to be the true and proper last will and testament of Vincent Treat O'Kelly. It had O'Kelly's lifesig and the usual notary holoseal. It was timestamped the morning of his admittance to the Opus Refurburator Clinic on Dinero Dinero. It all looked legal and proper, at least to my unpracticed eyes. But the meat-and-potatoes part was these two lines on the second page about the dispersal of bequeathed funds:

•   St Coriander University Endowment Fund (in formation): 522,164,467.00 teros

•   Benevolent Trust for Fiscal Atonement (on deposit at Misterioso Bank of Dinero Dinero): 522,164,467.00 teros.

"Who the fuck knows, Mayarino? I sure don't. But I don't see our names on it so far."

I flipped to the last page. Just below the last line of blather was something else: a miniature comtab with my codepic. I peeled it off, held it against my forehead until it chimed. I retrieved my slate, unfolded it and slapped the tab on the surface. What popped up was on letterhead of the Benevolent Trust for Fiscal Atonement.

Maya took the liberty of reading it over my shoulder. It purported to be the minutes of the trust's organizational meeting. Mostly legal blah-dee-dah, but the important thing was the nomination by Vincent O'Kelly of the three permanent members to the Board of Trustees: Hildi Mazarian, Maya Ng, and Travis One-Shoe. The other interesting item was that the starting stipend for all confirmed trustees was 20,000 teros per month. Oh, and there was a signing bonus of 500,000 teros, payable at the first official meeting of the Board of Trustees, set for two weeks from yesterday.

"Do you think mine says the same thing, One-Shoe?"

"Be real surprised if it didn't."

"You going to do it?"

"Sure am going to think about it."

Maya looked at me like I might or might not have suddenly acquired a cognitive defect. Then she shrugged and said, "What do you think is going to be in these skinny little white boxes?"

"Dunno, but let's find out." Mine weighed almost nothing, but when I shook it, something rattled a little.

Maya sniffed hers first, which says something about something. "Smells like flowers."

"Bet they're black," I mumbled, mostly to myself.

Maya gave me a quick squint, then unsealed her box. Inside was a folded square card of heavy, textured paper that looked suspiciously like one of the handmade papers we'd seen at the Purple Pen. Inside was a small dragon.

Petals of black dahlias, black calla lilies and bat orchids — the flowers I'd seen in O'Kelly's funeral spray — had been arranged to form a stylized black dragon and somehow pressed into the paper. It was like an impressionist watercolor in petals ... and I recognized the artistry from similar works in a gallery inside Hildi's Palace. Expensive ones.

Maya just stared at it while I opened mine, which turned out to be similar in technique, but a different pose.

There was nothing in the boxes that said who sent them, but it wasn't a hard mystery to puzzle out.

Sometimes when the mood strikes me, I still wonder exactly why. Even now.

34
EPILOG

16 MONTHS LATER — The outside view from the Third Overhang wasn't much different from the first time I sat here. Well, that's if you don't count today being a chirpy spring day instead of a winter night back then. The obelisks and their sparkly reflections weren't quite as mysterious, but I couldn't complain.

The big difference was the inside of the Falling Frog Pub: it was alive. The planners, architects and engineers had set up shop at the St Coriander Institute of Additional Knowledge a couple hundred yards down the way because it had some large working spaces, but the Frog's common room was the gathering place for meals and blowing off steam.

"Fascinating eavesdropping," said Malkovich, more to himself than to me. "The future life of St Coriander is unfolding right down there ... and I get to listen in on every single conversation. It's a nosy Librarian's dream.

"Do you think they know, Travis?"

"If they did, I don't think they'd turn around and go home, Malkovich. They're so charged up about being able to create something brand new in this decaying world that I really don't think they give a shit what ghosts might be looking over their shoulders. I wouldn't."

"Not to put too cynical a spin on it, but you're possibly still in the thrall of being a purveyor of foodstuffs. Your judgment may be clouded by taco euphoria."

That comment would have earned a love tap to the shoulder if the Malkovich Semblance had something other than hyperdense photons for substance. It was also true. Owning a small fleet of food trucks was fun at the moment. Would I feel that way in six months? Nope. In my occasional moments of introspection, I could tell that the fun factor was shrinking already ... and faster than I expected. Every night I would hear walkabout calling a little louder.

"To change the subject, is our friend Maya Ng still enjoying her new life as a tropical do-gooder?"

"That and the new madness of Dinero Dinero ... and all the erotic entanglements that go with it. It's even money whether she or Hildi will wear the other down first." I chuckled, but it wasn't exactly my happiest chuckle on record. For all their pleasures and intensities, my entanglements with women always seem to last on the shy side of long enough.

I said goodbye to Malkovich and went for a long walk, being sure to wave at all the people standing in line at the New Azteca Grill. I'm something of a hero to the gullets of those folks.

The planners called it St Coriander Memorial Park, so that's what the temporary painted sign on Outbound Road at Saw Creek Trail says. To me, it's just the cemetery. It's where I go to escape the busy-ness around here. I walked up the hill to where the forest ends at the former Fatherhood Revelation Retreat. For the last two weeks construction crews have been repurposing the retreat buildings into a museum of St Coriander history. But the place I always plunk myself down is at a trio of graves, the last resting places of the Chan-Zita family.

The Librarian (and now Master Curator) invited me to participate as one of the first survey crews after the minefield clearance was completed. I accepted.

Maya had decided to accept Hildi's offer to stay in Dinero Dinero and this was the only offer on my plate. I sure wasn't going to spend one second longer in Hildi's domain than I absolutely had to.

Anyway, on my first day of surveying I came across three skeletons in rotting clothes just outside one of the overgrown mazes. My genetagger said the remains belonged to Carlos, Mika and Varley Chan-Zita of 111 Blue Sky Lane in West Village. I recorded the scene, marked the site for future removal and was about to head north along the thornmesh when I found my feet glued to the ground. Not literally, but I had this strange sensation in my gut that there was something else I needed to do here.

So I just stood looking at the three of them until my eyes finally found a reason to settle on the smallest skeleton. It had been lying face down for enough years that it was now half-buried in windblown detritus and grass. The child's once living form was the usual skeletal curves, but my eyes finally found the little radiused corner that had never been alive.

I broke all the survey party rules and excavated what turned out to be Varley's slate. Never turned it over to anthro, either. My favorite comtech guy in Ishernot refurbed it for me and pointed out the Dragon Hoard game the user had been playing on the night of his death. I always have that slate with me when I come up to visit the Chan-Zitas and talk to Varley. I keep wanting to tell him that he actually won in the end ... even though he didn't. But I don't.

THE END

242

ACKNOWLEDGMENTS

I WAS CONTEMPLATING the wrong ends of a couple of leaf-munching mule deer this morning when I was hit by one of those completely unrelated "oh crap" moments: the Dedication and the Acknowledgments pieces of this book had gone missing. More accurately, they were still lost in the future: I'd neglected to write them. Oops. One of the excellent things about indie publishing is that the author can usually remedy such gaffes before anybody finds out about them. You know, of course, but you'll probably let that just be our secret and not go tweeting about it.

People-wise, I'm grateful to the author of the deliciously original *Thodkin's Spear* (aka Scott Ellison, aka my brother) who read several of the early drafts of *Treasure* and had his usual gentle-but-accurate critiques. The book is better as a result. Two ladies also contributed substantially to its betterment: Jacque Greenleaf, who critiqued and edited last year's draft (and suggested including a map) and Sharon Ellison Rhine (yes, one of my excellent sisters), who stepped up at the last minute and handled the final copyediting and proofreading duties. Any leftover errors, however, are mine alone and I encourage readers to find them and tell me about them. Call it Crowd-Sourced Betterment.

Geographically, I'm particularly grateful to the expansive American Southwest. I've never lived there in Real Life, but I've logged thousands of 4-wheel vehicle miles through that unique countryside during my wandering years. And I've spent quite few years of Fiction Life writing about the world of the Last Nevergate Chronicles, much of which is set in the northern New Mexico high country in the vicinity of Chama (albeit in the 26th century). Coincidentally, it's the same place Travis One-Shoe does his thing a few centuries earlier. Prequels are allowed to do that ... even if they're only sort-of prequels.

Most of the geographic locales I describe are as real and accurate as I could make them. That said, Tony Hillerman's marvelous Leaphorn and Chee mysteries are more vivid in real geography and Native American culture than anything I'd ever be able to create. I miss Mr Hillerman. Not mysteriously, I have (wisely, I think) taken refuge in the future, where anything is possible and reality is a road hazard that can usually be avoided.

ETE

May 1, 2020

www.etellison.com

ABOUT THE AUTHOR

E. T. Ellison is the author of nine novels. His genre-busting first book, *The Luck of Madonna 13*, is a two-time book of the year winning epic that according to one reviewer "tackles the nearly impossible challenge of seamlessly knitting together persuasive technological realism with such high fantasy staples as castles, dragons and magic in a 26th century future Earth that is not wildly different from our own." Another reviewer wrote that "Ellison writes with a gleefully whimsical style that pulls you through the book like a tiger on a leash; half the time you're having the ride of your life, while the other half you're wondering if you're going to survive."

The Luck of Madonna 13 is the first book in the six volume Last Nevergate Chronicles. A new 2020 edition of *Luck* and most of the final five books of the sextet are being published in 2020. Also in simultaneous release are *The Deadly Crocus* and *The Well of Life*, the first two books in Falling Sky, a YA series, and the first Travis One-Shoe thriller, *Treasure of the Holy Quincunx*, set a couple centuries earlier than the Last Nevergate Chronicles in Ellison's richly imagined future Earth of the Last Nevergate Chronicles.

In his pre-fiction decades, Ellison was a consultant on hundreds of diverse projects that were often fascinating and challenging, but no match for the surpassing joys of making stuff up and writing it down.

He currently lives in Northern California, where he claims to be employed as Chief Unscientist for the Institute for Perplexive Amusement.